SPELL
SWEEPER

Also by Lee Edward Födi

THE BOOKS OF ZOONE
The Secret of Zoone
The Guardians of Zoone

SPELL SWEEPER

LEE EDWARD FÖDI

HARPER

An Imprint of HarperCollinsPublishers

Library of Congress Control Number: 2021937025
ISBN 978-0-06-284532-0

Typography by Jessie Gang
21 22 23 24 25   PC/LSCH   10 9 8 7 6 5 4 3 2 1
❖
First Edition

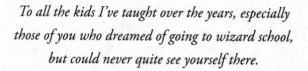

*To all the kids I've taught over the years, especially
those of you who dreamed of going to wizard school,
but could never quite see yourself there.*

Maybe now you can.

There's nothing magical about a broom

It's one of my earliest memories, vivid as a full moon. I'm only four or five, and Su is walking me to school like any good big sister. We stop at the crosswalk and I see an old woman sweeping the pavement, just a few feet away. She wears a frayed sweater, grimy jeans, and maybe a second-hand pair of sneakers. Her broom is wisps of straw, the handle fashioned from a twisted stick of wood. Everything about her is ordinary. Mundane. But as I watch her, the morning sun catches her just right, and for an instant she ignites with a golden luster, frozen in a perfect moment of magic—a fairy sweeping away the shadows of the night.

Then she vanishes. Maybe it's a trick of the light, maybe my childish frame of mind, but I'm convinced she's a witch, that she has leapt upon her broomstick and taken to the clouds. When I tell Su this, she doesn't laugh or chide me for having an overactive imagination. Instead, her eyes dance with wonder.

"Well, there *is* magic in the world, Cara. That's what Dad always says. Right?"

I nod dramatically in agreement.

Of course, that was a long time ago. A lot of things have changed since then—with me, with my sister, with everything.

I know now that you can't fly away on a broomstick. It's not that I grew up and stopped believing in magic—actually, I believe in it *more*, which is what happens when you're chosen to attend one of the most prestigious wizard schools in the world. But here's the thing: when I was given my own broom, it wasn't so that I could soar across the skies, read prophecies in the stars, or fight dragons in wand-to-fang combat.

It was because I'm a failure.

Trust me. It doesn't matter if you're some old lady on a street corner or a kid with a whisper of magic in her blood—a broom is for one thing and one thing only: sweeping.

Yay, me. I'm going to wizard school.

And it's terrible.

CHAPTER 1

Meet the Star of Our School
(Hint: It's Not Me)

THERE ARE A LOT OF things worse than being late for school. One of them is being late for wizard school.

I should know. I'm late almost daily, but I can't blame school buses, alarm clocks, or even the weather because, like any good educational institution for the magically gifted, Dragonsong Academy is a boarding school—which means my only excuse for being late is my attitude. My teachers stopped asking for excuses a long time ago and just went straight to assigning detention. And trust me, detention doled out by a wizard is *horrendous*.

Which is why I'm completely out of breath when I arrive at the auditorium. Classes officially began last week, but today is the first assembly, and I'm determined to make a strong start to seventh grade after a disastrous first two years here. Of course, arriving late isn't a good start at all—it's just that I wanted to wear the fancy hairpin I "borrowed" from my sister, but it took forever to find it (turns out, it had rolled underneath my bed). By the time I slip through the back door of the auditorium, the assembly is well underway. The entire school—four hundred students—is packed inside and, because it's late August, it's as hot as a cauldron of basilisk blood on full boil. I lean on my broom, taking a moment to collect myself.

It's dark, with a single spotlight shining on the stage, but I know my place—it's at the back. I skirt the perimeter and scramble into the chair next to Gusto. My crewmate is sitting there attentively, his polished goggles nestled perfectly atop his luxurious crop of black hair. Then I spot the vacant seat on the other side of him. Master Quibble is late, too.

"Where's the Q-Man?" I ask, nudging Gusto.

He purses his lips and stares intently ahead, not wanting to talk during the assembly—that's Gusto for you, a straight broomstick. But if the Q-Man isn't here, he can't punish me for being late, so maybe I've dodged some dragon fire. I turn my eyes to the stage, where Headwizard Singh is blathering on about something to do with the tenets of magical education.

"Maybe I wasn't late *enough*," I mutter. Gusto sighs, and I remind myself that I'm supposed to be adjusting my attitude.

"And now, the moment has arrived for our annual Student Stunt!" Singh announces.

I audibly groan. A few heads swivel in our direction, prompting Gusto to sink into his seat with embarrassment. Then someone else appears on the stage, and I don't have to worry about drawing *any* attention—because it's all handed over to Dragonsong's star student.

Harlee Wu.

She has the type of reputation that demands you regularly use both her first and last name. She's only fifteen, but you'd think she was a seasoned wizard by the way the school treats her. Her mystique is probably helped by her height; Harlee is so tall that most of the school population has to literally look up to her. Her dark hair is cropped short, except for the two long locks dangling down either side of her face. Those locks, along with the tips of her bob, have a dash of red dye, which I begrudgingly admit is very cool, and matches her uniform. I say *begrudgingly* because, in case it isn't apparent yet, Harlee Wu and I are sworn enemies.

At least we would be if she knew I existed.

As Harlee assumes center stage, whispers of admiration rise out of the audience, along with murmurs of "the Chosen One." Most students at Dragonsong believe that Harlee is going to grow up and save us—though from what, nobody knows—because of some famous wizard prophecy, which, like in every fantasy book I've ever read, is conveniently vague.

It's tradition that the top student from the previous year performs a magical stunt to welcome everyone during the first assembly—but it's the same student every year, so they might as well just call it Harlee Wu Day and end the charade. After receiving a round of applause, the queen of the school offers some remarks about how honored she is to be chosen to perform the stunt. Then she closes her eyes, a thrum rises in her throat, and her cheeks begin to shine. (This is a wizard thing—you perform a spell and your cheeks glow.) She raises her arms, snaps her wrists, there's a crackle of lightning between her fingers, and—

WHAM!

The whole auditorium quakes as an enormous statue of Riva Dragonsong, the school's founder, appears next to Harlee. Everyone knows that sculpture—it's located in the garden right outside the auditorium. Correction: it's *normally* located there. Harlee has translocated it to center stage, which is an ability unheard of for someone our age. Then the statue suddenly begins dancing around, sparks crackling at its feet. Everyone oohs and aahs, which prompts me to stick my finger in my mouth and make a gagging motion.

"Stop it," Gusto hisses.

I scowl at him. Most students don't have the faintest idea how much work it'll take to clean up an over-the-top spell like this, but Gusto does. He should be taking my side.

After her performance, Harlee snaps her wrists again, and the statue disappears—presumably returning to its rightful location. The glow of wizardry fades from her cheeks, restoring her flawless golden-brown complexion; the stunt hasn't even caused her to break a sweat.

As she exits the stage, all the students and teachers are on their feet, madly applauding. I sure wish someone would cheer for *me* like that. But does Cara Moone ever get any praise? *Nope.*

The lights switch on, indicating that the assembly is officially over. The students rise, stretching, showing off their colorful uniforms. Each grade level at Dragonsong has its own fancy color scheme, but because Gusto and I are rejects, we have the distinction of wearing the same boring shade until we graduate: mop-water gray. It's officially known as "ash," but it's nothing compared to the other grades' colors, which are based on precious gemstones. You start with pearl in fifth grade, then topaz, emerald, amethyst, citrine, ruby, sapphire, and finally moonstone. Very cool—and very irrelevant to me.

Everyone begins filtering out, heading off to class, but Gusto and I stay behind because even though our teacher is nowhere to be found, this *is* our class: Spell Sweeping 101. (Okay, it's not actually called that, but whatever.) Today's assignment? Clean up Harlee Wu's mess.

After the auditorium has emptied out, I stand up with a melodramatic sigh, lower my goggles, adjust my utility belt, and follow Gusto to the stage, broom in hand.

Spell dust is pouring over the sides like sand. We climb up to see the stuff is everywhere; some of it's even swirling in the air, red and slightly phosphorescent. Craning my neck to peer upward, I spot more of it settling on the rafters high above. Way up there, nestled in the belfry above the dome, is the school bell. And by bell, I mean an actual giant old-fashioned medieval bell. Which is why I can't blame a malfunctioning alarm clock for being late, because when that bell rings you can hear it clear across Dragonsong Island. I bet the bell is now covered in spell dust, too.

"What a disaster," I mutter.

Gusto is already gnawing on a stick of candy extracted from his utility belt. The candy looks like licorice, but it's called witch's delight—it's delicious, but if I ate as much of it as Gusto, I'd look like a six-hundred-pound dragon slug. Gusto, though? He's as thin as a wand.

Gusto cheerfully surveys the situation. "It's not so bad. Bet we can finish by—"

A loud rumbling emanates from above, causing the entire auditorium to quake. The sound isn't coming from the bell, I realize. It's too deep and . . . unearthly. An empty auditorium can be creepy even in the normal world, but here, at a magical school?

"Wizard ghosts *have* to be worse than regular ghosts, right?" I ask Gusto.

His only response is to take a nervous bite of witch's delight.

When the sound finally comes to an end, I realize something is butting against my leg. Quibble may have decided not to show up, but at least his familiar came to do his part.

Zuki is trembling head to tails—he's got three of them—and he's ghost white. Well, I mean, he's naturally white, but right now he's so pale he glows. He's a magic fox and, apparently, he's spooked. Which doesn't exactly make me feel better.

"Nice of you to show up," I say.

"I think I'll unshow up," Zuki whines.

"What was that sound?" Gusto wonders.

"Do you think it's a bandernock?" Zuki moans. He crouches low and peers out between his tails, which are so long that he can easily fold them over his snout.

The lights shut off, casting us into immediate darkness. I slip my goggles to the top of my head. They're mostly for detecting certain types of spell dust, and they definitely don't help in the dark. Thankfully, we have Zuki's moon fur—it's our only source of light until Gusto and I find our flashlights and switch them on. Still, they don't do much to negate the darkness in the cavernous auditorium.

"What's going on?" I mutter.

"It's a bandernock," Zuki insists. "Maybe a whole nest of them, maybe an infestation, maybe—"

"You talk too much," I snap at the fox. "Especially when you're nervous."

"Yeah, well, when you're nervous, you . . . you stink," Zuki yips.

I roll my eyes. Zuki really needs to work on his burns. "I don't stink. And I'm not nervous."

Which is the truth. It's one of the few things Quibble says I'm good at: staying clearheaded in a "purge situation." Zuki continues rambling, but I tune him out. He could go on for hours, and by then it'll be dinnertime. I mean, not for us. For whatever's prowling in the rafters of the dome.

I tap my fingers on the handle of my broom, pondering. My grandma says brooms are symbols of good luck because they can sweep away bad spirits and protect against evil. I wish. If I were allowed, I'd tell her a thing or two about my broom, like how it's good for sweeping up spells, but that it won't do a thing when it comes to confronting a monster. Except maybe giving it something to use as a toothpick when it's done with its main course.

"I wish I had a wand," I mutter, though admittedly, given my inferior wizarding abilities, it would probably end up as a toothpick, too.

"Maybe this is a training exercise," Gusto suggests, already on a second stick of witch's delight.

I frown. "Would Quibble really—"

"*Master* Quibble," Gusto corrects me.

The rumble sounds again; this time, it's even louder, causing the walls to shake.

"Quibble—sorry, *Master* Quibble—wouldn't purposely put us in danger," I argue, although I have second thoughts as I stagger to keep my footing. "Uh, would he?"

"Not me!" Zuki insists, twitching his tails as if they're exclamation points to his sentence. "I'm more important to him than sleep. More important than food. More impor—"

"Okay, okay," I cut him off. "Enough messing around."

"What does *that* mean?" Gusto asks.

I roll my shoulders. "That means I'm going up there."

How magic works
(and why we have to clean it up)

In books and movies, wizards stroll around, flicking their wands, turning people into toads or zapping recalcitrant dragons into submission. In reality, it's not that simple.

Magic is messy.

It's like when you squeeze toothpaste onto your toothbrush—there's always a bit that ends up on your brush handle, the counter, or dripping down your chin. Magic works the same way.

The first thing you learn in wizard school is that there is a Field of Magical Matter. When wizards want to perform a spell (or, if you want to get all official about it, a Magical Occurrence), they have to access the Field. Basically, they have to squeeze a giant magical toothpaste tube. And, like I said, it's messy, always leaving something behind. We usually refer to it as spell dust, but it's essentially leftover enchanted residue. How much depends on the Magical Occurrence. A wizard utters a simple spell? You just circle your broom around her feet and go for lunch. Someone magically relocates, let's say for the sake of argument, a giant statue of the school's founder? You better strap on your full spell sweeper kit because it's going to be a *loooong* day.

But you *do* need to strap on the kit, because spell dust is definitely not the sort of thing you want to leave sitting around for very long. It causes ALL sorts of problems.

First off, spell dust is visible to normal, non-wizarding people. (We call them "Blisses" because they are ignorant to the existence of wizards and, as the saying goes, ignorance is bliss. I should point out here that I come from a Bliss family, so I know all too well about the finer points of keeping magic secret from non-wizards.) If Blisses see green floaties trickling down the side of the local school, they tend to panic and call 911 or the local news station. The last thing wizards need is attention drawn to their activities, because that usually leads to official investigations (awkward), interrogations (even more awkward), or—in the old days at least—getting tied to a stake and tested for flammability (extremely awkward).

But wizards aren't just worried about self-preservation. Unpurged spell dust can harm wizards and Blisses both. It morphs, expands, and takes on a life of its own, performing unsupervised magic. (Imagine leaving a two-year-old unattended in the chainsaw section of your local hardware store. Now give that two-year-old magic powers).

We call it "feral magic." You think your lost car keys

simply disappeared? Of course not. You've probably got feral magic in your house, hankering for a taste of metal (I don't know why, but feral magic has a thing for keys). You can't find that cool pizza place, the one you went to last summer, then you turn around and it's sitting right in front of you? That's feral magic, toying with the dimensions of time and space. Crop circles? That's feral magic, too.

I haven't even mentioned the various beasties who have a magical sweet tooth. Leave spell dust sitting around for long, and you're sure to have a squix or a bandernock on your hands (though you tend not to worry about your hands when you are being slowly digested inside one of a bandernock's nine stomachs).

Of course, there are many wizarding activities that *don't* involve using the Field. Brewing potions, divining the future from the stars, communicating with animals—these are all Field-free activities. But mention that to a wizard and most of them shrug and say, "What's the fun in that?" As far as they're concerned, if you want to get *real* wizarding done, you've got to use the Field.

Which takes us back to the unfortunate fact that wizards DO NOT clean up after themselves. The closest they ever get to cleaning is sweeping the room with an ornery gaze.

Which is why you need someone to do the dirty work.

In other words, someone like me.

CHAPTER 2

A Spell Sweeper's Gotta Do
What a Spell Sweeper's Gotta Do

GUSTO NEARLY DROPS HIS CANDY. "Are you crazy?! You can't go up there!"

"Sure I can," I say. "I'll just take a quick snoop. Stay here—see if you can get the lights working."

Before he can protest further, I sling the strap of my broom across my back, head to the ladder built into the backstage wall, and begin climbing. Maybe this *is* a test—but I'm not going to give Quibble the satisfaction of failing. Not today.

By the time I reach the rafters, I'm huffing. The ladder continues upward to the belfry, but I decide to stop and investigate. When I shine my flashlight around me, I don't see anything except cobwebs and spell dust. Lots of spell dust. Gee, thanks, Harlee Wu.

I heave myself onto the nearest crossbeam. While I'm up here, I might as well clean up. I unsling my broom, stick my flashlight in my mouth, and start sweeping. My broom sucks up the spell dust like a vacuum, the straw turning increasingly red as it absorbs the waste. The wooden beam is a couple of feet wide, ample enough, but the tricky part is carefully step-ping around the braces and not plummeting to my death. Not exactly easy with all my gear, but I don't have a choice—this is the job.

"Cara?" Gusto calls from below. "Are you okay?"

"Mrmph mrhrmp." Right. Flashlight. I pull it out of my mouth. "Yeah, I'm fine. No ghosts up here. Not sure where that sound came from."

"Maybe it was an earthquake," Gusto suggests, his voice sounding distant and echoey. "Maybe we should leave."

"Yeah," Zuki adds. "What if there are aftershocks? What if—"

"Ugh, just be quiet and let me concentrate!" I shout down. "What about the lights?"

"Switches don't work," Gusto replies. "Need to find the breaker. But I really think we should get help."

"Just hold on . . ."

"What is it?"

I don't respond. There's black gunk dripping from above, like a long string of saliva. Even though I've only been a spell-sweeper-in-training for less than a year, I've seen all kinds of magical residue. It comes in various colors, textures, and lumi-nosities, especially if it's gone feral—but this is something new. Something *different*. Trying to hold my flashlight at the same time, I cautiously reach out with my broom and touch it to the slime. The straw immediately starts to smoke and *sizzle*. Which is definitely, one hundred percent *not* what's supposed to happen. The gunk smells rotten, prompting me to lift my scarf up over my nose.

This isn't just something new. It's something *wrong*.

"Do you see black stuff down there?" I call down.

"*Everything* is black down here!" Gusto retorts. "It's dark."

"Zuki! Whatever you do, don't touch it with your tails."

"Don't touch *what* with my tails? Is something wrong with my tails? Ah! My tails! My beautiful tails!"

The straw on my broom has turned the color of ink and, for lack of a better description, is recoiling, like the slime is slowly dissolving it. I exhale in confusion. What is going on?

"Cara?" Gusto calls. "Come on! I think—"

This time it's not a rumble. It's a *roar*, so loud and violent that the entire dome shakes. I cling to the nearest brace and manage to hang on to my broom—though my flashlight goes spinning away (a couple of seconds later, I hear a pronounced "OW!" from Gusto below). The roar is coming from above, so I muster the courage to stare upward. The darkness is somehow *rippling*. This is no earthquake. This is . . . magic.

I consider leaping for the ladder, clambering down, and fetching the nearest teacher. That's what the spell sweeper manual says to do when you encounter an unusual entity. I mean, I *think* it says that.

Darn. Maybe I should have read the manual.

It's too late now—to read the manual, and possibly to do a lot of other things, like graduate from seventh grade—because that's when I see the giant, puckering mouth open up above me.

It's even drooling—this is where the black gunk is coming from—but there's no face, no body. Whatever it is, it's suspended in the *air*, and I can only really see it because the cavity—or throat?—beyond glows with a toxic purple color.

I hear Gusto and Zuki screaming and scampering around below—basically being useless. Which means I'm going to have to do this on my own. I swing my broom at the slime, catching it before it can splatter against the crossbeams or the stage. The goo keeps gnawing at my broom head. Soon, there will be nothing left.

"What's going on?" someone shouts from below—someone who isn't Gusto or Zuki.

Harlee Wu has returned. I've heard her voice at enough assemblies to recognize it anywhere.

"Get out of here!" she orders.

"I'm a little busy!" I snap.

"I'm talking to these two!" she yells at me. "They're freaking out!"

She makes me want to scream. Sure, Gusto and Zuki are acting like idiots—but they're *my* idiots. Who's she to boss them around? But I guess they're happy to bow to her, because I hear them quickly exit.

"I'm going to find the breaker box," Harlee calls up.

I continue swiping my broom through the air, capturing all the toxic spit, but my broom head is still smoking, and the handle is growing red hot. I should have worn my gloves, though I doubt it would make a difference. I could just drop my broom, but that would mean the mouth-thingy wins, and that's annoying. But I can't hold on to my broom any longer—I need to do *something*.

The thing belches at me, which gives me an idea. If it *is* a mouth, its gullet has to lead somewhere—hopefully to some vital organs. I pitch what's left of my broom into the entity, and it's swallowed whole. Next comes a loud, irritated grumble.

Yes! Point for Team Cara! In a moment of inspired rage, I begin pulling things from my utility belt—every vial of neutralizing potion and stain remover I have—and chuck them at the mouth-thingy. Its grumbling turns from frustration to anger and possibly pain—then, just as it gulps down my bottle of qilin powder, it vanishes.

In that instant, every light in the auditorium flares back to life. The sudden brightness is so blinding and shocking that I stumble, sway . . .

And fall.

It's like every atom in my body has been smashed and rearranged. It's painful, but not the kind of painful I was expecting. I suddenly realize my throat is full of water—I'm drowning.

I thrash and claw, completely disoriented, until someone grabs me by the collar and yanks me from the water. It takes me a few seconds to comprehend that I'm lying alongside the ornamental pond in the garden adjacent to the auditorium. It's Gusto who has pulled me out, and now he and Zuki are staring down at me with eyes bulging like they're a couple of cartoon characters.

"What happened?" Gusto asks.

"Don't know," I gasp as I pull myself to my elbows, dripping wet.

Though I *do* know. Harlee Wu translocated me so that I'd land in the pond instead of slamming into the stage and breaking every bone in my body, a feat she probably accomplished with nothing more than a blink of her pretty brown eyes. If it were me, I would have conjured a giant feather bed or a massive trampoline—but nope, she sent me for a dip.

My broom is gone, and so are my neutralizing potions. My hair is wet and matted against my face, my sister's hairpin dangling awkwardly next to my ear. At least I didn't lose it—my sister would kill me, especially since I didn't ask permission to take it in the first place.

I realize there are other students congregating—a blink of fifth grade wizards (I can tell by their pearl-colored uniforms) has been drawn out of the nearby classroom by the commotion.

"You look like a drowned rat!" one of them says. I recognize him as Lucas, the younger brother of one of my other enemies, Georgia Dirk. He's a smug little monster, like his sister, and he soon has the entire group pointing and laughing at me. Is there anything more embarrassing than being taunted by kids younger than you?

"Hey!" I yell. "Do you know what happened in there? I just killed a—"

There's a boom as Harlee Wu suddenly appears, standing over me in a puff of scarlet smoke. Dratch, the girl knows how to make an entrance. Talk about being upstaged.

"Are you okay?" she asks me.

"Uh . . ." I'm so surprised to be addressed by the Queen of Dragonsong that my words evaporate on my tongue.

Harlee doesn't seem to notice—or care—that I haven't replied. Instead, she points at Gusto and Zuki and says, "You two can go finish the job. Seems safe now, except there's spell dust everywhere in there."

"I wonder whose fault that is?" I grumble under my breath. Like I said, translocation is messy.

Harlee wrinkles her nose at me. "You might want to shower."

She says it like I've had a lifelong aversion to soap and water, and I hear a couple of snickers from the assembled students. At the best of times, I'd look like a complete and utter loser in comparison to Harlee Wu. My hair has a weird reddish tinge and my face is painted with freckles—Mom's "Irish gift," as she likes to say. I certainly don't have any sense of style like Harlee or half the girls at Dragonsong, and nearly drowning in a pond full of goldfish doesn't help.

"What happened, Miss Wu?" Professor Plume asks Harlee (it's his class that is flocking around). He has to look up at Harlee when he speaks, partly because she's so tall, but mostly because he's as short and squat as a garden gnome. (His pointed beard only adds to this impression—the man really should take a look in the mirror, though he'll probably have to find a stool first.)

"Uh . . . I forgot this in the auditorium," Harlee says, plucking a tattered sketchbook from her pocket. "I went back to get it and that's when I saw her slip from the rafters. So, I translo—"

"What?!" I cry. "I didn't sl—"

"You saved her," Lucas says with a gasp. "You're a hero, Harlee Wu."

"She's more than that!" the girl next to him, Aleah Farhad, adds. "She's the Chosen One!"

Everyone surges forward, nearly trampling me to death in the frenzy to reach the Queen of Dragonsong. They want a piece of her, a glance, a word of acknowledgment—maybe an actual scrap of her robe. Lucas has the audacity to ask her for an autograph.

That's what happens when you're someone like Harlee Wu, someone who is the exact opposite of me. She's a star and I'm a set piece. She's award-winning and I'm remedial. She's a wizard and . . . me?

I'm just a plain old MOP.

It's as bad as it sounds

Yep, I'm a MOP. If I had an Instagram account, then my username would be @caramoone_MOP. (But I'm not allowed to use Instagram—not because of my mom, but because WIZARDS. Being a secret society, they have this thing about social media.)

MOP stands for a much fancier-sounding title: Magical Occurrence Purger. But no one says that. They say MOP. Or spell sweeper (which sounds slightly cool) or scrub (which does not). But, officially, it's MOP. I'd like to have a conversation with the wizard who came up with that acronym.

There is nothing glamorous about being a MOP. I can't rewind time, remove a zit hex from your chin, or erase your memory so that you forget that you saw a dragon pooping on your neighbor's lawn on the way to school. All I can do is scrub up that dragon poop—and the residue of magic left behind after a *real* wizard has dispatched said dragon.

And by real, I mean a wizard like Harlee Wu.

CHAPTER 3

Even at Wizard School, They Put the Janitors in the Basement

AFTER HARLEE AND HER LEGION of adoring fans disperse, I'm left alone in the garden. Which is fine by me. I prefer the school grounds this way; without the gaggle of students, they're serene and majestic. Magical, even—which sounds like a ridiculous thing to say, since it's a wizard school, but I mean it in a more aesthetic way. Dragonsong Academy is a realm of spires, towers, and stone walls decorated with gargoyles. There are different buildings and wings housing the various classrooms and facilities. There are winding pathways, terraces and courtyards, and even an extremely tricky hedge maze. And, of course, there is the tranquil walled garden, where I am right now.

I peel myself from the stones and stand up. I can see the dome and belfry above the auditorium; from the outside, you would never know that some evil mouth-thingy tried to devour me.

Strange.

I plop down on the nearest bench, tug off my wet boots, and contemplate the statue of Riva Dragonsong—which Harlee did indeed return to its pedestal. It stares back at me with an expression that I interpret as slightly judgmental.

It's said that Riva "created" this island centuries ago when she was flying over the Strait of Juan de Fuca on her dragon. Some nasty leviathan surged out of the sea to snack on her, and Riva counterattacked by transforming it to stone (I don't want to know how much spell dust that created). Instant island. Eventually, other wizards came and built the school here and, over time, Dragonsong Academy has expanded to become one of the premier wizardly institutions in the world. Technically, we're located in Canada (the closest city being Victoria), though wizards don't pay much attention to international boundaries. "A wizard is a wizard," Master Quibble is fond of saying, and we have students from all over the place.

Me? I'm from just around the corner. As the dragon flies, Dragonsong Island is only an hour away from my family in Seattle. Of course, they don't let us take dragon transport when it's time for a visit home, because seeing a giant flying lizard land in your backyard is the kind of thing that tends to give Blisses heart attacks. Instead, I'm left to get home by ferries and car rides. It's a five-hour quest to taste home cooking.

I wave a palm over my boots in an attempt to dry them with a spell, but they remain as soggy as my brain. I could try again, but I feel way too frazzled—I mean, I *did* just fight some mouth-thingy. Of course, Harlee came along and stole my thunder. Do I get any credit for vanquishing a monster? Nope. Just imagine if all those fifth grade kids had seen me in action!

Then everyone would be talking about me instead of Harlee.

"Whatchya doin'?"

"Ahh!" I cry, suddenly realizing that Zuki is sitting in front of me. I was so deep in thought, I didn't see him slip into the garden. "Don't sneak up on me like that!"

Zuki flicks his long tails. "Master Quibble wants to know why you haven't come back to class."

"Uh . . . because I nearly died?"

More tail flicking. "No, you didn't. Harlee saved you!"

"I'm not talking about that. I mean the mons—"

"Soooo," Zuki interrupts, "if you're done feeling sorry for yourself, let's head to class. By the way, what happened to your broom?"

"Got eaten," I mutter as I pick up my soggy boots and follow him.

"Eaten?" he says incredulously. "You mean you lost it? Your broom? The most important tool of a—"

"Just leave me alone," I interrupt. "I've had my fill of evil tricksters today."

"I'm not evil!" Zuki protests. "Or a trickster!"

"You can *shapeshift*. What's trickier than that?"

Zuki turns on me, flashes a smirk, then instantly transforms into a fluffy white poodle. "I think you mean, 'What's *cuter* than that?'"

I roll my eyes. In Japan, where Master Quibble found him as a pup, Zuki's kind are known as *kyūbi no kitsune*, foxes that can grow nine tails. Those nine tails allow them to shapeshift into humans, but Zuki only has three so far—the best he can do is transform into different canines. (What will he be able to do with four tails? Hopefully not become even more annoying.)

Zuki flashes back into his regular fox form. "What is it with you, Cara?" he asks. "You've got some extra pop in your potion today. Some sizzle! Some—"

"I'm wet and grumpy. I just need to go back to my room. Take a shower."

"I told you, Master Quibble wants you *now*."

"At least let me get out of these wet clothes. I've got a spare uniform in my locker—I'll be there in the blink of a gorgon's eye."

"You better," he mutters.

We separate once we reach the Crucible, which is what we call the main concourse of Dragonsong. It got its name because it's a giant round hall with concave walls that stretch upward into shadow—also, crossing it can be a real trial when classes let out. Spiraling staircases lead to different levels, while the walls are decorated with paintings of different shapes and sizes, all hung slightly askew (on purpose—it's a wizard thing). Back in fifth grade, I was convinced that the subjects of the pictures secretly moved about when nobody was looking—I mean, isn't that what artwork is *supposed* to do at a magical school? I even spent one afternoon staring at a painting of a sasquatch, determined to catch it in the act, but the only thing I discovered is that my Rune Reading teacher, Professor Leon, didn't think that my experiment was a good excuse for being late.

"One day, I'll get you," I tell the sasquatch in that same painting as I hurry past it.

It's possible it winks in response.

My locker is tall and skinny, like one at a regular school, but that's where the similarities end. The door is thick oak, carved with an intricate floral pattern and featuring decorative metal hinges, giving it the appearance of an old-fashioned wardrobe. There are no combination locks either; you open them with personal spells. Regular students just say the spells in their minds and the doors creak open. Being remedial, that rarely works for me and I have to say my words out loud—which is kind of embarrassing and more than just a little risky. Ella MacIntyre's locker is right next to mine and I'm pretty sure she's been trying to overhear my spell. I can only imagine what type of mischief she's cooking up.

Thankfully, the Crucible is currently deserted, and I can utter my spell with impunity. I unstrap my utility belt, hang it on a hook, and grab my spare uniform. It has the same basic design as the other students' outfits: a white blouse, plaid skirt, and a robe-like cardigan with a hood. The difference, of course, is that my uniform is the color of sludge.

I also keep a spare set of socks and underwear in my locker (thanks for the sage advice, Mom), along with some flats, so I grab everything, scurry to the bathroom and change, then stuff my wet clothes back into my locker, at which point I'm *extremely* grateful that no one's around, because I happened to put on my pink unicorn underwear this morning. Yes, I'm really too old for them now, but I've always considered them lucky.

Correction: I *used* to consider them lucky.

Once I'm as presentable as I'm going to get after being translocated to a pond full of overfed carp, I make my way to the MOP department, which means heading down the nearest set of stairs and into the basement. The place is damp, the walls stone, and its nooks and crannies home to all kinds of scuttling critters. I pass by our MOP classroom, which is a combination of lecture room and workshop, and arrive at our master's office.

There's a plaque on his door that reads: *Patrick Quibble, Department Head, Magical Occurrence Purging.* The other teachers call him "Trick" for short, but that's way too playful to fit my master's somber personality. Which means that, as I place my hand on the doorknob, I take a moment to review the chain of events in the auditorium so that I can properly present them. Quibble has this way of turning me into a mumbling mess, but I'm not going to let that happen today. For once, it wasn't me who screwed up! I actually solved the problem, and this time he'll be impressed with me, and—

The door swings open from the other side and I stumble through, colliding awkwardly with Quibble himself.

"Caradine," he says quietly. "Do you mind explaining to me how you lost your broom?"

CHAPTER 4

Go Ahead, Drink the Queen of Dragonsong Kool-Aid

OF COURSE THE ONLY THING Master Quibble is concerned about is my broom. Not about *me*. There's no, "Are you all right, Cara?" Or, "Do you need to take the rest of the afternoon off?" He's only worried about my stupid gear.

The truth is, Quibble never wanted me in his program. I mean, I didn't want to be assigned here either, but at least I can look him in the eye, which is something he rarely does with me. Even now, as he levels his question at me, his gaze is fixed somewhere over my shoulder. I stare at him, hoping for some glint of sympathy in his expression, but all I get is the pulsing of the red, hand-shaped mark that mars his otherwise pale white face. For the longest time I thought it was a birthmark, but Gusto told me that it's from a fight that happened with some dark wizard years ago, when Quibble was the headwizard at Dragonsong. The fight did more than wound him, though—it caused him to quit his position and go on a three-year drinking binge. When he finally returned, it was to take a demotion and run the MOP department.

Quibble's ever-present disappointment in me is usually deflating. But today? Well, as Zuki says, I've got some pop in my potion, so I tilt my chin high, march into the room, and take the vacant seat between Gusto and Zuki, facing Quibble's massive desk.

"If you must know, Master Quibble, my broom was eaten by a monster that I single-handedly defeated in the auditorium." I keep my chin tilted upward as I speak because my sister once told me it's a way to project confidence.

The Q-Man shuts the door, shuffles around to the other side of the desk, and sits. He doesn't make a sound. He just stares into space. It's not unusual, but it *is* unnerving. Sometimes I wonder if he's a few straws short of a broom. He's obviously having a bad day, since he didn't show up for the assembly. Or maybe he's just trying to make me uncomfortable.

Shifting nervously in my chair, I glance around, searching in vain for something to distract me. You'd think that a wizard's office would be cluttered and eccentric, but maybe Quibble missed an important memo or something because the room is bare and bereft of magical items. There are no leering skulls, no haphazard stacks of books. At the very least, he could have a candle or two, maybe a jar with a pickled claw. *Anything.* But nope—other than the desk, the chairs, and us, the office is completely empty.

"Monster?" Quibble asks at last. "What are you talking about, Caradine?"

"This humongous belching mouth appeared and tried to eat

me—it wasn't feral magic, it was something different, like I've never seen before, and . . ."

So much for a calm and collected presentation. I'm blabbering, but I don't care, because at least I've got momentum. No one interrupts, not even Zuki. Eventually, I run out of steam and Quibble leans back in his chair and strokes the single white hair that sprouts from his chin. I guess he doesn't know that, in addition to a cluttered workspace, he should also have a messy white beard (I mean, has he read *anything* with a wizard in it?). The lone hair *is* long—I'll give him that—but it doesn't make him look wise, just negligent with a razor.

It seems like forever before Quibble speaks again. "Kazuki and Augusto didn't see any of what you describe," he says. (He refers to everyone by their full names, whether they like it or not.)

Big surprise: he doesn't believe me. I've been railroaded into the MOP program, probably because I'm from a Bliss family, but as far as Quibble's concerned, I'm barely qualified to swing a broom across the floor—let alone to identify a toxic spell dust monster, even when it's trying to gnaw my face off. To him, I'll always be the disobedient failure who got thrust into his department against his wishes. But I'm not going down without a fight.

"They weren't up there with me!" I protest, before turning to my so-called crewmates and firing a dragon-hot glare at them. "Are you saying I made it up? How do you explain what happened to my broom?"

Gusto frowns. "I can't."

"Knowing you, you threw it away," Zuki adds.

"Why would I do that?!" I cry.

"Because you like to goof off?" he retorts.

"No, I don't," I argue.

"You snuck feral magic into Ryan Kang's locker at the end of last year," Gusto reminds me.

"That wasn't m—"

"I saw you do it," Gusto interrupts. "And his locker exploded."

I try to stifle a chuckle—and fail. "Yeah, well, he deserved it. Calling us MOPs."

Gusto sighs. "We *are* MOPs."

I shrug. "It was the way he said it."

"And then you blamed Gusto," Zuki piles on.

"He told on me!" I cry. "We're supposed to be a team."

"Exactly," Gusto says. "And then I had to clean it up. Just because you were too busy trying to sneak into the unicorn stable—"

"Why do only the seniors get to go there?" I wonder. "I mean, if we're sweepers, shouldn't we get to sweep up unicorn hair, too?"

Gusto doesn't respond. He's too busy grimacing at the sight of our master, who now has his chin hair wrapped around his finger. Gusto can't stand that hair. He keeps claiming that he's going to slip into Quibble's quarters one night and pluck it out, but as a general rule, I don't advise sneaking into a wizard's personal space. There's a rumor going around

Dragonsong that Ariel Morales broke into Professor Ska's laboratory last spring to alter her Transfiguration score and ended up a newt for a week. Just to be clear, that's seven days living in a terrarium and being fed insects for snacks. I think that's why she's a vegetarian now.

Gusto shakes his head and turns his attention back to me. "You're always complaining about spell sweeping duty. Always late. Always trying to get out of it. Let's face it, Cara. You're a . . . *slacker*."

He utters the word like it's the worst possible insult on planet Earth (like Zuki, he needs to work on his burns). But I'm feeling extra fragile at the moment, so the burn actually lands. "Th-that was last year," I sputter. "This year, I—I'm *telling* you. This monster mouth exists! It tried to devour me. It—"

"Caradine," Quibble says, finally deciding to rejoin the conversation, "did you throw away your broom?"

"NO!" I shout. "It got eaten. By that thing. Everyone's attacking me, but I was the one who went up to face it. If Harlee Wu waltzed in here saying she fought a monster, everyone would be—"

"ENOUGH!"

It's a rare outburst of passion from our master, and it makes me shiver. Zuki releases a quiet whimper. Gusto sinks in his seat.

Quibble takes a deep breath. "I do not think, Caradine, that it's your best move to compare yourself to Dragonsong's finest wizard."

Finest wizard? Harlee's only fifteen—she hasn't even graduated yet! But, like everyone else, Quibble can only see her as the Queen of Dragonsong. Like everyone else, he absolutely adores her.

"This is so unfair," I mutter, crossing my arms.

"Caradine," Quibble says earnestly, "whether they're real or imagined, I don't need you to face monsters."

Because only real wizards get to do that is what he means. "But—"

"I need you to sweep," Quibble emphasizes. "*That's* your role, Caradine. And you need to take it seriously. Like Augusto. Like Kazuki."

"All they did was run around, freaking out," I scoff.

"Hey! At least I didn't lose my brooms," Zuki counters.

"Seriously?" I snort. "Holy dratch! Your brooms are attached to your butt."

"Language, Caradine," Quibble chastises, though I'm not sure if he's referring to the use of *butt* or *dratch*—which just means dragon poop, so I'm not sure what the big deal is.

"Yeah, and I've still got them," Zuki taunts, waving his tails in my face.

"Ugh—gross!" I groan, swatting him away.

"It's time for a full review of the manual," Quibble announces. "And a quiz. Tomorrow."

"Thanks a lot, Cara," Zuki growls. He's not a fan of quizzes, which may have something to do with having to hold the pen in his mouth. "Do you know what I hate more than tests?"

"Enlighten me," I mutter.

"*You,*" he snarls.

I roll my eyes. Zuki isn't capable of sustaining any given feeling for very long. In an hour, he'll probably be begging me to scratch his ears. At least, I hope so.

"Dismissed," Quibble announces, but as we start to file out, he adds, "One more thing, Caradine."

I turn around, shoulders slumped. "Yes, Master?"

"Your broom?"

"Honestly, it's gone."

He sighs dramatically. "You will construct a new one. A week from today, at sundown, meet me in the broom workshop. Remember, a broom is to a spell sweeper as a wand is to a spellcaster."

I slog out of the office. A broom is nothing like a wand. For one, I wouldn't complain if I were given the opportunity to build a wand. I've got a notebook full of designs for how mine would look and what type of wood I would use.

But it doesn't matter how much I want it; it's pretty clear I'm never going to get my wand. For the umpteenth time since coming to Dragonsong, I think: *I should never have picked up that broom.*

How I became a spell sweeper (a.k.a. a wizard fail)

Let's rewind to a pivotal scene in my failed wizardly career. I'm halfway through sixth grade, my second year at Dragonsong Academy, loitering outside the Apothecarial Arts lab (I wish they would just call it "Potions Class," but no one consulted me), trying to catch a glimpse of what the eighth grade class is doing. That's when I see Ian Flynn bump over a vial of dragon snot.

Not a good move, because dragon snot is explosive. There's a boom. *Fireworks*. Ian's hair is on fire and the rest of the students are screaming and running around in a panic. In other words, no one is doing anything useful, not even Professor Kane because, instead of putting out the fire, she's trying to put out Ian. Okay, I guess that's important, but someone needs to make sure the entire school doesn't burn down.

So I leap into action by charging into the lab and grabbing a bottle of unicorn tears to douse the flames. But then Kathleen Sketcher decides she'll try to clean up the disaster with some ill-advised spellcasting—which is *not* how you clean up a magical mess, which means she makes everything worse. Andy Kuber raises his wand to help, but before he can escalate the situation even further, I snatch up the emergency spell sweeping broom in the corner and have the catastrophe contained within a minute.

When I'm finished saving Dragonsong from turning into Inferno Island, I realize everyone is staring at me—even Ian, who's now sporting the school's worst haircut.

Then Professor Kane speaks, which is like listening to a spell, because she only ever does so in rhyme. "You are brash with a broom, young Caradine Moone. For once, not a complete vexation! Can it be that we've finally found your station?"

Shortly after that incident, I failed the wizard standardized test. I guess they don't believe in late bloomers in wizard school—no sense in tiptoeing around the cauldron, right? Because I was immediately reassigned to the MOP program—or, as I think of it, Remedial Wizardry.

For the record, I'm not completely talentless. Being good in a sticky situation (and I mean that literally) is a strong wizardly characteristic. I also have a way with magical creatures (though don't tell that to Zuki, because he'll want to argue about it). Obviously, I've got a strong basic knowledge of potions (not brewing, which I'm not allowed to do, but how to use them to clean up or nullify disasters). And, of course, I can conjure up enough magic to open my locker.

Most of the time. Some days it feels like what little magical essence is in my blood is evaporating.

But don't worry, kids. That's the message Dragonsong tells students before they take the sixth grade standardized test: if you fail, you can still harness your tiny glimmer of talent and find all sorts of "important" roles in the magical world. Maybe you'll be a recruiter, identifying magical kids who come from Bliss families. Maybe you'll work in magiculture, milking hippocampi, collecting dragon eggs, or harvesting broomcorn. Or maybe you can scrub up magical garbage for the rest of your life.

Yep, there are all kinds of tracks for remedial students, but Dragonsong doesn't let us choose—though even if I *could*, I don't know what I'd do. I'm not a people person (so recruiting is out of the question) and who wants to milk a monster? But at least the kids in other remedial programs get to wear the same uniform as everyone else. It's only us scrubs who stick out like dirty thumbs in our sludge-gray uniforms.

If you ask me, I was rushed into the MOP program. My teachers saw a Bliss with a broom, and their minds were made up. Okay, I'm not a Bliss, but I come from a Bliss family and, for some wizards, it's the same thing. (There are probably two dozen of us "Bliss kids" at Dragonsong—I don't have the actual statistics for how many of us are in remedial programs, but I bet it's a lot.)

Not many MOPs stick it out to the end of wizard school.

Currently, Dragonsong's MOP department consists of only three students—if you count Zuki, who Master Quibble "volunteered" to join us. It's no mystery why so many kids drop out of MOP. To reiterate: there is absolutely ZERO glamour in spell sweeping. Besides, it's not like you need to finish high school to work as a janitor, even a magical one. You might as well abandon your wizardly education and get on with your dismal destiny.

Of course, I don't have that luxury, because there's no way Mom would let me quit Dragonsong—she thinks it's a prestigious private school for Blisses, that I've finally accomplished something exceptional, something to make her proud. The disappointment of me dropping out would probably kill her.

Plus, if I'm being really honest, I'm clinging to this hope that there's still a chance for me. That, one day, everyone around here will wake up and see that I'm something more. Something great. Or at least something better than a MOP.

Like I said, I should never have picked up that broom.

CHAPTER 5

A Familiar Scene around Here

THAT EVENING, AFTER THE REST of my classes, I slog to the dormitories. I'm overcome with a sudden desire to call home, but that would mean trekking to the "Vault" in the administration tower, where our phones are stored because of wizards' technology paranoia. (The magical world prefers summoning mirrors, which don't leave pesky digital trails.) I only see my family during vacation or on designated weekends, which is not *that* big of a deal. I've gotten use to boarding school life. Except, when I do miss home, I *really* miss it.

As soon as I step through the doorway to my dorm, something swoops at me. I instinctively duck, only to feel tiny pinpricks tickle my scalp.

"Another bat infestation?" I wonder, casting an inquisitive glance in my roommate's direction.

Yuna is sitting at her desk, surrounded by book skyscrapers, with the Flaunette (a famous wizard composer) cranked on her phonograph. As soon as she sees me—or more accurately, what's on my head—she kills the music and scurries toward me in a panic.

"Agi! Bad owl! Bad!" She reaches up and plucks the cutest bird I've ever seen off my head. "Sorry, Cara! We got our familiars today, and I haven't managed to quite train mine yet." Unlike me, Yuna's on track to becoming a top wizard, and she takes her studying seriously—it's so like her to think she can train her familiar in half a day. "This is Agi," she announces, placing the owl on her shoulder. "It means 'baby' in Korean and—"

"Today was Familiar Day?" I interrupt, jealously eyeing Agi. I immediately identify her as a saw-whet owl. I know all the different familiars available to students—I spent the first year and a half at Dragonsong dreaming about the day when I would get mine. I could never quite decide between owl, ferret, or hedgehog. Turned out to be irrelevant because, of course, spell sweepers do *not* get familiars. Sure, I get to hang out with a talking fox, but he's not *my* familiar. Maybe if he was, he wouldn't argue with me so much.

"You should have seen the ceremony," Yuna says, stroking Agi's chest feathers. "Every student in seventh grade was there!"

I snort. "Well, not *every* student."

Yuna sighs in resignation. "I didn't mean anything by it, Cara," she says. "I won't talk about it anymore."

Now it's my turn to sigh. Yuna and I have been roommates since we first came to Dragonsong in fifth grade. We used to be close, but things have become extremely strained between us since I was demoted to the spell sweeping program. It's just so hard to sit by and watch all the cool stuff Yuna gets to do every week. Of course, Yuna's not to blame for that, and the crestfallen expression on her face clobbers me with a wave of guilt for not being appropriately enthusiastic about her big day.

"Sorry, Yuna," I tell her. "It's not your fault I'm remedial."

"Don't use that word," she admonishes me, honey-brown eyes flaring. "It's insulting."

"To . . . me?"

"To Blisses," Yuna explains. "You're in wizard school! Even if you don't like it here."

I blush, which always makes my freckles shine. I can't cast a spell strong enough to make my cheeks glow with *magic*, but when it comes to *embarrassment*? I'm top of class. "I like it here," I mumble unconvincingly. "But Blisses don't know we exist. So, you know—by definition, they're never going to hear me 'insulting' them."

"All I'm saying is you could be a little bit more compassionate," Yuna lectures, turning away with Agi.

I know Yuna doesn't mean to sound patronizing, but it's really hard for me to take her tone any other way. We've had a version of this argument *so* many times since I became a MOP. But I guess she has a point. Plus, she's recently dyed her hair silver, and it seems to add to her air of wizardly wisdom.

"Go ahead and tell me about the familiars," I say. "I want to hear."

She whips around, a hopeful smile tugging at the corners of her lips. "Really?"

I plop onto my bed and nod.

"All kinds of familiars were there—toads, ravens, even skunks!" Yuna gushes. "We were called to the front, one by one, and you had to sit on the floor, beckoning in your mind. The first familiar to answer your call was yours."

I do my best to swallow my envy—it tastes like sour milk. "Owls are the best," I tell her, contemplating Agi. Her giant eyes are simply adorable.

"I think so, too," Yuna says, stroking Agi's chest. "They can fetch things, deliver messages—well, after she's trained. Simone Hunter got a scorpion. Ugh."

"That suits her," I say.

"Be kind, Cara," Yuna chides. "I thought you were trying to—well, *your words, not mine*—'improve your attitude.' Something happen today?"

"Harlee Wu."

Yuna groans. "Come on, Cara. It's always someone else's fault with you. What imaginary thing did Harlee do to upset you?"

"It wasn't imaginary. You'll hear all about it. Don't worry. And Quibble—"

"Master Quibble," she corrects me, like everyone does.

"—took her side, of course."

"Cara, Master Quibble is always going to take her side. They've got history."

I grimace. She's right (as usual). Harlee has been at Dragonsong as long as anyone can remember, since before she was even old enough to formally attend classes. She worked one on one with Master Quibble back when he was headwizard of Dragonsong.

"Honestly, I think Master Quibble was like an uncle to her," Yuna continues. "Harlee spent *years* under his wing. They were so close, until—well, you know." She gestures vaguely to her face, referencing the mysterious catastrophic wizard duel that maimed Quibble and sent him on his three-year sabbatical. "He obviously still has a soft spot for her."

"I wish he had a soft spot for *me*," I mutter.

"Cara, don't you think—"

"What do we know about Harlee?" I interrupt. "Like, *really* know? Why did she come to Dragonsong so early?"

"You know the rumors floating around here. Some people say her parents couldn't handle her talent, so they put her in school early."

"So why don't they ever visit?" I wonder. "I've never seen them, not even on Family Days."

Yuna shrugs. "Maybe they live too far away to visit. Or . . ."

"What?" I urge after she trails off.

Yuna sits down beside me on the bed and her voice turns to a whisper; it feels like we're having something remotely akin to a roommate moment, the kind we used to share all the time, when we could call ourselves friends. I'm almost tempted to reach out and clutch her hand, like we used to do when we both first arrived at Dragonsong and felt homesick.

"Hanna Koval told me that Harlee's parents died protecting her from a dark lord's attack," Yuna tells me. "She's an orphan."

I frown. That rumor is new to me, and I instantly hate it—mostly because it just adds credence to Harlee being the so-called Chosen One. Orphaned due to an evil wizard's attack? That's *exactly* how hero stories work. The next thing you know, people are going to be saying she has some special birthmark.

Yuna sighs. "I feel sorry for her."

"Pfft!" I snort. "She's the Queen of Dragonsong!" I swing off the bed to curl up on the ledge of the single round window in our room. It offers a spectacular view of the ocean and Vancouver Island to the west—too bad it's ruined by Yuna's sympathy for Harlee. Lots of people lose parents, and it clearly doesn't make them special.

"Well, what if she *has* lost her family, Cara? You of all people should understand—"

"Me?!" I spit.

Yuna swallows. "Because, you know, your dad—"

"This isn't about me," I proclaim. "And don't feel sorry for Harlee. Chosen One? Have you actually read the prophecy?"

Yuna casts me a withering look.

"Okay, don't you find it a little vague?" I ask. "Some young hero will rise, vanquish the forces of darkness that threaten wizardkind—blah, blah, blah. I think you're conveniently ignoring the fact that there is no dark force threatening us. What's Harlee supposed to save us from? Low test scores? *Acne?*"

"Cara, why does it bother you so much anyway?"

"Because . . . because . . . you know, maybe the Chosen One is someone else."

"You just said you don't believe—"

"You know," I interject, "maybe it's *you*."

Yuna laughs so raucously that Agi flutters away and takes roost on my bedpost. I don't blame the owl—Yuna has a really awkward, snorty sort of laugh. Still, embarrassing laugh aside, Yuna is already on her way to being a fabulous wizard.

"You've got skills," I insist. "And your name! *Yuna Bang*. Even your name sounds cool."

"Oh, whew, then I can stop working so hard," Yuna declares, brushing a silvery strand of her hair aside. "I mean, if a cool-sounding name is all it takes, then maybe *you're* the Chosen One."

"What's *that* supposed to mean?" I demand.

"Seriously, Cara? Your last name is *Moone*. Caradine Moone has a pretty magical ring to it, don't you think?"

I frown. Caradine was my mom's maiden name—which means I have a last name for a first name, which is kind of weird and a little bit annoying. As for Moone, it's from my dad's British side, and I've never considered it to be *magical*. Especially given how kids in Bliss school made fun of it (use your imagination).

"This might be the first time you haven't had a comeback," Yuna tells me.

I give her a halfhearted sneer before closing my eyes to

disappear into my imagination. What would it be like being someone the whole magical world considers to be special? Just the thought of it is intoxicating. What if I were the one standing onstage during assembly, performing the Student Stunt, shifting statues around with the power of my magic, while someone else was skulking around to clean up after me? What if every time I prowled the grounds of Dragonsong, students would turn and whisper, "There goes Cara Moone"?

My life would be so different. So easy. So much better.

Then I hear a chirp and I open my eyes to see Agi fluttering over to land on my knee, as if she's somehow intuited that I need cheering up. But she only makes me feel worse. Agi's not my familiar, just a living, breathing symbol of the glorious path that lies before a *real* wizard, like Yuna.

Maybe there *is* magic in my name—but far too little in my blood.

The Dragonsong Academy
grade seven syllabus
(not for the faint of magic)

Dragonsong Academy offers a rigorous set of classes for students with a wide range of magical abilities. Of course, those abilities dictate your curriculum—regardless of what *you* want. Here's a list of exciting classes that I'm NOT allowed to take:

Astronomy, Professor Althea Paradigm
Dragonsong doesn't go by a normal school schedule, but from 1:00 p.m. to 7:00 p.m., with curfew at 1:00 a.m. (wizards tend to be more nocturnal than your average Bliss). Yuna gets to stay up past curfew on Astronomy nights and use telescopes that are so powerful that you can see the litter left behind by the astronauts on the surface of the moon. But no matter how messy astronauts are, they've probably got nothing on wizards in the slob department.

Talismanic Studies, Professor Devona Drake
The class I want to take more than any other.

Apothecarial Arts, Professor Chickory Kane

They've got things burbling, smoking, exploding—all the exciting stuff.

Spellography, Professor Galen Vitrix

How to invoke spells, though the most talented wizards don't need to vocalize their magic or even recite enchantments in their mind—they just will their desires and draw on the power of their talismans.

Metaphysical Arts, Madame Dona Kree

This is painting with sound, tasting noise, touching color—it sounds cool, but it's not for remedials, so, basically, I'm also being deprived of a formal arts education.

Translocation, Professor Hisao Akari

When wizards want to get somewhere quickly or secretly, or drench someone in a goldfish pond, they use translocation. As we all know, it leaves behind a giant mess.

Transfiguration and Metamorphosis, Professor Nadia Ska

This also leaves a huge mess. And a SMELL. Like, if magic could have diarrhea, this would be it.

Magical Mending, Dr. Selma Glimm

My sister broke her arm a couple of years ago, and she had to have a cast on for two months. Gusto busted his leg in a training exercise and Dr. Glimm fixed it in about five seconds. (What didn't take five seconds was sweeping up the residue afterward.)

Familiar Husbandry, Professor Theodore Perrandor

This sounds completely sexist to me, but Yuna assures me it's a course on how to take care of your familiars. This might be the one class she's failing, given the number of times Agi has already pooped on my pillow.

Clairvoyant Studies, Madame Chandra Aslam

This includes prophecies, so another good title for this class would be: How Harlee Wu Is Going to Save All of Wizard-kind Because She Is the Best Thing Since the Invention of the Cauldron.

CHAPTER 6

My Freckles Work Overtime

"SHALL WE DISCUSS TALISMANS?" PROFESSOR Tam asks as we file into the Ethics of Magic classroom for our last block of the evening.

It's two days after the auditorium incident, and the sun is filtering through the windows to cast a warm glow on the room. It's a cozy and inviting place—or it would be if it wasn't for Professor Tam's officious demeanor. He speaks mostly in questions, which is extremely irritating.

Gusto heads to the front of the class and settles in next to Yuna; since we're MOPs, Ethics of Magic is one of the few classes we have with her. I don't sit next to her because I'm not a front-row sort of student. Besides, Gusto has a crush on Yuna, and the one time I did try to sit near them was the most excruciating hour of my life. He turns into a pandering idiot when he's around her, and she's either completely oblivious or she's purposefully "giving him the wart" (that's an old wizarding expression I've decided to resurrect).

With Zuki tagging along behind me, I saunter to my usual

seat at the back of the class. Because it's located in a tower, the chamber is circular in shape, and the configuration of desks results in my "row" containing only one seat. But I don't mind. I'm not exactly alone, not with Zuki by my side. As predicted, his anger at me about the pop quiz quickly evaporated. (Master Quibble said we all passed, though he wouldn't tell us our scores. Maybe he thinks I'll be embarrassed to find out I scored lower than a fox.)

I'm especially grateful for Zuki's company now that all the seventh graders have started bringing their familiars to class. With a magical fox at my heels, I can almost pretend I'm on the same level as Yuna.

I get comfortable in my chair, which means leaning back and sticking my boots on the desk.

"Is that where your feet belong, Miss Moone?" Professor Tam wonders, strumming his beard, which is so long it's tied around his waist. I'd say Tam is at least seventy years old, though that's just a guess. Wizards don't tend to retire unless they're forced to (like, for example, by losing a staring contest with a gorgon).

Georgia Dirk and Simone Hunter, sitting directly in front of me, smirk at me over their shoulders.

"MOP," they mouth at me in perfect unison, which, of course, Tam doesn't notice. I'd try to cast a mascara-running spell on them—something to blotch their perfect ivory cheeks—but every classroom is curse protected (and my spell would probably fail anyway).

Thankfully, Zuki lifts his chin and issues a low, threatening growl at the girls, which causes Georgia's hedgehog familiar to squeal and burrow into her hair. Even Simone's scorpion seems to cower.

"Thanks," I tell Zuki as I obediently lower my feet. "Those two could compete with my sister for the Cruel Cup."

"What's that?" he wonders.

"Something I made up. I'm keeping a mental list of competitors. Right now—"

"Sounds like an enemies list," Zuki says.

I shrug. He's not wrong.

Tam begins his lesson. "Should you use a talisman to save a Bliss if it means risking that same Bliss seeing it? What are the ramifications . . ."

He prattles on, but I'll never be in the situation he's talking about, so my attention drifts to the many shelves that line the walls. They're filled with books and sculpted busts of famous philosophers, and nothing is arranged in any kind of order, chronological or otherwise. I suddenly spot a pair of bulbous eyes staring at me from one of the book spines—it takes me a moment to realize it's only Tam's familiar, a chameleon named Skimble. I lean in for a closer look, and she shoots out her tongue to smack my cheek.

"Hey!" I cry in surprise.

"Miss Moone, are you paying attention?" Tam asks.

"Huh? Oh. Yeah."

Georgia and Simone titter. Possibly, so does Skimble.

"Then why don't you tell us what you know about talismans?" Tam says.

Really? Could he ask me something *more* basic? "It's something a wizard uses to amplify her innate magical ability," I explain. "A tool."

"Wow, you'd need the biggest tool in the world," Georgia murmurs, just loud enough for me to hear.

"*You're* the biggest tool in the world," I snap.

The entire class turns to stare at me, prompting my stupid freckles to glow like fireflies. Picking on a MOP is like catching pixies with a melting Slurpee and a summoning spell: easy. Still, I always fall for it, always bite back.

At least Zuki's on my side. "Good one, Cara," he whispers with a chuckle.

"Miss Moone, why don't you continue with your explanation?" Tam prompts.

I roll my shoulders, try to collect myself. "Common talismans are wands, amulets, or rings. But they can be anything. There's a story that Riva Dragonsong once used a wet noodle to repel an entire horde of hydras."

Yuna, simply unable to contain herself any longer, pipes up, "Some talismans only produce specific spells—like a wand that petrifies objects, or a stone that hypnotizes animals. The most powerful talismans are the ones that a wizard constructs or forges herself."

Yuna is such a show-off sometimes. I notice that Tam doesn't bother to reprimand her for speaking out of turn, though. He nods approvingly and says, "And haven't most of you been hard at work on your talismans in Professor Drake's class?"

"Most of us," Simone declares. She brushes the shoulder of her emerald-colored uniform—her way of pointing out that I wear mop-water gray and don't get to take Talismanic Studies with Professor Drake. "I'm fashioning a wand of birch wood."

"I'm smelting a ring inlaid with a sapphire," Georgia adds with a tone of superiority.

All the other students begin chiming in with descriptions of their chosen talismans.

Josh Greene: "Skeleton key."

Lakisha Stewart: "A dragon fang I excavated with my grandfather."

Jayden Zhang: "The feather of a phoenix."

This is my entire life at Dragonsong: listening to kids gush about all the stuff they get, the stuff that I would love to have, like owls and talismans. Gusto should feel the same way as me, but he doesn't seem the least bit perturbed. In fact, he contributes to the conversation by saying, "Yuna finished her talisman this morning. A medallion."

"It's no big deal," Yuna says, shrinking in her seat.

She's such a weirdo sometimes. She loves sharing something she's learned—but if it's something's she's *done*, then she's as shy as a unicorn. If I made my own talisman, especially ahead of the rest of the class, I'd be shouting about it from the tower tops.

"Why don't you show us, Miss Bang?" Tam encourages Yuna.

Agi gives her a persuasive cluck from her shoulder, so Yuna stands and pulls a chain from beneath her robe to reveal her talisman: a thick disk of polished metal, embedded with a giant gemstone that swirls with purple and gold. It's my first time seeing it—I guess Yuna didn't want to rub one more thing in my face this week—and it's so gorgeous I nearly stop breathing.

"I'd use that in a heartbeat," I announce.

Yuna gasps and quickly tucks her medallion away. "That's . . . Cara, you can't—every wizard knows . . ."

"What?" I ask, my freckles burning bright—*again*.

"Have we forgotten that Miss Moone comes from a Bliss background?" Tam addresses the class. "She may not understand what so many of you have intuitively learned by growing up in magical environments—but which is something we must review here tonight, something that must be absolutely clear in all your minds and hearts." He pauses theatrically, building the gravity of the moment. "The bond between a wizard and talisman is *sacred*. Talismans must not be shared, bequeathed, or borrowed. It is forbidden."

When Tam doesn't phrase something as a question, then you know it's super important, like a cardinal truth of the universe. Everyone begins vigorously writing in their notebooks. Except me, of course—I'm not much of a note taker. But I am a *thinker*. Which prompts me to do something I've never done before in Tam's class: I thrust my hand into the air.

Tam blinks at me like he's on the verge of a heart attack. "You have a question, Miss Moone?"

"Why exactly *can't* you use someone else's talisman?" I ask. "I mean, I get it's a rule, but is it *possible*?"

Tam doesn't say anything. He just twiddles with his beard, as if he's trying to fathom how to answer such a ridiculous question. Or maybe, it suddenly occurs to me, he's hiding something.

"Cara," Yuna chastises me. "What you're saying—it's blasphemy. A talisman is a *part* of a wizard. Like a limb or an organ."

"Isn't that a bit overdramatic?" I ask. "Some wizards don't even use talismans to—"

"Like Harlee Wu!" Georgia shrieks excitedly.

"It's unheard of in someone so young," Simone adds.

"I heard she was just a baby when she first revealed her powers," Josh says. "Her parents walked into her room one morning and all her toys were swirling above her crib." His dimpled dark brown cheeks glow as he levitates all the items from his desk in demonstration—and to show off (which is *so* inconsiderate— someone is going to have to sweep up the resulting spell dust after class).

"It just proves Harlee's the Chosen One," Georgia declares.

Excited murmurs ripple across the classroom. Just my luck— on one of the rare occasions I try to participate in class, everyone ends up raving about Harlee. Yes, she's the only student in all of Dragonsong who doesn't use a talisman, but that was *not* the point I was trying to make. What I *wanted* to say was that there are other ways to perform magic—like brewing potions.

Professor Tam finally recovers from his uncharacteristic silence and manages to calm everyone down. "What is a talisman except an invisible cable to connect a wizard to the Field of Magical Matter?" he says. "A wizard who requires no talisman has established a pure and direct bond with the Field, one that cannot be broken. Miss Wu possesses the purest of all magic."

"The exact opposite of *you*, Moone," Simone taunts over her shoulder.

"Put a toad in it," I mutter.

"What toad? Your familiar? Oh, right. MOPs don't get familiars!" Simone says, petting her scorpion again.

"Maybe you can get a fish," Georgia says. "You know, since you like hanging out in the pond so much."

That. Does. It.

Leaping to my feet, I yell, "Frakkle it, dratch-hags!"

Tam sighs. "Miss Moone, how do you feel about detention this evening?"

If he wants to converse in questions, FINE. "How do you feel about sending the snicker sisters, too?"

"Are they the ones who cursed in class?" Tam asks.

"Well," Zuki begins, climbing to all fours, "she was just—"

Tam silences him with a single raised finger. "Do you know where to report when we're finished here, Miss Moone?" Tam asks me.

I slump back into my seat, nodding. Georgia and Simone are grinning like a couple of sirens at a shipwreck.

"Now, how about we get our discussion back on track?" Tam suggests. "When it comes to making talismans, you want to consider . . ."

"Hey, you'll get to make your own broom soon," Zuki whispers in a feeble attempt to make me feel better.

I cross my arms and glare at the ceiling. To Morgana's hearth with making a new broom. (See? I'm a real wizard—I know all the lingo.) I want a *talisman*—and there's clearly something Tam wasn't telling me about them.

Something I'm going to find out.

The Dragonsong Academy grades seven to eight syllabus (for remedials—in other words, me)

Remember the list of exciting classes that I'm not allowed to take? Compare those to the ones on my current (boring) schedule.

Beastology, Master Torolf Tandrot

Okay, not that bad, but it's mostly book learning. After this year, the "real" wizards will get to move on to training and riding different creatures, while I'll still be stuck reading about them. Sigh. If I could ride a dragon, even once, I would die happy.

Calligraphy, Master Silas Ortiz

Wizards take this because they need to write down spells in fancy books. Apparently, I need to take it because it will teach me calmness and patience, even though I will never, ever get to craft my own spell because, you know. REMEDIAL.

Ethics of Magic, Professor Kuan-lin Tam
An alternate title could be: All the Exciting Things That You Can't Do with Magic If You're a Moral and Upstanding Person, Cara Moone.

Oology, Madame Arabella Strong
Yay, look at all these preserved dead eggs. Though, last year, some prankster—okay, it was me—swapped in an actual living egg and a dragon slug hatched as Mason Matthews was examining it. He was so shocked, he fell flat on his butt and I think he even peed a little. Which of course made my day. Until I was sent to detention.

Ancient Tongues, Professor Crispin Plume
This would be cool if it involved actual tongues, but it just refers to language. Wizard spells use words from tons of extinct languages, and I guess they want spell sweepers to learn them so that we can know we're being turned into a toad five seconds before we grow webbed feet and a long ... okay, I guess tongues are involved after all.

History of Wizardry, Master Peregrine Steele
Actually, I *love* magical history. Fine, call me a nerd.

Rune Reading, Professor Emylie Leon
This is deciphering magical symbols—just in case we come

upon a cursed tomb or something during a spell sweep. It's kind of important to know that a series of stones arranged in a certain way is warning you not to disturb the mummified corpse of a two-thousand-year-old zombie witch queen.

Secret Geography, Professor Keisha Hart
A lot of cities have secret wizard quarters that Blisses don't even know about!

Wizard Yoga, Madame Kressida Stone
Heavy on meditation. Show-offs like Georgia and Simone levitate while doing their moves, which is cheating, if you ask me. Plus, levitating entails using magic, which means—you guessed it—someone (ME) has to sweep up at the end. So if you've ever complained about putting the mats away after gym class—stop it.

Magical Occurrence Purging, Master Patrick Quibble
Also known as the Janitorial Arts, Remedial Wizardry, or MOPing—which I think is particularly appropriate because I've done my share of moping under Quibble. You can say my attitude adjustment is a work in progress, but can you blame me? I spend most of my class hours in the basement with a teacher who hates me.

CHAPTER 7

What's So Bad about a Little Forbidden Magic?

STRAIGHT AFTER ETHICS, I TRUDGE down to see Miss Terse and serve my detention. Miss Terse is the gazillion-year-old school caretaker and her office is conveniently located near the MOP department.

"Already?" she huffs when I arrive at her door. "We're not even through the second week!"

No kidding. I was supposed to be a new me this year, not back to serving detention like Sixth Grade Cara. Miss Terse sets me straight to work, scrubbing the teachers' lounge toilets—which are horrifically disgusting, especially since Professor Perrandor likes to gorge on hippocampi cheese (it's a thing), even though it doesn't agree with him (as I've said, wizard detentions are terrible).

After I finish, I find Zuki sleeping on a bench outside the bathrooms. My hands are sprouting blisters from a night of scrubbing and here he is, snoring away. I make sure to "accidentally" bump into him.

"What?" he mumbles, lifting his head. "Oh! You're finally done."

"No thanks to you," I mutter.

"It wasn't *my* detention," he says defensively, following me outside. "Where you headed to?"

"Library. Shouldn't you be with Quibble? You *are* his familiar."

Zuki flicks his tails in a kind of shrug. "You're more fun than *Master* Quibble. You know, because of all the trouble you get into."

"That's not fun!"

"It is for *me*," Zuki claims with a wide grin. "Were you like this in Bliss school, too?"

I shrug. "My sister used to keep me out of trouble. Mostly."

"You could really use her around here, then!"

"No!" I say a little too quickly. "I mean—she's, uh, a Bliss. And totally different from me."

"How?"

"Pretty, smart—look, we're just different. Okay?"

"Okay, okay," Zuki says. "So, what trouble are you stirring up tonight?"

"Nothing. I just want to do some research on talismans. Don't you think it's weird that Harlee doesn't use one?"

"She's Harlee Wu! Super talented! All powerf—"

"Yeah, yeah."

We enter the library, a gorgeous building that I absolutely adore. It has thirteen stories, if you count the ones belowground (which a wizard always does) and all kinds of niches and nooks. Numerous artifacts are sprinkled throughout, and in the very center is a rotunda where an elaborate display case showcases items that belonged to Riva Dragonsong. The collection includes her wand, a gem that looks like a dragon eye, even a book of her spells.

As usual, I pause to ogle the relics, to Cara *Moone* over them. The wand is particularly beautiful, a stick of wood curling in places like a corkscrew. It's no coincidence that the wand in my notebook looks very similar to Riva's.

Eventually, my pining is complete and we head upward, because that's where I know the more obscure books are located. At the top of the first set of stairs, we encounter Miss Epigraph, the librarian.

"Cara!" she greets me warmly. "It's a beautiful night on the grounds. Most everyone is outside, enjoying the moonglow— why not join them?"

"No thanks," I tell her. "You can go, though—I'll watch things around here."

It's something I often tease her about, because Miss Epigraph *never* leaves the library. She can't, because she's a book dryad, bound to the ancient grimoires that populate the bookshelves. She never complains about her confinement, though, and I don't blame her, because if I had to be stuck in one place for all eternity, I'd probably pick a magical library, too.

"Suit yourself," Miss Epigraph says, hovering before me. The bodice of her dress is ribbed with book spines, while the skirt consists of parchment pages—though I don't think it's really a dress, but just a part of her. I mean, she *is* a book spirit. Even her hair feathers out in layers like the pages of an old tome. "Remember, curfew is at one," she adds. "I don't want to catch you sleeping here again."

She flutters away, leaving me to continue through the library with Zuki pressed against me like a little kid clinging to his parents on Halloween night. I guess you could call the library creepy, though I like to think of it as delivering the appropriate ambience for a wizardly institution. Miss Epigraph says that once you put so many magical books in one place, they start to affect one another and behave weirdly. I believe it; I've heard some books whisper, others sing, and, one time, I even heard a shriek during a late-night visit. (Okay, admittedly, it was more like early morning; this was the time Miss Epigraph caught me sleeping in the library, and the shriek came from her.)

After a few twists and turns through the aisles of the library, we arrive at a tower door that reads: *Restricted.*

"It's spell-locked," Zuki informs me.

I nod. "So, what's the spell?"

"How would I know?"

"Because you're Master Quibble's familiar. You're telling me you've never been in here with him? Not even when he was headwizard?"

Zuki nervously licks his lips. "I'm not letting you in there. It'll mean trouble!"

"I thought the whole reason you came with me was for trouble!"

I can see the internal battle rage behind Zuki's violet eyes.

"Fine," he says at last, glancing back over his tails. "Plug your ears."

I don't, of course, but I still can't make out what he says. The most important thing is that the door opens.

We hurry through, up a spiraling set of stairs, round and round until we arrive at a chamber that smells like dust, mold, and mystery. Given the number of stairs we've climbed, we must be high up, but I don't know exactly *how* high because there are no windows. There are no lights either, but I came prepared with my flashlight, so I switch it on and beam it around the cramped, circular chamber to see dozens of books chained to shelves.

"Cool," I murmur. "All the best books are locked up. That's Magic Library 101."

I trace my fingers along the ancient spines. The books grumble and moan in response, which only adds to my feeling that I'm in the right place. My eyes pause on a spine that reads: *Occuli: Forbidden Magic.*

In other words, it's got Cara Moone written all over it. I tug it out and plop down on the floor, which is as far as the chain will let me go. I shine my flashlight on the cover. Books in Dragonsong's library come in all shapes and sizes; this one is octagonal in shape and has a heavy metal clasp. I crank it open and use a bit of Cara-level spellcasting to turn the parchment pages without actually touching them. The book is old and handwritten (though wizard handwriting is typically so neat, it's easy to assume it's typesetting).

There is a long-winded introduction, but then the book gets to the good stuff: a picture of a gruesome skull with the obligatory candle perched on top of it and a definition of what an occuli is. I read out loud: "Occuli—a talisman that is used to summon magic by a wizard other than the one who originally forged, built, and/or bonded herself to it."

Zuki gasps. "You can't do that. The bond between a wizard and his talisman is—"

"Yeah, yeah—I know, sacred," I interrupt, though what I'm actually thinking is: just as I suspected, using another's talisman *is* possible. I continue reading: "After a lifetime of use, a talisman retains vestiges of a wizard's magic, thus containing considerable power. Throughout history, there have been cases of lesser wizards craving to possess talismans utilized by more talented spellcasters."

Lesser wizards. That's *me.*

"No wonder this book is restricted," Zuki moans. "I think you should put it back before—YIKES!"

On the next page, there's an illustration of a smug-looking guy with a wand. The image transforms before our eyes (it was obviously created with magic ink) to show the figure dissolving into a burbling pool of black slime. The animation keeps going in auto-loop and the page faintly whispers, "Beware . . ."

"Put it away!" Zuki pleads.

I give him a dismissive wave and keep reading: "When a wizard's talisman is used by another, it becomes known as an *occuli*. The magic cast by an occuli is extremely erratic and dangerous."

"No kidding!" Zuki says, eyes still glued to the illustration. "Cara, you can't seriously be considering this!"

I grimace. Zuki and most of my classmates would never be tempted by an occuli, because they don't think about what it's like to have remedial abilities. But I do. *All the time.*

"Let's get out of here," Zuki declares. "Enough joking around!"

"My life isn't a joke," I snap. "You go. I'm staying."

"Fine. Don't blame me when you're a pile of goo."

He skitters off, which allows me to concentrate on reading: *Because occuli are unstable, they can disrupt pure magic simply by being present during spellcasting. If an occuli user is someone with little or no magic, the results can be particularly devastating, and even damage the Field of Magical Matter.*

Great. So using an occuli might not only give me magic cancer or something, it could even damage the Field . . .

Wait a minute.

Even damage the Field.

I peer down again at the animation of the black-goo man. Then I keep flipping, searching for any illustrations of the Field itself dripping gunk. I don't find any, but . . .

"Is that what happened in the auditorium?" I wonder out loud. "Did the Field get damaged?"

I shake my head. It doesn't make sense. The only person who performed magic in there was Harlee, but she doesn't use a talisman, so . . .

I jump to my feet with a sudden realization.

What if Harlee *does* use a talisman? What if she uses an *occuli*? It could be anything: a feather, a pebble, something tucked discreetly in her pocket or the palm of her hand. Maybe she's a complete and utter fraud! Using an occuli might explain the appearance of that mouth-thingy. That day, when Professor Plume asked her why she was in the auditorium, she seemed to fumble for an answer. Which means she was up to *something*.

I'm pacing now. If Harlee can use an occuli, why can't I? She hasn't turned to goo, so maybe this book is just one of those excessive scare tactics adults like to use on kids.

My mind turns to Riva Dragonsong's relics in the rotunda below. They're just sitting there, unused. She was one of the most powerful wizards in history. If I snatched up her wand, the magic that would flow through me would be unbelievable! I would be as talented as Yuna—dratch, maybe even Harlee.

"Beware . . . ," the book whispers again, disrupting my ecstasy.

I slump down against the bookshelf. There's no way I can use Riva's wand—the idea feels wrong, even to me. In other words, unethical (happy, Yuna?).

But it sure feels good to fantasize about it. I stare down at my hands, raw and blistered from my night's detention. I have to do *something* to change my life—because there's no way I can spend the rest of my days scrubbing wizard toilets.

The test I didn't fail
(though, sometimes, I wish I had)

Let's rewind to another crucial moment in my life, back to when I was in Bliss school. I'm in fourth grade, but I've been pulled out of class to visit the downtown office of one Mrs. Raine. My family has been told she's a specialized learning assistant, but the truth is that she's a secret recruiter for Dragonsong. While Mom and my sister sit in the waiting room, Raine gives me a two-hour test. Some of it's written, some of it's visual, and some of it's telekinetic—at that point, I know something's going on. Yes, I'm not normal— but maybe I'm not normal in a *good* way. A magical way. As the test progresses, I'm sure there's a door opening for me.

Then the literal door opens, and I'm introduced to the most peculiar person I've ever met: Saraya Singh, headwizard of Dragonsong Academy. She saunters into the room, dressed in elaborate robes with diaphanous layers of black and purple, and embroidered with gemstones and strange emblems. There is hardly a wrinkle on her warm brown face, but her hair is stark white.

Singh sits in front of me and says, "A dragon steals a princess and promises to return her if—and only if—the queen can correctly guess what the dragon will do with her. The queen guesses that her daughter will *not* be returned. How should the dragon respond?"

Her stoic eyes offer me no clue as to the correct answer. After thinking for a while, I ask, "Whose side am I meant to be on?"

"That's not quite the point."

"Isn't it?" I wonder. "Because the dragon is totally planning to roast the princess. But if the queen says the princess won't be returned, then she's right—which means the dragon *has* to return her. But if it does return her, then it didn't actually do what the queen said, which means it shouldn't have to return her. It's a loop."

Singh offers me a vague smile. "Technically, it's a paradox. Do you know what a paradox is?"

"A fancy term to describe *thinking* about saving someone from becoming a dragon's marshmallow instead of actually doing something about it?"

Singh laughs out loud (something I haven't experienced since). "Do you have any questions for me?" she asks.

"Yeah," I tell her. "I'm assuming I'm the princess in your story. So, does that make you the dragon or the queen?"

Singh levels her gaze at me. Her eyes glint. Possibly like a dragon's. "Welcome to wizard school, Caradine Moone."

CHAPTER 8

Home Is Where the Dragon Is

IT'S THE LABOR DAY LONG weekend and the dragon den is sweltering. I haven't built my new broom yet, and I don't even have my utility belt. Right now, my kit consists only of a battered tin bucket and a pocketful of grain. Not exactly a recipe for success, but if there's one thing I know, it's how to trick a dragon. I narrow my gaze at the beast, listen to the threatening rumble in its throat and the snap of its maw. Its pupils flare with the keen desire to sink its claws into me and gouge my eyes out.

No big deal.

I reach into my pocket, snatch a handful of seed, and scatter it onto the ground. While the dragon and its minions are distracted, I dart into the nest, snatch the precious eggs, then zoom out before they're any the wiser.

Mission accomplished.

I stride into the house, kick off my shoes, and carry the bucket of eggs into the kitchen for cleaning. My sister's there, making herself a cappuccino with the fancy coffee machine that's a new addition to the house. How chic of her.

"Back from dragon fighting," I announce.

Su turns around slowly and glares at me. We couldn't look more different—she has a freckle-free complexion, raven-black hair, plus she's slender as a shadow. There's only one physical trait we share, and that's our dark brown eyes. There was a time when I would lose myself in the comfort of those eyes—but now? Her expression lingers somewhere between contempt and murderous intent.

"What?" she snaps.

"Chickens are descended from dinosaurs," I tell her, elbowing her out of the way so I can reach the sink. "And dragons are basically dinosaurs with bad breath. Which means going into the chicken coop is the same as venturing into a dragon's den. So: dragon fighter."

"Ugh. That school is making you worse."

Of course, there are people who collect actual dragon eggs for a living, but I keep this information to myself. I mean, I have to. That's the deal when you're the only one from a Bliss family attending wizard school. There's an entire part of my life that is a lie—which can make my visits home, like the one this weekend, more than a little challenging.

"Do you help out with the chickens when I'm not here?" I ask Su, even though I already know the answer. She wouldn't be caught dead going near chicken poop.

"They're Grandma's chickens," Su says. "She likes looking after them. There's only four of them."

I shrug. Because we live inside Seattle's city limits, we're not allowed to have a rooster (too much noise too early in the day), but one of the hens has taken it upon herself to be alpha and she's a mean piece of business, pecking the other hens to the skin. I'd be curious to see how she would fare against a real dragon. Like Su.

"You've got to start growing up," Su lectures.

She looks pale and drawn, which makes me wonder if she snuck out last night after I got home and partied into the wee hours of the morning. I mean, that's what teenagers do in the movies—I don't really know what Su does because it's not like she shares her social calendar with me.

"Get your head out of the clouds," she continues. "You're not a little kid anymore. Dragons don't exist. And there's no witch on the street corner."

I grimace. The Cara-thinks-she-saw-a-witch incident has evolved into a family legend over the years, and Su loves bringing it up to make me feel stupid.

"You're so juvenile," she rants.

For most of my life, I've worried about being compared to Su. She used to be so put together, earning perfect grades in school and behaving politely and respectfully at every social occasion. She was the model daughter.

This last summer, something happened.

It was like a switch flicked. Overnight, Su became moody, hostile . . . edgy. This morning, for example, she's wearing ripped jeans, a crop top, and thick eyeliner and black lipstick.

Plus, since I last saw her, she's had her nose pierced. It's not subtle—she's got a giant hoop through her septum. I can't believe Mom let her get away with that. I begged to get my ears pierced before going to Dragonsong, but the answer was a very adamant no.

But at least when Su was the model daughter, she still liked me. I really miss the old Su.

"Hey, do you want to do something later?" I ask.

"What? With you?"

"Well . . . yeah," I say sheepishly. "Maybe a movie or . . ."

I trail off and my request hangs there, awkwardly, like a little kid who has started across the monkey bars and now realizes she's not strong enough to make it to the other side. Su is definitely *not* coming to the rescue. She takes a long and luxuriant sip of her cappuccino, and lets me dangle.

Thankfully, Mom wanders into the kitchen, wraps her arms around me, and kisses the top of my head. "It's so nice to have you home for the weekend, Caradine."

"Yeah, a real joy," Su scoffs.

I wriggle out of Mom's grasp and she heads to the coffee machine and starts pushing buttons like she's programming the launch of a space shuttle. Apparently, this machine has become the focal point of the household—for everyone except Grandma, I assume. She's purely a tea drinker.

"Mom, can I dye my hair?" I ask. "I'm thinking red. Or maybe silver. No, red."

Su snorts. "You've clearly thought this through."

"How much did you think about it before you had someone jab a hole through your schnoz?" I retort.

"Mom, we really have to pull her out of that school," Su says. "It's giving her brain damage."

Before I can launch a comeback, she saunters out of the kitchen, a swagger in her hips. That's Su for you. She exits with flair.

With a sigh, Mom turns and contemplates me.

"Well?" I ask. "Can I? Dye my hair?"

She brushes a lock of hair out of my face. "Your hair already has a tinge of red. Why do you want to change it?"

"I mean cool red," I tell her with a scowl, "not weird ginger red." As soon as I say it, I realize how mean it sounds—because I get my "tinge" from Mom. Thankfully, I'm saved from an awkward apology by Grandma shuffling into the kitchen. She's still wearing her slippers and robe, but her hair is freshly braided, a hibiscus (my favorite flower) tucked behind her ear.

"Where's my latte?" she demands, a slight twinkle in her eye.

"Seriously, Grandma?" It feels like the entire household has flipped upside down, and I've only been away for two weeks. "How about a nice cup of tea?"

"I'm into lattes right now," Grandma says as she cranes her neck forward to examine the three thousand buttons on the coffee machine. "Hashtag delicious."

"Hashtag . . . what?"

Grandma stands to her full height, which means she has to tilt her head to see me eye to eye. She waves her phone in my face. "What's your Instagram? Give me the deets. I want to keep track of my granddaughters."

"First of all, Grandma, don't say 'deets,'" I tell her as I wrap my arms around her in a hug. "How about a good morning?" I got in so late last night that she was already in bed.

"Good morning, Caradine," she says, hugging me back. "I still want your Instagram."

"Since when are you on Instagram?" I wonder.

"Suzannah set her up," Mom says. I catch a hint of disapproval in her voice.

"Honestly, Grandma, I don't have Instagram," I tell her. "Dragonsong discourages social media."

"Good for them," Mom says.

Grandma snorts. "You have a secret account, don't you?"

"That would be Suzannah you're thinking of, Grandma," Mom says (she calls her "Grandma" because Grandma isn't *her* mom and I guess it's too weird to call her "Eleanor"). "If you find *that* account, let me know."

I detect the tension in the air. My sister has clearly been causing drama in the house; it should make me smug, but when I notice the bags underneath Mom's eyes, it just makes me worried.

"Don't worry about Suzannah," Grandma says. "Hashtag puberty. Am I right?"

I laugh in spite of myself.

"So, how's school, Caradine?" Mom asks, as she starts a latte (a latte!) for Grandma. "Getting along better with Yuna?"

"Uh, sure."

"That sounds like you're not."

"No. We're fine. I mostly hang out with Zuki."

"Zuki?" Grandma says.

I give myself a mental facepalm. Why did I bring up a talking fox? Sometimes it's *so* hard to keep my lives separate. "Uh, yeah. He's an exchange student. Visiting. Temporarily."

"I'm glad you're making more friends," Mom says with an approving nod.

"Oh, yeah, tons more," I lie. Then, eager to change the subject, I ask, "So, what are we cooking tonight?" I always get something special when I come home for a weekend. The food at Dragonsong is okay, but it never compares to anything Mom or Grandma can whip up. "I've been craving comfort food, Mom. Can we make chicken pot pie? Or something—"

Grandma pats my arm. "Tomorrow, we'll make whatever you want, Caradine."

"Why not tonight?"

Grandma casts a glance in Mom's direction and my internal alarm bells begin blaring.

"Uh, what's going on?" I ask Mom.

The coffee machine dings, but she ignores it. Instead, she takes a deep breath. "Actually, we have a special guest tonight, so Suzannah chose—"

"What?!" I cry. "Su can choose anytime. It's my special weekend! I nearly died!"

Mom's brow furls. "You nearly died?"

Whoops. I definitely *cannot* tell them about the auditorium incident. "Uh . . . coming here," I say for the save. "It takes forever. And I've been subsisting off cafeteria food for two weeks."

"Don't exaggerate, Caradine," Mom chastises me. "I've toured your school. Cafeteria? It's more like a banquet hall in a palace. Look, your sister is going through some things."

I throw a warning look at Grandma, in case she's considering another "hashtag puberty" comment.

"Tonight's important to her," Mom continues. "Brad is coming for dinner."

"I don't care—wait, who's Brad?"

"Suzannah's boyfriend. He's a vegetarian," Mom explains.

"Hashtag no chicken pot pie," Grandma contributes.

"Who cares?" I protest. "Who in their right mind would go out with Su? She's—"

"Caradine!" Mom scolds.

"Fine," I mutter as I trudge out of the kitchen. In my mind, there's a cartoon image of a mouthwatering chicken pot pie sprouting wings and fluttering away.

CHAPTER 9

Topics We Shouldn't Discuss at Dinner

SU MAKES A GRAND PRODUCTION of preparing for her big evening. If she isn't doing her nails, she's soaking in the tub or strutting around slathered in face cream. Mom and Grandma fuss over her like she's a princess. It's basically the Su Show, and I'm just shuffled off to the side. If anyone in my family *did* know that I nearly died, would they actually care?

Apparently, Su and Brad have been an item for a while, but Mom just unearthed the truth last week. At first, I assumed Mom pressured Su into bringing Brad for dinner, but apparently it was *his* idea.

When the doorbell rings at quarter to seven, Su's still preening in her room, so Mom sends me to answer the door. I swing it open and my jaw hits the floor. You'd think Su would go for the jock type, but while Brad is tall, he's also gaunt, with skin so pale that it looks like it could pick a fight with chalk over copyright infringement.

"Uh . . . come in?" I say.

He wanders in and sits on our wooden bench to unlace his

battered combat boots. The rest of his outfit consists of ripped jeans, a leather jacket, and a black T-shirt. He has multiple piercings—mostly in his ears, but also one above his left eye. "You're Cara?"

I nod, still gaping. His cheeks are so hollow that I have the impression that he subsists solely on drinking coffee and vaping. Mom caught Su vaping this summer and freaked out. My sister swore it was only one time, but she still does it—I *know*, because when I was "borrowing" her hairpin, I found a vape pen in the secret gap behind the top drawer in her bureau. It looks fancier than the one Mom confiscated, which tells me this is a habit Su has decided to embrace. I've been saving this discovery to use against Su when I really need it—but now that I've met Brad, I don't think I'll need to redeem the Su-is-still-vaping gift card anytime soon. There's no way Mom and Grandma are going to like him—he's clearly the one who introduced her to her addiction.

"You attend that fancy school," Brad says. It's an accusation more than a question, and his gray eyes dart up and down as if he's appraising me. "Su tells me it's expensive."

"I, uh, got a scholarship," I mumble, which is more or less the truth.

"Good for you," Brad says, though I'm pretty sure he doesn't mean it.

I lead him into the living room, where awkward introductions take place. Mom is gracious, and I can tell she's really trying hard to be open-minded, but I can also tell that she's making all sorts of internal judgments. Grandma is . . . Grandma. Let's just say there are a few hashtag references.

Su finally swoops down and I have to admit she's stunning, somehow casual and elegant at the same time, which is something only my sister can pull off. She's wearing a black blouse patterned with white flowers and jean shorts. Her hair has a slightly tousled look, and she's reapplied the eyeliner and dark lipstick.

When it's time for dinner, we sit around the table in our usual spots, with the addition of Brad next to Su, which makes me hope that they don't try to hold hands or something because that would be extremely cringey—to be clear, romance isn't cringey, but he is. Still, maybe that would be a better alternative than the way they sit across from me, cool and calculating, as if they have some sort of agenda.

We dish up our salad and meatless pasta and start eating. The conversation is stilted, even though Mom does her best to make small talk.

"So, Brad, graduation is around the corner, right?" she says. "What are your plans?"

I notice him glance at Su before answering. Then he clears his throat and says, "I'm interested in helping the underprivileged."

His answer takes me by complete surprise. Is it possible I've misjudged him?

Mom seems equally hopeful. "Very admirable," she says, nodding in approval. "Are you thinking of a specific society or NGO? You know, when I was younger, I worked for Doctors

Without Borders. It was—"

"I believe there are bigger injustices to address than those any traditional charity can fix," Brad interrupts.

I drop my fork. Mom has always been extremely proud of her time with Doctors Without Borders, and he's just stuck the sharpest, longest pin in her balloon. I glance over at Su, but she's just sitting there, demurely batting her eyes as if her boyfriend isn't being completely rude.

Mom maintains her composure and asks a few more questions, but every one of Brad's answers seems to be even more terse and cryptic than the one before it. I can tell Mom is drawing upon every fiber of her being to remain calm and polite, but it's like he's trying to provoke a reaction from her. She doesn't fall for it—but I do.

"What do you see in this dratch-bag?" I finally ask Su in exasperation.

Su levels her gaze at me, her black lips twisted into the hint of a smile. For some inexplicable reason, she's enjoying the most uncomfortable dinner ever.

"Dratch-bag?" she asks in amusement.

"Uh . . . it's just a made-up term. From school."

"Well, excuse those of us who don't attend a school for the exceptionally gifted at basket weaving," Su says. "Some of us have to live in the real world."

Great. I love getting picked on at school *and* at home. "Excuse *me* for getting an opportunity for once," I snap. "You get everyth—"

"Girls," Mom warns.

"Hashtag pass the bread," Grandma says. I'm not sure if she's trying to avoid conflict, or give it an extra stir.

"You don't have the faintest idea of what I do at school," I mutter, poking at my pasta.

Brad reclines, draping an arm around Su. "Why don't you tell us?"

"Yes," Mom says, grasping for any excuse to calm the conversation. "Cara, tell us more about your exchange student friend." She glances at Brad and smiles, almost apologetically. "I'm sure Su has told you; Cara's school starts earlier than regular ones."

I feel my face flush hotter than a cauldron's belly. How did this dinner turn into an interrogation of *me*? And now my earlier mention of Zuki is coming back to bite me in the butt and . . .

"Cara?" Mom prompts.

I fiddle with my food. Continually hiding the truth from my family is exhausting.

"I guess private schools can make up their own schedules," Brad proclaims.

"Apparently, they make up all kinds of stuff there," Su adds.

Mom swoops to my defense. "It's a prestigious school. They don't let just anyone attend."

"So it's for the elite," Brad says contemptuously.

"Oh—well," Mom sputters in embarrassment. "It's not like we—it's— Cara earned a scholarship. I'm sure your parents—"

"Brad's parents are dead," Su interrupts.

"Oh," Mom says. "Brad, I'm so sorry. I—"

"It's okay," he interjects calmly. "Losing them caused me to look at the world differently. To see things for what they really are. Do you know what I mean?"

He's staring at me, which is completely unnerving. For a brief moment, I feel like a fish caught on a line.

Mom feverishly scoops more pasta onto his plate. "Maybe this isn't the best topic of conversation for—"

"It's like what happened with Su's dad," Brad says.

The room goes silent.

"What do you know about my son?" Grandma asks after what feels like an eternity.

Brad's pale eyes are still fixed on me. "I know he didn't need to die."

"It was a car accident!" I blurt. "How dare you—"

"What do you know about it?" Su snaps. "You were just a little kid. You don't even remember him."

"I was six! Of course I—"

"And I was ten."

"So what?" I snarl. "You lost him *more*?"

"Girls," Mom murmurs, her voice catching. "It's not a competition. We all—"

"How about Mom, then?" I yell at Su, standing up and leaning across the table so that I can really get in her face. "How about Grandma?"

"I . . . I don't feel well," Grandma says. She stands up, accidentally knocks over her chair, then stumbles over it and crashes to the floor.

"Grandma!" Mom cries.

We all rush toward her, but Su gets there first.

"Grandma," she murmurs, squeezing her hand and helping her to her feet.

Grandma is not someone I associate with being frail, but she suddenly looks like a helpless old woman, completely bewildered. All the color has drained out of her and she clings to Su's arm like it's a lifeline.

Mom, ever the doctor, takes over. "Let's go lie down," she says, putting her arms around Grandma.

"I'm coming," I say.

"No," Mom says tersely over her shoulder. "Go finish your dinner. Both of you."

She can't be mad at *me*, can she? I didn't start the fight. Before I can defend myself, Mom escorts Grandma out of the dining room, leaving me to awkwardly stand next to Su. I turn to snipe at her, but the words die in my throat as I catch the worried, contrite look on her face. In that moment, she's the big sister I used to know, the sister I love. The shock of it—the longing for that person—stabs at me.

"Su?" I whisper.

She looks at me and seems about to say something, but then Brad calls out, "Hey, girl. I'm lonely over here."

And just like that, my sister is gone. She blinks, turns, and rejoins the dratch-bag at the table, his arm curling around her like a pale serpent. It's like she's under his spell or something. She can't see it, but he's wearing the smuggest of all smiles.

Rage explodes through my chest. I point a finger at Brad and feel my cheeks flush—for once with magic, not embarrassment—and prepare to zap Brad with the best spell I can muster.

"What are you doing, freak?" Su snaps.

Her jab prompts my second thoughts to kick in and, with a scowl, I lower my hand.

I can't punish Brad.

Yes, my magic is so meager that my spell would probably fail anyway, but the main reason? Dragonsong students aren't allowed to spellcast on Blisses. Magically wiping Brad's smile from his face would mean definite expulsion. Which means all I have are words. "Listen up, you giant—"

"Calm down, Cara," Su says. "You're so easily triggered."

I don't even think about it; I just pick up the nearest plate and hurl it at her. It sails past her head—she barely flinches—and shatters against the wall. Half the fettuccini noodles stick there, dripping sauce.

"I don't even know you anymore," I hiss as I turn and storm out of the dining room.

"Run away, sister," Su mutters. "Leave me to clean up after you. Like always."

I don't dignify her comment with a response. That plate is the least broken thing in our family.

Meet my sister, guardian angel (now retired)

Su's wrong. Yes, I was only six when Dad died, but I remember him as clearly as the image in a wizard's summoning mirror. He had a laugh that filled the entire house. When he smiled, his dark eyes danced. He could cure any hurt, especially when he hugged me and called me "Supernova." (That was his pet name for me, because I was his "tiny ball of energy.")

What I *don't* remember is anything surrounding Dad's death. Maybe it's my brain's way of protecting me. Because I can't conjure up the memories of the police coming to our door to inform us of the accident, or of Grandma locking herself in her room for a week (she had just moved in with us the year before), or of Mom having a massive breakdown—and blowout—over the phone with her own mom (the one we call "Gran"—except we don't, because we don't see her anymore). Su assures me all these things happened when Dad died, but it's like they've been completely erased from my mind, like I wasn't even present.

There's one exception, one thing I do remember, and that's being at the hospital. I'm not even sure why we were there; everyone is always vague about that part, maybe because it involves details that are too gruesome to talk about, like Mom having to identify Dad's body, or maybe because he wasn't pronounced dead until he reached the ER. In movies, when people are waiting for bad news about their loved ones, they pace the waiting room, surviving off bad coffee and vending machine snacks. That's not a part of my story.

Instead, here's me, six years old, scrambling through the hospital corridors, lost and alone—somehow separated from my family, and desperate to find them. The walls loom over me, impregnable and claustrophobic, and the harsh fluorescent lights bleach everything of color. I fumble past preoccupied nurses and ghostlike patients. As a little kid, I feel completely terrified.

Until Su shows up. She calls my name, and I turn to see her standing behind me. Her eyes are red with exhaustion, but she's dressed nicely, with her hair clumped into a pair of neat buns. Even in a crisis, she knows how to look beautiful. She might as well be an angel. *My* angel.

Then I notice she's holding Jingles, my favorite stuffed unicorn, and I instinctively reach for it.

"Come with me," she says calmly.

"I want to see Dad."

Su draws in a deep breath. "So do I."

She steers me down a hallway, and we duck into an empty room. "Let's rest for a minute," she says, curling up with me on a chair.

"Where's Mom? Where's Grandma?"

Su's eyes flutter. There's a lot in that flutter—though I don't know quite what. It's like she's pausing to come up with an excuse for why they aren't here. Why they aren't the ones hunting me down in the maze of hospital corridors.

"*I'm* here, Cara," she says eventually, gazing intently into my eyes and brushing the hair from my forehead. "Okay? You've got me right now."

"But . . ."

"I'm your sister. I'm going to be here for you. Always. *Always.*"

Then, before I can persist with my questions, she draws me close, into her warm embrace. She's not Dad, or Mom, or Grandma, but I feel protected. Safe. *Okay.*

So . . . yeah.

There was a time when my big sister was all kinds of awesome.

CHAPTER 10

Into the Witch's Den

I NEVER GET MY CHICKEN pot pie. After the meet-the-boyfriend catastrophe, everyone in my family spends the rest of the long weekend slinking around the house, avoiding each other, and sustaining ourselves on whatever can be scavenged from the fridge.

It's a relief when Mom and I climb into the car late Monday afternoon and she drives me to Port Angeles. It's a long and silent journey, and I feel the distance stretching between us, just like it has with my sister these past couple of years, since I started at Dragonsong. Once we arrive at the ferry terminal, Mom gets out of the car and hugs me tightly.

"About Suzannah. She's just . . ."

"I know. *Going through some things,*" I mimic my mom.

She sighs. "She's just really angry these days."

"Yeah, must be hard to be perfect and beautiful," I mutter under my breath. "I can't believe you let her pierce her nose."

"I—I didn't," Mom says, voice hitching. "This is my fault.

After your dad died . . . I spent too long in a daze. I put too much on her. And I . . ."

There's a lost look in her eyes. It's not something I'm used to seeing in Mom. She's a doctor; if there's one person you want next to you in a crisis, it's her. But now she seems overwhelmed and drained. Which is why I decide not to pester her about getting my hair dyed—or to rat on Su about her secret vape pen.

I'll give my sister this: she knows how to command the whole family's attention. It used to be by outshining me—now it's by making more trouble than me (and I'm the one failing wizard school!). So everything has changed, and yet nothing has. When Su's in the room, her fire sucks up all the oxygen so that there's none left for anyone else.

Especially me.

I say goodbye to Mom and trudge onto Dragonsong's private ferry, which will shuttle me across the strait to the island. I find a seat near a window, away from the rest of the returning Dragonsong kids. I spot Gusto still standing on the dock with both his parents fawning over him (they live in Portland, and obviously all made the drive up together). When he eventually wanders onto the ferry, he glances around as if he's searching for someone—probably Yuna—but when his eyes land on me, he smiles and heads over and sits next to me. He's wearing the slightly dazed expression of someone who has just experienced a weekend of family bliss. But Gusto's family is not Bliss in the wizard's sense of the word—his moms are both magical and so is his biological dad. That's about as much as I know about his family, but I'm guessing *everyone* related to him is a wizard, down to his second cousin a gazillion times removed.

In other words, he has *no* idea what it's like to spend a weekend trying to pin a secret to the ground like it's a two-year-old throwing a tantrum.

"Good weekend?" he asks.

"Disaster," I grunt. "My sister's the worst."

He nods, which is followed by a long silence between us.

"Look," he finally says, "I'm sorry about what I said in Master Quibble's office. About you being a slacker."

I sit up. "So, you believe me? About the black gunk?"

He takes a deep breath. "I never saw it, Cara. So I can't tell Master Quibble that I did."

I slump back in my seat and cross my arms. He definitely doesn't believe me. Maybe he sees me as the girl who has cried "Dragon!" one too many times.

"How about we turn the page?" he suggests. "Start fresh?"

I try to fire a sidelong spell at him, just something simple that will give him a nosebleed. He twitches his nose, then wipes his sleeve across it—no blood. *Great.*

"Look," Gusto says, "I'm an only child, so I don't get the whole sibling thing. The closest I have is . . ."

"What?" I prompt after he trails off.

"Well, uh, *you.*" His face turns crimson—for once, at least it isn't me who's embarrassed. "We don't exactly get along, but we're supposed to be on the same side. You know?"

I sigh and stare out the window again. The ferry has started moving, and we're out on the strait. Behind me is one world I don't fit into, and ahead of me is more of the same.

"Hey," Gusto says. He tugs out a stick of witch's delight and offers it to me, like a truce. He's trying—which is more than I can say for Su.

Or myself, I guess.

"Thanks," I tell him, taking the candy. "I'm sorry I let you take the rap for Ryan's locker last year."

"New page," Gusto says simply.

I nod and bite into the witch's delight. It's the best thing I've eaten all weekend.

As we ascend the stairs to the school from Dragonsong Island's dock, everyone else is still bubbling with excitement about their weekend. Gusto sees Josh, his roommate, and rushes over to catch up with him, leaving me on my own again.

I pass through Dragonsong's grand and imposing gates, into the front courtyard, which consists of a meandering stone pathway lined with maple trees. It's a beautiful, awe-inspiring sight, but I feel the need to escape everyone's exuberance, so instead of entering the Crucible, I shoot off toward the safety of the garden.

As soon as I step through the doorway, I scowl. So much for peace and privacy—Harlee Wu has stolen my favorite bench, near Riva Dragonsong's statue, legs curled up beneath her as she doodles in her sketchbook. I've been so focused on Su all weekend that I almost forgot about my *other* nemesis.

I guess Harlee didn't leave Dragonsong for the weekend. Maybe her parents live too far away (I'm still not willing to go with the orphan theory). For a moment, I just linger there, watching her from across the pond, but she must sense me because she suddenly glances up. Her normally stoic facade seems to briefly flicker. Then she closes her sketchbook and quickly slides it beneath her cape, almost as if she has something to hide.

What if Harlee *is* using an occuli? What if there's evidence in her book? What if the occuli *is* her book? I take a tentative step toward her, and she's on her feet in an instant. With a flourish of her cape, she turns and exits the garden through an opposite doorway. She's up to *something*, so I decide to follow her. I go as quickly as I can without being obvious that I'm tailing her, only to turn a corner and arrive at a dead end: the locked entrance to the Poison Patch. That's not its official name, but that's what everyone calls it because the plants inside are super dangerous; some of them can knock you flat just by whiffing them.

There's no sign of Harlee anywhere. I rattle the gates, but they're locked. Harlee might know the spell, but I didn't hear the gates open. So where did she go? I turn and scan the way behind me. She could have translocated, but I don't see any spell dust.

I hurry back to the nearest stone wall. There's probably a secret passage somewhere—Dragonsong's rumored to have tons of them. Even though I've logged some serious investigative hours, I've yet to discover one—but there's a first time for everything. I feverishly start pressing on the various stones in the walls, seeking that telltale click. Nothing happens, but I'm not about to give up. I keep pressing.

"Whatchya doin'?"

I whirl around to see Zuki sitting there, his long white tails swishing nonchalantly.

"Nothing," I say.

"Good weekend?"

"Why does everyone keep pestering me about it?"

"It's called small talk. That's what people do."

"Yeah, you're not exactly a person."

"I will be as soon as I get nine tails," Zuki retorts. "Anyway, come on."

"Where?"

"It's past sundown! You were supposed to see Master Quibble to make a new broom!"

"Oh, right—how could I forget such an exciting appointment?"

Zuki has already turned, so, with an extra-loud sigh, I follow him into the depths of the school, past the MOP workroom, past Quibble's office, and down another flight of steps. I've never been down this low; it feels extremely dungeon-like.

Eventually, we reach a thick wooden door and I push it open to find a warm and dimly lit chamber filled with the musty smell of straw. There's a fireplace in one corner, a cauldron suspended above its glowing embers. There are shelves lined with a variety of vials, jars, and canisters and a workbench covered with all the stuff to make sweepers: tools, bundles of broom-corn, twine.

If this isn't a witch's lair, then I don't know what is. The chamber clearly doesn't fit the Q-Man's personality; he must have inherited it from his predecessor, and I guess he hasn't gotten around to sucking all the fun out of it yet.

Quibble himself is sitting on a simple wooden chair positioned near the fireplace. He doesn't turn to look at me, doesn't even nod. He just says, "Let's get to work, Caradine."

Well, at least he didn't ask me about my weekend.

The science of sweeping

When I was first put into the MOP program, I was given a broom. It never occurred to me to wonder how or where it was made. I didn't really care and, to be honest, I still don't. But after my time as a spell sweeper, I know a lot about what brooms *do*.

To begin with, it should be obvious that spell sweepers don't use any old broomcorn. There's an entire magicultural sector devoted to the cultivation of enchanted grain, and that's what makes our brooms so different from the ones you keep in your pantry or on your front porch.

Want a more detailed explanation? In an ordinary, non-magical chemical spill, acids and bases are used to neutralize each other. Enchanted messes need to be neutralized, too. The remedy depends on the mess (please refer to the time I used unicorn tears to extinguish the dragon snot explosion in the Apothecarial Arts lab). When it comes to spell dust? The best way to neutralize it, to prevent it from turning feral, is to sweep it up with magical broomcorn. As the broomcorn absorbs the dust, it changes color, usually red, blue, or purple, depending on the type of residue—definitely *not* black, like what happened with my broom in the auditorium.

Spell dust (at least the nontoxic kind) also causes the broomcorn to *grow*, which means we have to continually give our brooms haircuts. Which is pretty easy, since you just trim off the part that's turned a color. At that point, since the broomcorn has already neutralized the residue, the cuttings are safe and can go into a designated compost heap (ours is located near the Poison Patch).

Incidentally, there's another material that turns out to be good at purging spell dust: the tails of a magic fox. We trim the hair from Zuki's tails after each purge, like we do with our brooms—if we don't, Zuki gets a little too hyper after a spell sweeping, kind of like a little kid after eating too much sugar. Sometimes I wait a little bit to give him a haircut, just to watch him bounce off the walls. (I mean, spell sweeping has to have some sort of perk—right?)

CHAPTER 11

A Clean Sweep

AS I LINGER BEHIND MASTER Quibble, I remind myself that a bad attitude is definitely not going to help me escape the MOP program. Maybe if I can make a good broom, I can make a good impression—and someone important, like Headwizard Singh, will notice.

It's not like I have another choice at the moment, anyway. So, with a sigh of resignation, I say, "Where do we start?"

"We soak the fiber," Quibble says, gesturing to a workbench where there are bales of broomcorn. "Grab a bundle. Enough for your sweep."

I see that the fiber has already been trimmed just past the knuckle of the corn, where the head meets the stalk. I bring a thick handful to Quibble. He swings the hanging cauldron out on its arm, then sticks the broomcorn in vertically, so the stalks are immersed, with the brushy tops sticking out. He pours the contents of a nearby kettle into the cauldron, then swivels the whole contraption back over the embers and stirs them into flames.

"What are we soaking the fiber in?" I ask. "Jackalope blood? Basilisk venom?"

His only reply is to turn around and use the last dribble in the kettle to top off his teacup.

"Oh, just water," I say with disappointment. Glancing around again, I realize that the containers on the shelves don't contain anything quite so exciting as bat wings or newt eyes, but your more pedestrian items such as stains and varnishes.

"Tea?" he asks as he refills the kettle in what looks like the first sink ever invented. The water comes through a handpump.

"Uh . . . no thanks," I reply as I notice a cringey sign above the sink that says *Home Sweep Home*, decorated with flowery brooms. I suddenly wonder if this is going to be me in fifty years, bumping around in the equivalent of a dungeon, drinking tea and discussing broom making with a student I can't stand.

Dratch. I hope not.

"We need to soak the broomcorn to make it pliable," Quibble explains. "For now, we wait."

He returns to the chair and I take the one next to him, Zuki curling at my feet. Big surprise: broom making is boring. An awkward silence hangs in the air, and I do my best to avoid fidgeting, waiting to see if the Q-Man will engage with me.

He doesn't.

It's *so* frustrating and, for the kajillionth time, I wonder why he has such a problem with me. Sure, I'm not some star student like Harlee Wu, but I'm still worthy of polite conversation.

Then, thinking of Harlee makes me realize that I have the perfect person sitting in front of me to provide intel on my sworn enemy, and I decide to speak up. I mean, who cares if it upsets him? It's not like he can hate me *more*.

"Master, I want to ask you something."

He nods vaguely, his gaze lost in the flames.

"Where are Harlee Wu's parents?"

He doesn't reply; just fiddles with his chin hair.

I'm not going to let him get off that easy. "I'm just curious. I know you used to personally mentor her, and . . ."

Zuki lifts his chin from his paws, his tails twitching frantically. I'm pretty fluent in magic fox tails, and they're saying: "Abort! Abort!"

"Caradine," Quibble says, somehow quietly and sternly at the same time. He leans forward and adjusts the broomcorn in the cauldron. "Harlee's story is not mine to tell. Or yours to gossip about."

"I'm not gossiping! I just thought that—because you're so close to her—"

"Not anymore," Quibble murmurs. "Come, let's speak of other things."

"Ooh! Let's talk about *my* story!" Zuki yips excitedly.

What could be construed as a smile flickers across the Q-Man's face. It's possible that the one thing that brings joy to his life is Zuki.

"Tell the story of how you found me," Zuki begs. He's like a little kid, asking to hear about the day he was born.

Quibble scratches the fox behind his ears. "It was a long time ago. Professor Akari and I were visiting Tokyo when we caught wind of someone smuggling magical animals, so we decided to investigate. Ended up in this depraved den tucked away in the Golden Gai district. There were so many creatures. A phoenix, a qilin foal, even an assortment of eggs."

"And me!" Zuki contributes.

Quibble nods. "I found you hidden in a barrel with a false bottom. You were in rough shape, but you instantly bonded with me."

"And you nursed me back to health."

"You had one tail then, but Professor Akari and I suspected you to be a kitsune," Quibble explains.

"There are all kinds of fox spirits, Cara," Zuki takes over. "They're called *gumiho* in Korea, *Jiǔwěihú* or *húli jīng* in China, and—"

"Yeah, yeah," I mutter, irked by how much he's loving the attention. "I take Beastology, you know."

"Your fur was white as the moon," Quibble tells Zuki. "That's why I decided to call you 'Kazuki.'"

"It means 'brightness' and 'hope,'" Zuki informs me.

"Makes sense," I quip. "Because I often hope that you won't annoy me."

Quibble sighs and rises from his chair. "I think that's enough reminiscing. Come, Caradine."

He guides me over to the corner of the room, where there are several barrels containing long branches.

"Pick a handle for your sweep," he instructs me.

Hanging on the wall nearby is Quibble's own broom. It has a handle that branches like a Y at the end, which means it has two heads and admittedly looks very cool. I begin poking around the barrel, wondering if I can find a similar piece of wood. I don't—but I do find various shapes, colors, and lengths. Some are straight and true, some twisty with natural knots and grooves.

"I don't know which one to choose," I confess. "Does it matter?"

"All things matter."

I roll my eyes at his cryptic answer. I know for a fact wood selection is ultra important when it comes to fashioning a wand—I've done my research. Different woods have different strengths, different symbolic meanings. But I'm not sure how—or if—any of this relates to broom handles.

"Bamboo or birch for flexibility," Quibble explains. "Fir for lightness. Hickory for strength."

I sigh. So, basically, there is zero *magical* significance to the type of wood you choose for a handle. But I'm not about to give up quite yet, so I root deeper into the barrel; there has to be an option that's not quite so mundane. That's when I find it. Hiding down below, almost cowering behind the other branches, is a shorter, twisted stick. I pull it free and set it on the workbench. It's curved in the middle and has two prongs jutting out from either side.

"What kind of wood is this?" I ask.

"Ah . . . dragonwood."

The base of my neck tingles; this is more like it. "For heat? For power? For extra *magic*?"

The Q-Man grunts. "For having something with stumps and knobs that gets caught on your cuffs."

I stare at him, heartbroken.

"The branches are twisty, like a dragon's body," Quibble proceeds to explain. "That's how the tree got its name. A rare tree, known only to wizards. If you're looking for something with a little more practical—"

"I'll take it," I breathe, returning my gaze to the wood. Forget practical—this branch looks almost as cool as the Q-Man's broom handle.

He has me polish the wood, which brings out its vibrant red and tawny colors. By the time I'm done to his satisfaction, the straw has finished soaking. Then comes the hard part—and by hard, I mean physically hard. We attach several stalks of broomcorn to the handle, below the knuckle of the brush, securing them with twine, which we unwind from a metal spool.

Quibble demonstrates on a separate handle, but makes me do my broom myself. The whole time I have to keep the twine taut between my handle and the spool, twisting the broom as I go. I brace my leg against the spool carriage and lean back to get as much tension in the twine as I can while I wind it round and round the broomcorn. It takes a lot of exertion, and because I don't know what I'm doing, I have to start over a few times.

Eventually, I settle into a hypnotic rhythm, the straw

crackling softly as I labor. That and Zuki snoring his way through a nap are the only sounds in the workshop. The earthy smell of the broomcorn fills my nostrils and there is a slight flicker of warm light emanating from the hearth. You could almost say it's a magical moment.

By the time the head of broomcorn is attached, I'm sweating. But that's just the first part; next comes stitching and plaiting the tops of the stalks, then more stitching. Who knew making a broom was so complicated? The final step is attaching a strap, so I can carry it across my back.

When we're done, Quibble inspects my work. "Caradine, I believe that's the longest I've ever heard you go without sass."

I grunt and wipe my hand across my brow. I'm exhausted.

Quibble holds my broom on two open palms and extends it to me. There's an air of ceremony in the moment and maybe even a slight thrum of magic, though I'm so tired I'm probably just delusional.

"Well?" he asks. "What do you think?"

I take the broom, running my fingers along the dragonwood and across the plaited straw at the top of the head. Next, I twirl it across the floor and feel the whisk of the broomcorn against the old and worn stones. I finally look up and grant Quibble a nod. I know a broom isn't a talisman, that I can't have a bond with it the way a wizard does with her wand, but here's the thing: it's possible I love my broom.

It's almost too bad I don't plan on staying a spell sweeper.

CHAPTER 12

Some Lockers Are
Messier than Others

"I WISH I COULD MAKE *my* own broom," Gusto says as we climb the stairs after our evening MOP class. It's Friday, and he's been enviously eyeing my sweep all week.

"Want to speed up the process? Try losing yours."

He gapes at me, appalled.

When we arrive at the Crucible, it's buzzing, mostly because it's Friday night. Josh calls to Gusto, then tosses him a moon disc (the wizard version of a Frisbee), and they race away to the courtyard. At least I have Zuki by my side.

"Want to go to the library later?" I ask as we approach my locker. "I could use your help. If you know what I mean."

"No way!" Zuki says. "I'm not helping you break in ag—OWWWW!"

His ear-piercing yowl causes the entire Crucible population to freeze—except for me. I whirl around in a panic.

"Someone stepped on my tails," Zuki moans. "My luxuriant tails! My gorgeous sweeps! My beautiful brushes!"

I lift my eyes to find myself staring at Harlee Wu.

"Be careful with those tails of yours, Spooky," she chides softly.

"It's Zuki," I retort impulsively.

"It's okay, Cara," Zuki says sheepishly, curling his tails around his legs. "It's just a pet name."

"You're not a pet," I snap—though, as soon as I say it, I realize that if Harlee used to be close to Quibble, then she probably also spent a lot of time with Zuki. The idea of her having history with *my* magic fox buddy makes me feel near dizzy with jealousy.

Then I realize that Harlee is looking at me—though not in a good way. It's like she's getting the sum of me, and the number isn't very high, which makes my stupid freckles shine.

I back up, cradling my books like a shield, until my heels bump against my locker.

"I know you," Harlee says.

"She's just a MOP," Georgia titters.

As usual, she and Simone are lurking around Harlee, fangirling and hoping to pick up her scraps. Which is actually not the best analogy, because currently the scraps are *me*.

"Don't you have something to sweep up, Cara?" Georgia sneers as a bunch of other students begin to gather. "Maybe some *freckles*? They seem to be *everywhere*."

People start to snicker, but I notice that Harlee's not one of them. What she *is* doing is narrowing her gaze at me. "You're the one from the auditorium," she says.

"Yeah, you saved her from face-planting into the stage," Simone pipes up.

"Too bad, might have improved her," Georgia adds.

"Put a toad in it, Georgia," I blurt.

A smile flashes across Harlee's face. I'm not sure if it's because of Georgia's insult, or my comeback (which would be a typical villain move, because villains don't care if their minions get mistreated). Then she flinches, as if she's suddenly realized something, then turns to leave, which she does with a flourish of her crimson cape. (Dratch! Why is she so cool?!) I just stand there like an idiot until Zuki whimpers again—he's such a baby when it comes to his tails—and I'm snapped into action.

I slam my textbooks to the floor. "Apologize to Zuki, Harlee," I command. "*Now.*"

The snickering stops. It's so quiet you'd be able to hear a speck of spell dust drop.

Harlee slowly turns back around. "I . . . what? It was an accident."

I roll my shoulders. I know the best thing to do at this moment is to stand down, stop stirring the cauldron. But I've had enough.

"Maybe *you're* the accident."

Now there is a lot to hear in the Crucible—gasps and nervous mutterings. It might be the first time in the history of Dragonsong Academy that someone has called Harlee a name.

As for Harlee herself, there's no flicker of emotion now—a

full scowl rises on her face. "What did you say?"

I touched a nerve. I'm not sure why exactly—but *good*. "Just trying to open my locker," I say as nonchalantly as possible. "Oh, and you're an accident."

Harlee's lips tremble, but she doesn't say anything. Instead, she steps right in front of me and seems to inflate in size, like a volcano on the verge of eruption. The fire of magic rises in her cheeks. An intricate pattern of swirls and sparks blossoms on her skin, causing it to shine with a radiant light. It's so mesmerizing I forget to breathe.

Next, she snaps her fingers, and my locker door springs open behind me, which sends me stumbling to the side. Then things explode out of my locker, and by things, I mean *everything*: books, my broom, my spare clothes, my utility belt, and my pink UNICORN UNDERWEAR. (Because, yes, it's still stuffed in there from three weeks ago.)

Harlee is subtly twirling her finger, making my stuff whirl around her like it's caught in a slow-motion cyclone, which means it's on display for the entire school population to see. I really, *really* should have taken my dirty clothes to the laundry room.

"Dratch!" Simone cries. "When was the last time you bought underwear, Moone? When you were six?"

I don't say anything; everyone is killing themselves with laughter and all my nerve has shattered like imitation witch crystal.

Harlee retracts her finger, and everything collapses to the

floor. The broom ends up standing on its head, my pink unicorn underwear dangling from it like a flag on a pole. Harlee's cheeks return to their normal beige color, then she turns on a heel and stalks away. Everyone else lingers, jeering and pointing while I slouch there, completely mortified, my freckles burning. But eventually the fun of humiliating me wears thin and they wander away.

Zuki grabs the handle of my broom in his mouth and lowers my underwear toward me—I quickly snatch it and cram it into a pocket of my robe.

"It's okay, Cara," Zuki says. "I'll help y—"

"Just leave me alone," I tell him, trying to stifle tears.

"But—"

"Go away!" I roar, which makes him jump back in surprise. "OKAY?"

He releases a quiet whimper. Then, tails drooping, he slips away, leaving me to collect my stuff, which is scattered everywhere. In addition to my belongings, there is a healthy coat of spell dust everywhere. One more thing for me to sweep up.

Su's hairpin, which had also been stuffed away in my locker, has rolled up against a pillar. As I retrieve it, I look up to see our school crest, which features a friendly dragon (the one Riva was flying on when she made this island). Below the crest is a banner with a motto that reads: *Dragonsong Academy—where young minds soar.*

Yeah, I think glumly. *And sometimes your underwear, too.*

★ ★ ★

I linger beneath the Dragonsong crest, trying to compose myself. Despite my best efforts, the tears come, rolling in thick streams over the freckled landscape of my cheeks.

Eventually, I shuffle back toward my locker, collecting more of my possessions as I go—and that's when I hear it: a faint and familiar grumbling. It's quieter than the one I heard in the auditorium, but there's no mistaking it. I spin around, desperately hunting for the source. Because it's Friday night, the entire Crucible is deserted.

The lights flicker.

Great. I'm alone. With whatever this thing is. Why is this happening *again*? And only to *me*? The grumble repeats, and this time I realize it's coming directly from my locker.

Where Harlee spellcast.

Occuli may even damage the Field. That's what the *Forbidden Magic* book said.

Both times I've encountered this mouth-thingy, it's appeared *after* Harlee's performed magic. Which means she's the common denominator. Which means my theory that she's using an occuli must be right . . .

Right?

My churning thoughts are interrupted by more belching from my locker. The door is still ajar, so I creep forward, brandishing Su's hairpin like it's a sword. Dragonsong lockers may look like old-fashioned wardrobes, but I know I'm not going to find anything so wonderful in there as Narnia. I yank the door fully open to see a slit hovering in the air, just like the one I confronted in the auditorium. The first time around, I thought of it as a mouth, but now I see it as a wound, a lesion on the Field of Magical Matter. And, just like a wound on a body might ooze pus, this one's dripping with black slime. A smell of rot punches me in the nose.

My first instinct is to race off and find Gusto—or better yet, Master Quibble—so I can prove I'm not making this up, so they can see for themselves that this isn't just a case of extra-feral magic. But the gunk is starting to trickle onto the bottom shelf of my locker and drip onto the floor. It's more important to deal with this. Like *right now.*

There's no way I'm touching the gunk with my new broom, but I remember from my last encounter that I threw an assortment of neutralizers and cleaners into the slit, and that's when it closed. Maybe it's one of them that solved the problem.

I retrieve my utility belt, lying nearby on the floor, jam Su's hairpin into a spare slot, and begin running my finger along the vials tucked away in the various loops of leather (thankfully, I restocked after the auditorium incident).

"Griffin tears, caladrius gland secretions, qilin powder . . ."

I pretty much threw them all into the mouth-thingy last time, but now I want to be a bit more methodical in my approach. Putting on my goggles, I decide to start with griffin tears and dribble some on the gunk. It hisses in response, but keeps oozing forward. Next, I try the qilin powder (it's ground up from the antlers they shed annually) by casting a handful into my locker. The slime seems to slow down, releasing a noxious odor, and the slit snarls, but it doesn't disappear. Undaunted, I use the gland secretions from a caladrius, a magical bird that can draw the illness right out of a sick person. The vial already has a nozzle apparatus attached to it, so I begin misting the poisonous goo—and the mouth-thingy.

It has an instant effect. The slit emits one last groan, then shuts, and the slime solidifies into an ash-like dust. I keep misting the remaining slime, but it doesn't quite have the same effect—it stops spreading, but remains viscous. After a bit more experimentation, I realize it takes a combination of the gland secretions and qilin powder to neutralize it. I make a mental note to brew a proper mixture later, but for now I perform the job by layering both substances until all that's left is neutralized dust. It's still a mess, but at least a safer one—which I confirm once I cautiously touch my broom to the nearest pile of dust and the only thing that happens is regular old absorption.

I collapse against my locker and exhale in relief.

It worked.

But now there's a bigger problem gnawing at me. If Harlee *is* responsible for these ruptures, if she *is* using an occuli, what am I supposed to do about it? I can't confront her (clearly, that goes badly!). I can't just stroll into Quibble's office and accuse her of using an occuli—he doesn't believe me about the toxic slime, so he's definitely not going to believe this.

I close my eyes in concentration. I need to figure this out. And if I can prove that Harlee's responsible, then everyone will finally see the truth about me—that I'm not just some useless MOP who's only good for being picked on.

What I need is more evidence.

Brooms aren't for flying,
not even when it comes to wizards

These are the essential items in a spell sweeper's kit:

Broom
Most people think broom + wizard = flying. But take it from someone who actually attends wizard school—no one straddles a broom and jumps from the top of a Dragonsong tower unless they've drunk too much of Madame Kree's secret-recipe Halloween punch (which apparently happened with Chloe Quill one year).

Goggles
Good for protecting your eyes from residue splatter or from the venom that an attacking creature might spray in your direction. I only use them when absolutely necessary because even wizards don't seem to have conjured up a solution for preventing fog-up.

Sweeper scarf

These are woven from the fiber of elf's breath (a very purple and very pretty plant), which has excellent properties for filtering out toxic fumes. We wear our scarves around our necks and pull them up around our faces when required.

Steel-toed boots

Because when dragons stomp, they apparently don't mess around.

Gloves

Made with special residue-repellant material. A pretty good idea, because you definitely don't want magical gunk under your fingernails.

Utility belt

Next to my broom, this is my most important piece of equipment because it's where I store my broom snippers and vials of stain removers and neutralizers. It also includes a collapsible containment box—in the event that we encounter small magical entities, we can unfold the box and use it for transporting the entity to a proper wizard for inspection.

(Side note: This doesn't really make sense to me, because the sweeper code of conduct explicitly states that we should not interact with a magical entity.)

(Side note 2: It's really hard not to interact with a magical entity when it is trying to eat you, in which case the last thing you're thinking about is how to fit it into this tiny containment box.)

Barricade tape

You're probably familiar with the bright yellow "caution" tape for securing the scene of an accident. When we do a purge in Bliss territory, it's procedure to rope off the entire area to ensure no one stumbles upon any magical activity. Our tape reads: *Chemical Spill Containment Site: Do Not Cross*—because no Bliss would take *Danger: Feral Magic at Work* seriously.

Miniature dustpan

Useful in both the wizarding and the Bliss worlds.

Flashlight

Same.

CHAPTER 13

My Day Is a Train Wreck

THANKS TO THE LOCKER INCIDENT, I'm the laughing-stock of the school (I mean, more than usual), so I decide to lie low for a few days. I eat in my room (Yuna, sympathetic to my plight, brings me meals) and skip classes once the weekend passes. Zuki and Gusto knock on my door twice a day to check on me, but I chase them away each time, preferring to stew, sulk, and read wizard fairy tales. (They're mostly about dark wizards such as Theradune the Betrayer and Eurybia the Eradicator, and are the equivalent of Bliss horror stories.) I also spend some time mixing together a concoction of qilin powder and caladrius gland secretions—though I have to wait until Yuna's not around because, technically, I could get in serious trouble for mixing my own potion.

By Wednesday night, my cabin fever has reached its limit. The sooner I start investigating, the sooner I can figure out exactly what is going on with the Field's ruptures and if Harlee is responsible. I decide the first step is to break into the chamber of student records in the administration tower. There *has* to be something in there about Harlee's magical abilities (or lack thereof). I wait for Yuna to fall asleep, then sneak out of the dormitory.

The moon is a crooked smile in the night as I tiptoe across the courtyard. I take a few detours to avoid the sight lines from certain windows, but eventually arrive at the thick wooden door of the administration tower. I give the handle a turn because, hey, it's worth a try.

"Who disturbs this dragon's slumber?"

The crackling voice comes from the door—more specifically the metal dragon ornament in the very center. I must leap three feet into the air. I had no idea the dragon could talk or move. Then again, I've never tried to access the tower after hours. Besides, I should have known—there's probably some wizardly bylaw making it illegal to build a magic school without at least one talking door.

"So, you're like the sentry?" I wonder. "What do I have to do? Answer a riddle or something? Is it: *What walks on four legs in the morning, two in the afternoon, and one when the moon comes up?* Answer: a wizard. Okay, let me in."

The dragon flares its nostrils, then squints at me, causing the streaks of rust and grime on its metal surface to crackle.

"Uh, you know. Because she's standing on one leg, casting a spell. It's a famous—"

"Are you feeling any mental or emotional distress?" the dragon inquires.

"Uh . . . *yes!*" I reply in a moment of inspiration. "I *really* need to call my mom, and my phone's in—"

"Then I will hail an administrator for you."

"No! Can't you just unlock the door? Because—"

"Whatchya doin'?"

Another three-foot leap in the air. At this rate, I'll make the Olympics. When my heart has returned to my chest, I turn to see Zuki swishing his tails at me.

"Why are you always lurking behind me?" I demand.

"Because Master Quibble is always looking for you!"

"It's the middle of the freakin' night!"

"Exactly. Why weren't you in your room? Come on—Master Quibble wants you. *Right now.*"

As we descend into the subterranean levels of the school, a new dread overtakes me. Quibble's definitely angry that I've been skipping classes, but that's hardly enough to beckon me at such a weird hour. What if he found out about the Locker Incident? If he thinks I picked a fight with Dragonsong's cherished student, then I'm going to get it.

"Did you tell Quibble about, you know, what happened with Harlee?" I ask Zuki.

He glances at me with his violet eyes. "I don't talk to *Master* Quibble about Harlee. He finds it . . . upsetting."

"Why?"

Zuki frowns. "I don't like talking to you about Harlee either."

"Because?"

"You *also* find it upsetting."

I snort, mostly because I don't have a good comeback. We

★ 123 ★

enter the office to find the Q-Man pacing behind his desk, teasing his white chin hair. For some strange reason, Gusto is also present.

"Caradine," Quibble says, without looking at me. "You've missed my classes this week. Augusto and Kazuki said you've been ill."

"Well, I . . . uh, I'm okay. Now."

"Then pack your things."

I freeze. "Wh-what? You're expelling me?"

Quibble grants me a rare and startled look. "What? *No.* We're all packing. We're going on assignment. *Tonight.*"

"Assignment?" I ask, throwing Gusto a puzzled glance, but all he does is nervously finger the pouch on his belt where he keeps his supply of witch's delight. I turn back to Quibble. "You mean, like a training exercise?"

"I'll explain on the way," he says. "Bring your gear."

It's still dark when Quibble pulls the battered old van off to the side of the road. The vehicle belongs to the school, but it's unmarked—when you're a secret society, it's best not to advertise. We took the van across the Strait of Georgia on one of Dragonsong's private ferries to land at Horseshoe Bay, near Vancouver. Then it was another two hours up the Sea-to-Sky Highway to where we are now—which, if you ask me, is the middle of nowhere. So, basically, we've been up all night, and I'm exhausted. Wizards have quicker ways of traveling, but I guess MOPs don't qualify for first-class dragon travel.

We climb out of the van and stretch. A blush of pink is just beginning to show in the sky.

"You still haven't told us what we're doing," I say to Quibble after a long yawn.

"That's because you fell asleep," Zuki informs me.

I shrug and stretch again.

"We're going to a site that represents a dark stain on wizard history," Quibble replies solemnly. "One of Dragonsong's History of Wizardry classes took a field trip here in August; everything was fine then, but now Bliss news has been reporting some irregular happenings."

"Irregular how?" I ask.

He's already crossing the deserted road, heading toward the trees, his double-headed broom slung over his shoulder.

"You think someone from Dragonsong cast a spell here?" Gusto asks me as we buckle on our belts.

"If they did, and didn't clean up, then we've got a feral spell dust situation," I reply.

By the time our brooms are strapped across our backs, Quibble is at the head of a forest trail, roping it off with caution tape to dissuade any snoopy Blisses. As we catch up to him, I spot a sign marking the trailhead: *Train wreck site and suspension bridge.*

"Train wreck?" I wonder aloud, but Quibble is already off, so we hurry after him. Gusto is soon gnawing on a stick of witch's delight; he must catch one of my pining glances, because he tosses one to me. Mom would have a heart attack if she saw how I'm starting my day, but candy breakfast is better than no breakfast at all.

After a half hour of walking (and me complaining about the walking), we arrive at a short suspension bridge. There's an information board nearby, describing the site we're about to enter, but the Q-Man doesn't pause, so neither do I. Once we're across the bridge, a quick trek up a slope brings us to our destination, just as the sunrise is making its full display. It's as if the shafts of light are doing their best to cast a magical filter upon the place, but it doesn't really work.

A catastrophe happened here.

Train cars are strewn haphazardly about the forest floor, their mangled forms slumped amid the trees. They seem simultaneously solemn and garish because even though they're battered and rusted, they're also covered in graffiti. Obviously, some industrious Blisses tried to brighten the site up with their colorful artwork, but it only adds to the eeriness of the place.

"They could film a zombie movie here," I tell Zuki.

"Or your biography," he quips.

"Huh?"

"You know—it's a train wreck. Get it? Because of what happened with H—"

"Yeah, yeah," I say, swatting at his precious tails.

"What? Too soon?"

Too *true* is more like it.

"What happened here?" Gusto asks Quibble.

"According to Bliss history, a train was overloaded and going too fast, so it derailed," he answers.

"But the *wizard* story?" Gusto asks. "This was a Magical Occurrence, wasn't it?"

"Yes," Quibble replies. "In 1956, a wince of unsavory wizards was on the run, hiding out in the small town of Pemberton, just north of here. They were casting magic with reckless abandon, but had no way to purge their spell dust. So they just hid it in the train cars at the station and waited for it to get hauled back down the mountain."

"A spell dump!" I shriek.

We've studied spell dumps, which happen when wizards recklessly store their spell dust (in quantity) without worrying about purging. All that enchanted dust condensed and compressed in one place is a feral magic time bomb waiting to go off.

Quibble nods. "One of the trains packed with feral spell dust exploded as it was headed down the mountain. Cars flew right off the tracks, all the way here, into the forest."

"Wow," Gusto gasps.

Quibble begins working his chin hair. "Now something else is happening."

I roll my eyes—his air of mystique is growing a little tiring. "What kind of something else?" I ask as I unsling my broom.

More chin hair fiddling. Great. We're going to be here all day.

"Master, why not send, like—you know—a professional crew?" Gusto intervenes. "If it's something serious?"

"We don't know *what* it is," Quibble replies. "It has always proved impossible to completely purge this site, which means we consider it permanently infected. *Unstable.* Even the smallest spell might have reactivated something. If it was a Dragonsong student who was responsible, then it's Dragonsong's responsibility to deal with it. So: conduct an examination of the site. If you find residue, sweep it up, but if you encounter anything unusual, call for me. Immediately."

He slumps down on a nearby stump and closes his eyes. I suppose he might be meditating, but I have the sneaking suspicion that he's trying to catch up on his sleep.

Zuki, Gusto, and I head to the top of the site and begin working our way down between the train cars, methodically inspecting the wreckage. We climb inside each car and, in some cases, scramble up rusted ladders to the tops, but we find nothing. The morning light is growing stronger, sending the shadows into retreat, and I begin to wonder if Quibble contrived our arrival to sync with the sunrise. Maybe he *does* have a flair for theatrics—maybe, just maybe, we'll make a proper wizard out of him yet!

The daylight makes the graffiti shine brighter. It seems like every square inch of the trains has been painted—even the car couplings, which have been made to look like creatures with gaping, surprised mouths and stark yellow eyes.

"Train gargoyles," I dub them.

"Good one, Cara," Zuki says approvingly.

Gusto scowls at the gargoyles. "Like we need something to make this place creepier."

"Take it easy," I say as we approach the last boxcar. It's perched precariously over the edge of the steep riverbank, as if it's trying to lean down and take a slurp. "I think it's safe to say that gargoyles are the creepiest thing we're going to find here."

At that exact moment, because the universe likes to conspire against me, the entire forest rumbles.

Spell dumps are the worst

Throughout history, whenever wizards have behaved negligently, complacently, or outright delinquently, the results have been disastrous.

In 226 BC, the Colossus of Rhodes was destroyed by an "earthquake." In 1498, a "tsunami" ravaged the east coast of Japan. In 1666, London erupted into flames after a "fire" started at a bakery. And in 1956, here in Dragonsong's backyard, there was the Whistler "Train Wreck" incident.

By the way, I'm not saying ALL disasters are a result of feral magic (stand down, conspiracy theorists). I'm just saying there are some very famous cataclysmic events that were actually related to irresponsible magic disposal. I haven't even mentioned the sudden disappearance of entire towns. And if you think that's the sort of thing you probably would have seen on the news, well, I guess I only have one question for you: Ever heard of the Lost City of Atlantis?

CHAPTER 14

Things That Have Gone Off the Rails (Like My Life)

THE GROUND IS SHAKING SO fiercely that the mutilated train wreckage creaks and grinds. The trees sway like awkward kids at a middle school dance.

"What's happening?!" Zuki shrieks.

He loses his footing and begins sliding down the hill, taking me and Gusto out at the knees, so we all go tumbling. The only thing that saves us from slipping right over the bank and into the river is the giant tree we slam into. We cling to the trunk until the trembling stops.

I look up to see that we're right next to the open door on the side of the boxcar. A trickle of black slime is dribbling out. To the uninitiated, it might look like engine oil. But I am *not* uninitiated.

I suck in a deep breath. "Here we go again."

"Again?" Zuki whines. "What do you mean *again*?"

Master Quibble is suddenly beside us. I've never known him to move so quickly, and now he kneels to examine the slime.

"This is not spell dust gone feral," he pronounces. "It's something else."

"A rupture in the Field," I inform him, climbing to my feet. I peer inside the boxcar as the goo starts to burble and hiss. The back wall of the car is crumpled, allowing in a few streams of light, but I can still make out my old pal, a snarling line of purple hovering in the corner. "Yep, there it is," I say, turning back to the crew. "This black gunk? It's basically pus. Ugh. Smells like something died in there."

"Cara, what are you talking about?" Gusto wonders. "How do you know all this?"

"Uh, because I know how to read. Plus, I've seen it before."

I'm met by a wall of blank stares.

"Are you kidding me?!" I cry. "I *told* you! This is what I saw in the auditorium! And—wait a minute. Master Quibble, *which* class visited here last month?"

"The tenth grade history class," he answers. "Why?"

Of course! I bet Harlee Wu is in that class—everything is adding up. All my suspicions, all my theories are right! Harlee probably cast a spell when she visited here last month, which means every single instance of this black gunk I've encountered has involved her magic. There is no denying the connection.

I'm so lost in my thoughts that it takes me a moment to realize that Quibble is staring at me with his solemn blue eyes. It's so surprising, so unnerving, I take a step back.

"You weren't lying." The way he speaks, it's like he's reconsidering a foundational truth of wizardom.

For a moment, no one says anything. I just cross my arms and glare.

"I'm so sorry, Cara," Gusto says, reaching for my sleeve. "I should have believed you."

"Just so you know, I did believe you," Zuki says. "I, uh, just don't like to contradict authority."

I roll my eyes. Quibble has turned back to the slime and is pestering his chin hair. *He* hasn't apologized to me, but that's wizards for you—they like to admit they're wrong in the same way that owls like to swim.

"The Wizard High Council has been receiving reports of contaminated residue, just like this, happening all around the Pacific Northwest," he reveals. "No one understands why."

I can think of one reason: the Pacific Northwest just so happens to be where Harlee Wu lives. I decide to keep that opinion to myself—for now. I have to admit it doesn't quite make sense that her occuli use would be affecting places other than the ones where she is physically spellcasting, but that just means I've got some more investigating to do.

"It's more serious than I imagined," Quibble adds. "Now that I've seen it for myself, I need to contact the Council, make a report. And we need to call in a professional crew." He barely finishes his sentence before the train car quivers again.

"There's no time," I tell him. "Besides, I know how to counteract it."

He stares at me incredulously, so I decide to stop talking, lower my goggles, and simply demonstrate. With a roll of my shoulders, I pull out my bottle of self-made neutralizer (I've decided to call it "Moone Brew"—patent pending), and begin spraying the gunk that's dripping out of the boxcar. I obviously haven't had a chance to test my potion yet, and everyone is watching me intently, so I'm pretty relieved when the slime turns into a fine gray powder. But the job isn't done—the wound is still grumbling inside the car. Quibble protests as I climb inside, but I just ignore him and start spraying more neutralizer onto the laceration in the Field.

It curls like a scowling mouth, snarls one last time—then shuts.

"Ta-da!" I cheer before turning to examine the scene. There's more slime to attend to, but at least the source has been cut off. Everyone is leaning into the car, staring at me in disbelief, like I've just performed the annual Student Stunt. I guess that's what happens when people's expectations of you are so low.

"Amazing," Quibble murmurs in awe.

"Now that the wound is shut, we just have to deal with the rest of the black gunk," I explain.

"We can help," Gusto offers.

"Just stay there," I advise. "This car's not entirely stable. Too much weight on this end, and over we go." I don't bother mentioning that I'm the only one with a supply of Moone Brew, because I want to enjoy basking in the glow of Quibble's praise for at least a little while. Time enough later to get reamed out about making my own potion.

"Be careful," Quibble tells me. "Augusto, Kazuki, let's inspect the outside of the carriage."

I continue spraying. In the back corner, there's a pile of corroded metal. Slime is trickling into the debris, so I begin carefully shifting it—and that's when I discover the rock. It's bumpy and purplish in color, though it's hard to get a good look at it in the darkness. Did it come out of the wound, too?

I dare to touch the stone, and when nothing happens, I pick it up. It's not very heavy or big; it fits in the palm of my hand. I tuck it into a pocket in my robe, so I can better analyze it in the light outside.

Then I turn my attention back to the debris pile, and that's when I discover there's a hole in the floor of the car, which means I can see down to the riverbank. Slime is oozing through the crack, and as I lift my goggles and squint through it, I can see the rocks below are splattered with the tar-like substance. And there's something else down there.

Something huge. And *alive*.

"Uh, guys?" I call. "We need to—"

Whatever it is, it wallops the carriage with so much force that the whole contraption is lifted off the ground. I'm thrown backward as a giant, fleshy head rips through the metal at the end of the car, wriggling and clawing to get through.

Someone screams—it takes me a second to realize it's me. The other thing I realize? I'm being attacked by a squix, one of the most notorious beasties known to be attracted to magic.

It's the size of the entire train car. If it resembles anything, it's a caterpillar, because it has giant black eyes, a segmented body, and multiple fleshy legs. It's bluish, but also covered in long translucent bristles that shift and shimmer with color, making it seem beautiful, like something out of a dream.

Then its tongue shoots out, wraps around my ankle, and reels me toward its mouth and I realize: Nope, this isn't a dream. It's full nightmare.

The squix tugs me through the hole it has ripped in the floor of the car, but my broom, strapped across my back, catches on the metal, giving me a chance to collect my thoughts and kick ferociously. I manage to hit the squix's snout, sending it sliding back down the bank.

Using strength I didn't even know I had (thanks, wizard yoga!), I heave myself up and scramble toward the car's side door, but before I can dive outside to safety, the squix renews its attack and the entire car flips upward. I lose my feet and smash against a wall. I hear some of the vials on my utility belt crunch and shatter, and others go flying. The strap on my broom must snap because it spins away, too, along with my goggles. The squix has swelled back up the bank to thrust its meaty head through the floor of the car again, but this time it gets stuck, making it angry.

Correction: *angrier.*

The boxcar is like a huge misshapen collar around the squix's neck and it begins frantically thrashing, trying to shake free. There are pieces of metal—and me—flying around inside, like bolts in a tin can. Everything is a blur, but the squix must finally shake the boxcar free because it goes soaring through the air, me with it. And then—*wham*. We smash through the trees—I hear wood snap and splinter as the boxcar slides down through the foliage, coniferous whips smacking me through the gaps and holes. Then we lurch to a halt.

I collapse forward, completely disoriented. I lie there, eyes closed, trying to collect myself. But I can't close my ears, which means I hear all kinds of things: distant cries of panic from the rest of the crew (thankfully, they all missed Flight SQX from Bad to Worse), shrieks from the squix, the plaintive chirp of some bird (just how high up am I?), and—most alarming of all—the sound of branches groaning and bending beneath the weight of the car.

Moaning, I lift myself to my elbows and open my eyes. The entire right side of the car has been ripped off. We've been ensnared by the canopy of the forest, but who knows for how long.

A branch snaps beneath the car, causing it to lean ponderously to the right—where there is no wall—and I start to slide. I dig my heels into the metal beneath me, and, thankfully, it's just crumpled enough to give me some purchase. But now I can see out and that's not exactly a good thing, because I'm high up. Really high up.

My stomach turns to liquid. The bird chirps again, which is far from helpful. The branches continue to snap and splinter.

Dratch.

I piece together that the squix flung the car so hard that we hurtled across the river and into the forest on the other side. I can actually see the train wreck site from my vantage point— Quibble is there, cowering before the squix and trying to shield Gusto. There's no sign of Zuki, but I don't want to think about what that means. Quibble's voice is fraught with terror as he tries to shout down the squix. I watch him stretch out his hand and flip an open palm toward the monster. Even though I'm far away, I can see the power of wizardry begin to glow on his cheeks, his red hand-shaped brand blazing . . .

Then it fades.

Uh-oh. I have no idea what's happening with Quibble, but his sudden failure to spellcast means my crew's in trouble. *Huge* trouble.

And so am I.

Because at that moment another branch breaks, and the boxcar careens downward.

CHAPTER 15

Hanging by a Fox Tail (It's a Good Thing He Has More Than One!)

I'M SO DONE WITH TRAIN travel.

The car takes out more branches on the way down, but at least they slow our descent. Then we hit the ground, the car standing on end vertically, swaying like a poorly placed domino. It wavers like that for a few seconds, then crashes backward. We hit more rocks and the car starts to slide, scraping against stone.

When it stops, I'm lying stomach down on one of the car's structural beams—it's all that's left of the floor—arms dangling on either side. The bank is higher at this part of the river, more like a cliff, which means I'm *still* high up, and below me—way below me—is the river. So, if I fall . . . well, I *might* live.

"Cara?"

The car feels extremely unstable, so I respond without moving a muscle. "Zuki? You're alive!"

"You've got to get out of there, Cara," the fox quavers. "If that car falls, you'll be mulch. Ground meat. Pulveriz—"

"Got your point. Thanks."

"I'm going to reach down with my tails, so you can grab

them. But you need to turn around and climb toward me."

"You know what? I'm good. I think I'll just stay here. It's cozy, the view is decent and—"

The boxcar tilts again, teetering precariously on the rocks. Okay, maybe it's time to find a better neighborhood. After drawing in a deep breath, I slowly stand and balance on the beam. With the speed of glacier melt, I turn to face Zuki. His face is drawn and pale. I mean, it's always pale, but he looks completely spooked. Which doesn't exactly make me feel better. I begin inching along the beam.

I hear the chirp again.

I glance around, frowning. That chirp came from *inside* the car. Is it the same bird I heard before? How did it survive our epic fall? And what kind of imbecilic bird hangs out inside a death trap?

Then I see it. Wedged in the corner of the car is the rock I picked up earlier. It must have fallen out of my pocket, but now I realize it's not a rock, because rocks aren't known for their chirping.

It's an egg. A *squix* egg. Somehow, inconceivably, it's survived this entire train ride. Then again, I guess I have, too. It explains why the squix lunged at the boxcar. Not to attack me, but to protect her unborn baby.

"What are you doing?" Zuki asks fretfully. "*Come on.*"

"Just a minute."

I have to get that egg. It may have made it this far, but it won't survive if it winds up on the rocks or in the river. I start inching along the beam again, with a renewed sense of purpose. I'm headed to safety, but toward the egg, too.

When I close the gap, I stretch out, way out. But my fingers only brush the egg's surface. I'm just not quite close enough.

"Cara, hurry!"

I focus all my concentration on the egg. Maybe I can shift it with whatever meager magic I have murmuring in my blood. I reach out, but this time I don't try to grab the egg. I just try to *will* it toward me.

At first nothing happens. I try harder. Then something *does* shift—the boxcar.

A smart person would leap for safety, but instead I leap for the egg. I crash into the corner and the wall is so beaten and battered that it peels open, like the lid of a sardine can, and the next thing I know, my legs are swaying over the abyss as I hang on to the sheet of metal with one hand.

The other is clutching the egg against my side.

I did it!

But my joy is short-lived. The boxcar is sliding downward, so I thrust the egg back into my pocket and dive for the cliff. I slam against the rocks. Then, as I cling to them for dear life, I watch the metal contraption bash and smash its way into the riverbank below. It's quite the cacophony. I half expect the car to explode when it finally hits bottom. Which doesn't make sense, of course, but that's what would happen in a movie.

Zuki yelps at me, and I turn my gaze upward to see him wagging his butt over the edge of the embankment. I manage to scale the few feet to reach him, then wrap a hand around his longest tail.

"Ugh, you're heavy," he complains as I dangle there, scrambling to keep my foothold on the rocks. "Maybe you should lay off the witch's delight."

I yank. *Really* hard.

"Hey! Careful! I go down, we both go down."

All three of us, I think, feeling the egg nestled in my pocket.

Soon Zuki has pulled me over the lip of the rocks and I'm lying on flat ground, drawing in deep breaths. I can't hear anything from the other side of the river. Which is a good thing, I decide—if Mama Squix had won, she'd be rumbling toward us right now.

"Thanks," I tell Zuki. "You saved us."

"Us?" the fox wonders, sticking his snout into my face.

I exhale and close my eyes. I'm not sure I've ever been so exhausted.

Eventually, I find the energy to stand up and cross back to the other side of the river with Zuki and my secret egg. As I plod, I can feel every limb throb; I'm a walking mural of scratches and bruises. Quibble and Gusto are collapsed against a giant boulder at the train wreck site. A boulder that I immediately recognize as *new*. As in, not having been there before everything went full

Cara disaster mode. Gusto is clenching my hairpin in his hand, like it's a knife. I stuck it in my belt after the Locker Incident, but it must have flown out when Mama Squix attacked the boxcar.

"What happened?" I ask.

Quibble doesn't respond. He doesn't even open his eyes.

"He's wiped from performing magic," Gusto murmurs. "I don't think he's used to it."

"What are you doing with my hairpin?"

Gusto blinks at it, as if just realizing that he's holding it, then wipes a hand across his brow. The boy knows how to wear a smudge, I'll give him that. He should try being less of a neat freak around Dragonsong—it might catch Yuna's eye.

"The squix was coming right at me, and Master Quibble froze," Gusto says. "It was like he couldn't bring himself to hurt it. And I found this in the dirt, so I just picked it up and stabbed at the squix. But then Master Quibble's spell finally worked because at that moment . . ."

"That moment *what*?" I press as he hands the hairpin back to me. "Where's Mama Squix?"

Gusto's gaze flutters toward me. "Mama?"

"Uh, yeah. Where is she?"

"That's what I was telling you. *She* is now a boulder. Master Quibble petrified her."

I step back to gain a fresh perspective of the giant rock. Yep. I can catch details that betray its origin—it looks like Mama

Squix curled up like a caterpillar to try to protect herself from Quibble's spell. Which, of course, didn't work.

At least he didn't kill her—because now that I know she's the mama of the egg in my pocket, that's kind of heartbreaking. Presumably, he could de-petrify her and I could return her egg, but I know better than to ask about it. If Quibble finds out about the egg, he might destroy it. I'm not risking that.

A dribble of black is hanging in thin air: the telltale sign of another laceration opening in the Field. Which I guess makes sense—even though Harlee didn't perform any magic here *just now*, Quibble said the site is permanently infected and, besides, these occurrences have been happening all over the Pacific Northwest. I definitely need to do more investigating—but for now, I've got to neutralize the lesion.

"Everything on my belt got busted," I tell Gusto. "You have caladrius secretions and qilin powder?"

He nods, slowly, tiredly.

"Good—sprinkle the dust, then spray the secretions. I gotta find my broom."

"Since when do you care about your broom?" Gusto wonders.

"Uh . . . I don't," I lie. "I just don't want to get in trouble for losing another one."

I hunt the area and find my sweep way over by one of the train gargoyles. Thankfully, it's not snapped in two. By the time I return to the boulder, Gusto has started purging the area and I help him finish up. We explore the rest of the vicinity, cleaning up any remaining traces of residue. When we're finished, Quibble is still down for the count, so we decide to sit on the riverbank and take a well-deserved rest.

"What are we going to do if this is happening all over the place?" Gusto wonders. "Rifts in the Field, black gunk, monsters popping up . . ."

"It's a full-blown disaster," Zuki contributes. "A calamity. A catastrophe, a—"

"Yeah, yeah," I mutter, rubbing the back of my hand across my cheek. It comes away bloody.

"Hey," Gusto says to me, "why did you call the squix 'mama'?"

"Uh, no reason."

"Cara," Gusto insists. "New page. Remember?"

"You can't tell Quibble."

"Tell *Master* Quibble what?"

"Promise?"

Gusto runs his hand through his thick black hair and gives me one of his patented frowns of disapproval. "I'm too tired to argue with you. Sure, I promise."

I turn to Zuki.

"Oh, yeah," he says. "Cross my tails and hope to—"

"Good enough," I murmur, plucking the egg from my robe. It's vibrating slightly, and chirping softly.

"Whoa!" Gusto cries. "What is—"

"Shh!" I warn. "Don't wake the Q-Man."

"Is that a squix egg?" Gusto asks.

I nod.

Gusto sighs. "Cara, you have to turn that over to Master Quibble. Squixes devour magic."

"Then I guess I'm safe," I snap. "Since I'm remedial."

"Seriously, is that all y—"

"I'm not letting Quibble turn her to stone," I declare, clutching the egg close to my cloak. "No way."

Gusto considers me with a heavy gaze. "Aren't you tired of getting in trouble?"

I turn to Zuki and realize he hasn't said a word. Which is pretty unusual. I watch him wander in a circle around me, then sit down again, long tails curling around his body. "It's a living thing," he decrees.

"So?" Gusto says. "It's a monster."

"It's a baby," I retort.

"It'll *grow* up to be a monster," Gusto says. "*Evil.*"

"Some people say the same thing about *me*," Zuki says. "Fox spirits don't always have the most positive roles in human stories, you know! But I'm not evil."

"He's right," I tell Gusto. "Annoying—yes. Evil, no." Gusto still seems uncertain, so I add, "I'll look after it. You two don't need to do anything. Except keep this to yourselves."

"But there are rules," Gusto implores.

"You promised," I say. "And a crew sticks together."

"Yeah, when it suits them," he mutters, crossing his arms.

But maybe he feels guilty for not believing me about the black gunk in the first place. "Fine," he concedes at last. "But, for the record? I don't like it."

Later that morning, as we drive down the mountain, I sleep fitfully in the back seat of the van. One hand is in a pocket of my robe, nestled against the egg. It's warm, and I can feel the tiny creature stirring inside. I've already decided what to call her.

"Nova," I whisper, stroking the shell softly.

Do as I say, not as I bespell

There is a whole list of rules that comes with being a spell sweeper. Having recently taken a quiz on the subject, I know the Spell Sweeper Code of Conduct pretty well. It doesn't mean I'm going to follow it, though, and I'm not going to feel bad about it either. If there's one thing I've learned about wizards, it's that they love rules but they think they're for everyone else.

Rule #1
Do not attempt clean-up of a contaminated site unless directed to do so by your crew leader. *(Side note: Yeah, like I'm wandering around, looking for extra things to scrub.)*

Rule #2
Do not lose or damage your broom. *(Especially when it's a cool one made of dragonwood.)*

Rule #3

Trim your broom after each spell sweep. If an untrimmed broom is used on a different site, it could result in cross-contamination and possibly hazardous consequences. *(Ka-boom!)*

Rule #4

Do NOT keep any broom straw contaminated with spell dust for personal use. All residue must be deposited in the appropriate receptacles. *(I mean, haven't we all pined to keep just a little bit of that gray gunge we find at the bottom of the mop bucket?)*

Rule #5

Do not leave your gear unattended in Bliss areas. This includes when visiting the bathroom. *(Which is convenient if you have contracted Demon Orc Flu and have a sudden bout of magical diarrhea—you can just whip out your broom and make quick work of the mess.)*

Rule #6

Do not wander off on your own during a purge of a contaminated site. *(Spoken like a true wizard who has never actually had to deal with the results of a Magical Occurrence. The debris from a wizard's duel can be strewn across a six-mile radius.)*

Rule #7

Do not attempt explanation if you are accosted by a Bliss during a purge; summon the local wizard authority. *("Nothing to see here, folks—this is definitely not dragon egg yolk smeared all over your porch.")*

Rule #8

Do not be seen, heard, or smelled. *(They should add "tasted" to this list, because I'm not even a real spell sweeper yet, and I've already been nearly eaten twice.)*

Rule #9

If you cannot contain it, rope it off and summon the local wizard authority. *(Seriously, why don't they just scrap this code and replace it with the phrase: "Just call a wizard!")*

Rule #10

Do not attempt a purge if a magical creature is in the vicinity. If in doubt, summon the local wizard authority. *(You guessed it!)*

Rule #11

Secretions from magical entities—blood, mucus, urine, venom, yolk, etc.—can be as dangerous as feral spell dust. Ensure all surfaces are scoured and cleaned of these substances before departing a site. *(I've heard dragon pee leaves an odor that can last for decades.)*

Rule #12

All magical entities, or traces of magical entities, must be immediately turned over to the proper authorities. Do not attempt to keep these creatures as pets. *(I take this rule as more of a suggested guideline.)*

CHAPTER 16

The Care and Feeding of a Squix

WE DON'T MAKE IT BACK to Dragonsong until 10:00 p.m., which is still early by wizard standards.

"I'll report to the Council," Master Quibble says as we enter the main gates. "Everyone else, get some rest. Don't mention what's happening with the Field to *anyone*. No need to stir up a panic."

We begin to disperse, but Quibble says, "One moment, Caradine."

I freeze. Does he know about Nova? "Yes, Master?"

"You concocted something to neutralize the toxic dust."

I lock my eyes on my boots. "Well, I—"

"We'll discuss the recipe in the morning. We all need to be armed with it."

He turns and stalks away, leaving me to gape in surprise—because, let's face it. Anytime I *don't* get lectured by Quibble is a massive victory.

★ ★ ★

Yuna's not in our room, which gives me the opportunity to find a hiding place for Nova. I decide to build her a nest of socks beneath my bed, and just hope that Yuna won't hear the chirps. She usually listens to music when she's studying or sleeping—and those are essentially the only two activities she engages in while inside our room, so it should be safe. I'm still there, fiddling with the nest, when I hear our room door open.

"Uh, Cara?" Yuna asks. "What are you doing?"

"Oh," I mumble, scooching out backward. "I thought my quill fell un—"

"Spells!" she cries, and Agi, perched on her shoulder, contributes a surprised hoot.

"Huh?" Then I realize I still look like a mess. My uniform is coated in dirt and grime, there are twigs in my hair, and I've got scratches all over my hands and face.

"It's true, isn't it—you faced a squix?" Yuna says, clutching my arm.

"Ow," I say, wincing because she's touched a bruise.

"The whole school's talking about it."

"They are?" I gasp. "How—oh. *Zuki.*"

"You're so brave," she gushes.

Her comment makes me beam. I'm not used to Yuna (or anyone) praising me. Maybe, just maybe, I'll recover from the Locker Incident.

I shower, then head straight to the library to see what I can dig up on squix eggs. As I cross the grounds, I catch students staring and pointing at me, but not in a bad way. It's more with a sense of incredulity that a simple MOP didn't die when confronted by a squix. I'll take it—it's better than being jeered at.

Much to my disappointment, the library has a dearth of information about squixes and their eggs. I complain to Miss Epigraph, but she merely shrugs and says, "Why not consult Madame Strong?"

It's worth a shot, I decide. I track down the Oology teacher as she's leaving the dining hall. She's basically a walking omelet; her robe is dusted with eggshells and streaked with dried yolk. Her left cheek features a smattering of pink fragments, which really stand out against her dark skin. Good thing Gusto's not here; he'd go crazy trying to resist brushing those shells off.

"You missed my class this week," she declares as soon as I stop her.

"Yeah—um, I was sick." It doesn't look like she believes me, so I decide the best tactic is to press onward. "I have a question about eggs."

Strong gazes at me critically, crossing her arms, which comes with a crunching sound (because of the aforementioned eggshells). "Can it be that you're actually showing an interest in your education?"

Before I can reply, something squeals from her pocket. She plucks out a green egg lined with sharp ridges—it's grotesque, especially compared to Nova's.

"Here, hold this," she commands, thrusting the egg into my hands.

"Uh, is this hatching?" I ask. The egg is jiggling, and it's extremely warm.

"Yes, and we need to get it into a cage before that happens— follow me," she says, heading toward the Oology lab.

The egg is growing so hot that I have to juggle it as I hurry after her. "What is this thing?"

Strong snorts. "You'd know the answer if you had come to class on Monday. What's your question?"

"Do you know anything about squix eggs?"

She turns on her heel so suddenly that I'm peppered with bits of eggshell shrapnel. "Squix eggs? Did you find one? Yes—I heard what happened at the train wreck. If you have one, turn it over, Miss Moone. *Now.* So I can destroy it."

I audibly gasp, but cover it up by pretending it's because of the scalding green egg in my hands (it's not much of a stretch). "There's no squix egg," I lie. "I mean, there might have been— there was this strange purplish thing that got smashed in the river, so—"

"Good," Madame Strong huffs. "That's the best-case scenario for a squix egg. Though it's too bad you didn't retrieve any of the fragments; they would have made an interesting addition to my collection—and earned you extra credit. Merlin knows you need it."

She snatches the green egg from my hands, not seeming the least bit bothered by the heat radiating from its shell, and stalks off into the night. I release a long sigh. Of course she'd destroy Nova. Wizards think squixes are pests, something less than other magical creatures. It's generally how they think of me, too.

Well, teachers can give up on *me* all they want, but there's no way I'm giving up on Nova.

By the next morning, I realize I have a different problem: Nova might give up on *me*. When I check on her, her shell has faded to a dull, murky color and she's only faintly chirping. I sneak some of the broom clippings from the compost and add them to her nest. I figure if hatched squixes eat magic, then this should sort of feed her. But the clippings have no impact.

Undaunted, I search for other solutions. After restocking the supplies in my spell sweeping kit, I experiment by adding drops of various liquids into the nest or sprinkling powder around the perimeter. Nothing works. In fact, Nova just seems to get sicker.

By Friday evening, I'm really worried.

"If neutralizers and purgers don't work, maybe I need the opposite," I ponder aloud as I sit on the floor, slumped against my bed. Squixes eat spell dust, right? So, essentially magical garbage. Which means I need something toxic . . .

I turn my gaze toward Yuna's desk, where she keeps her potions kit when she's not in Apothecarial Arts class. I leap up and open a drawer to find the kit in its usual space (how often have I enviously watched her tuck it away there?). I begin rooting through her various bottles and eventually discover a vial of manticore venom—it's one of the most toxic substances known to wizardkind. Vial in hand, I return the kit to the drawer, then dive under my bed to dribble some of the venom over the sock-nest. The change is almost instant: Nova's shell starts to glow, and she emits a soft coo.

"Whew!" I murmur. Now all I need to do is keep feeding the venom to Nova's nest—and steal some from the Apothecarial Arts lab to replace what I've taken from Yuna.

"Uh . . . Cara?" Yuna herself asks as she steps into our room. "Why are you constantly under your bed?"

I stuff the vial of manticore venom into a pocket and extract myself from under the bed. "Uh, I can't find my—"

I stop as soon as I see the look on her face—which is extremely upset.

"Are you okay?" I ask, glancing nervously toward her desk. Does she somehow know about my theft? Stupid Cara! I never even considered that she might have placed some kind of alarm spell on her possessions.

"Have you seen this?!" she cries as she begins waving a piece of parchment in my face. She's in such a fluster that Agi hops off her shoulder and hides in the corner with a worried hoot.

I know that type of parchment. It's an official Dragonsong bulletin—usually, they're for announcing who's the top student of the year, or for advising us to keep our lockers tidy (in retrospect, I should have heeded that one). But this one is obviously something different. I snatch it from Yuna and read:

*All spellcasting has been SUSPENDED worldwide
until further notice. Transfiguration and translocation
are especially PROHIBITED—do not engage in
these practices under any circumstances, emergency or
otherwise—and limit all other activities, including use
of summoning mirrors, unless absolutely essential. All
spell-locked doors, lockers, and cupboards will be fitted
with padlocks and students will be supplied with keys.
This directive applies to both students and staff. Students
are required to turn in all talismans immediately.*

*—Saraya Singh, Headwizard, Dragonsong Academy
On the authority granted by the Wizard High Council*

Is this because of Quibble's report to the Council? Did they
hear what he had to say and decide to issue this edict?

"No one can use magic!" Yuna exclaims, interrupting my
thoughts. "Not even the teachers! Not even my parents!"

Well, mine never could, I think.

Yuna collapses into her chair. "I've already turned in my
medallion." She gropes at the base of her neck, like she's searching for a phantom limb. "What are we supposed to do without
our talismans? How are we supposed to study magic?"

"What about Harlee?" I wonder. "What does she turn in?"

"Nothing, I guess," Yuna replies.

Because no one knows about her occuli, I think. It suddenly occurs to me that I've barely thought about Harlee for the past twenty-four hours because I've been so consumed by Nova. I guess this is what it feels like to be a dedicated student with extracurricular projects.

"What about the Wizard Games?" Yuna continues fretting. "They're supposed to happen next month! How can we have them without magic?"

I scowl. The Wizard Games are Dragonsong's version of a track-and-field meet—though in our case, there's no track and a whole lot of Field—the Field of Magical Matter. Typical events include spellcasting, transfiguration, translocation . . . which means MOPs are automatically disqualified from participating (unless you count cleaning up after the event—which I don't).

"Maybe they'll do a version that doesn't involve the Field," I suggest. "You know, rune reading, yoga poses . . ."

Yuna releases a dramatic sigh. "I suppose that could work. Wouldn't be the same, though."

"Could be better. Hey! Maybe Gusto and I will get to participate! The playing field will be more even. Because, get it? No Field."

Yuna pensively toys with a strand of silver hair. "That would be one positive."

Her accompanying smile seems forced, though. I guess the upper class doesn't mind helping people up. They just don't want to take a step down to do it.

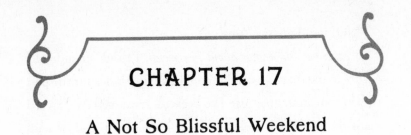

CHAPTER 17

A Not So Blissful Weekend

LIFE AT DRAGONSONG TAKES A definite turn for the worse. What do wizard kids do when they can't perform magic? Answer: pick on the resident MOP. Any credit I've earned for facing a squix evaporates like a dewdrop in a phoenix nest—let's just say I find myself reminiscing about how kind Georgia and Simone *used* to be.

Thankfully, I've got some Mom time on the way. The first Saturday of October is Dragonsong's annual Family Day, when parents tour the school and hang out with their kids. Of course, some students (like me) come from Bliss families, which means there is strict protocol put in place to keep the true nature of Dragonsong a secret. The Apothecarial Arts classroom becomes the science lab, the Rune Reading class becomes Language Arts, and only the main floor of the library is open (it's where we keep the "Bliss-appropriate" books). We don't have to worry about disguising the MOP department—no one wants to visit the janitor.

When Gusto and I make our way to the pier, I discover that

Mom has brought Grandma and Su. Grandma is in a cheerful mood, wearing a crown of pink blossoms, like she's on her way to a wedding, possibly to serve as the world's oldest flower girl. As for Su, she's dressed all in black and looks particularly anemic, which makes me wonder if Brad's convinced her to stop eating meat. But maybe she'll act half human, since he's not here. It's a hope that lasts approximately 1.5 seconds.

With a snarl, she snatches my—well, *her*—fancy hairpin from the top of my head. "Where did you get *this*?"

"I kind of borrowed it?" I wore it today to look nice for Mom, which I wouldn't have done, of course, if I had known Su was tagging along.

"Thief!" she hisses, stabbing the hairpin into her braided bun. "Do you know how long I've been looking for this? Mom! She's going through my personal things."

Mom sighs. "Suzannah, did it ever occur to you that your sister misses you? That she just wants to look like y—"

"No, I don't!" I snap, so loudly that a few other people on the pier glance in our direction.

"Let's move on," Mom announces. "Caradine, how about a tour of the school before lunch?"

"Sure," I mutter, my freckles blooming. Su has only been here for five minutes and she's already caused a scene.

Mom saw the school each of my first two years, but this is the first visit for Grandma and Su. We wander up the path toward the school grounds with other families, Mom making chitchat with Gusto's parents. It's cringey to hear her talk about me with such pride. As wizards themselves, Gusto's moms know he and I are both MOPs, but they're polite enough to smile at Mom's naive commentary. It's a relief when we reach the main gate and the families separate.

"Feels more like a resort than a school," Su mutters as we enter the garden.

She seems agitated, which is so unlike her. Annoyed and superior are her current go-to traits, not fidgety. Maybe she's just missing Brad. Or her vape pen. But then I wonder, for the first time ever, if Su might actually be jealous of me. She goes to a regular old Bliss high school and I "get" to go to Dragonsong. But I chase the thought away. The concept of Su being envious of *me* is too ludicrous to seriously consider.

"Do you even have a library?" she wonders.

I don't answer because at that moment I spot Harlee sitting on my bench, all alone and staring at the goldfish pond. She's not even sketching.

"Who is that?" Su asks. "Her uniform is even worse than yours. Full Halloween."

Su doesn't exactly have a cauldron to stir when it comes to commenting on how someone dresses—what's more Halloween than her goth outfit? But I let the comment slide; I'm not in the business of defending people who reveal my pink unicorn underwear to the entire world.

"She seems lonely," Grandma observes. "Why don't you introduce us, Caradine?"

"No way!" I blurt.

That catches Harlee's attention. She raises her chin and gives me an impassive stare that causes me to slouch where I stand. Then I see Zuki trot to her side. He's shapeshifted to appear like a dog, with a blunter snout and the requisite single tail. My heart swells with jealousy as I watch him affectionately lick Harlee's hand. Doesn't he remember she stepped on him?

"Dogs sense sadness," Grandma observes. "What a sweet pet."

"He's not her pet!" I snipe.

"They let strays roam wild around here?" Su asks, seizing any excuse to attack Dragonsong.

If only she knew some of the animals that normally prowl Dragonsong! But familiars—at least the ones that can't shapeshift—have been confined to students' rooms for the day.

"Ah, I get it," Su says, studying my face. "She's the one bullying you."

I whirl on her. "What?"

Su shrugs. "Someone is *always* bullying you."

"I just don't like her. And I don't like y—"

"Come on," Mom hastily intervenes. "Caradine, you're supposed to show me your display."

We make our way to the main concourse, where tables have been set up to showcase student work. I've prepared many "projects," including a dorky poster-board backdrop, which displays examples of my calligraphy, a "creative writing piece" (an essay I wrote for my History of Wizardry class), and a drawing of (traitor) Zuki with nine tails. My most cherished piece sits on the table: my broom.

"You made this?" Mom marvels as she runs her finger along the broomcorn.

"Yeah—for, uh, art," I say.

"Brooms are magical, you know," Grandma says. "They sweep away bad spirits. Hashtag helpful."

"Mom, I told you this was a basket-weaving school," Su complains.

"Suzannah," Mom says wearily, "you're the one who wanted to come today."

I gape at my sister. "You *wanted* to come?"

She only sneers, then says, "Is there a bathroom in this place?"

"I can show you," I offer.

"Never mind, freak," she says, flouncing away. "I'll find it myself."

Su doesn't turn up for lunch. At first, Mom doesn't seem worried, but once we're done eating, she sends Grandma and me on an expedition to find her.

As for Mom, she has to attend a parent-teacher conference, which means discussing my progress with Master Quibble. He'll fabricate all kinds of stuff about what I do here, because he can't exactly tell her that I got hurled across the river in a boxcar by a mama monster while I was trying to sweep up magic dust.

So, while Mom confers with the Q-Man, Grandma and I begin the quest for the long-lost sister. We eventually find her in the corridor outside the library. She's sitting on a bench, flicking the latch of the nearby window up and down. I can't tell if she's just bored, irritated, or a combination of both.

"This school is so pathetic," she grumbles. "There are all these little kid props, like wands and gemstones, on display in the library."

"Yeah, er, those are handmade by students," I lie—I obviously can't tell her they're items once belonging to Riva Dragonsong, one of the most powerful wizards of all time. But even if she thinks they are props, you'd think she could give them some cred for looking awesome.

"I'm done visiting Disneyland," Su snaps, sliding off the bench. "Grandma, tell Mom I'll be at the pier."

She saunters away without so much as a goodbye, leaving me to wish there was a spell to revert Su to her old self.

Grandma pats me on the shoulder, as if in condolence. "Why don't you take me up top? I want to see the view."

With a sigh, I lead her up the nearest staircase. It's a long climb, but Grandma is in good shape and we soon reach the open terraces and connected walkways at the top of the school. Here, we can gaze upon the lush forested landscape of the island and the ocean beyond. There are a few other people meandering around, so I guide Grandma along the walled walkway, past rows of potted trees, to a secluded spot.

"Your school is beautiful," Grandma tells me. "Like a poem."

We lean over the parapets, enjoying the autumn sun. Down below, we can see the pier and the black dot that must be Su, stalking back and forth. I fire imaginary missiles at her, but Grandma must notice because she says, "It's easier to feel anger than sadness. You miss her."

"No, I don't."

"Suzannah is going through a rough time. Be kind to her."

"Try telling that to *her*."

"Right now, I'm talking to *you*," Grandma admonishes. "Don't be jealous. Resentment is like drinking poison and waiting for the other person to die."

I cross my arms. "I'm really not in the mood for some old proverb."

"It's a quote from Carrie Fisher," Grandma informs me. "Princess Leia in *Star Wars*. Your dad's favorite movie."

I freeze. We've always had difficulty talking about Dad; usually, we just skirt around the subject like it's the edge of a cavernous hole, but the last time I saw Grandma was when Brad came to dinner. That night we all tumbled into the hole, and I'm not sure there's a way to crawl out.

Grandma puts a hand on mine. "I don't want to be afraid to talk about your dad. Not anymore. I wish he could have seen this place. Seen *you*."

I swallow the lump in my throat. "Me, too," I say, not daring to look Grandma in the eye. "But . . ."

"Tell me."

"I have so much of Mom," I blurt. "Her name. Her hair. Her freckles."

"What's wrong with that? Your mom is one of the best people I know."

I sigh. "What about Dad? What do I have of *his*?"

Grandma squeezes my hand. "You want to find your dad, don't look in the mirror. Look *deeper*. You're like him."

"How?"

"Clever. Resourceful. Magical."

I cough. If only she knew how unmagical I am. I know that's not what she meant by the word. But still.

"You're hunting for your place," Grandma says sagely. "I remember what it was like to not fit in."

I turn to her, gaping. She's hit the dragon right between the eyes. "You . . . you do?"

"I was a quirky kid, always standing out." She catches my eyes flitting up to her crown of flowers, and adds, "Okay, maybe I *still* stand out. Difference is, now I don't care. I'm just me."

I snort. Adults always say some version of this, like being yourself is the easiest thing in the world.

Grandma is unfazed by my reaction. "Caradine, you can take your feelings of inadequacy and feed them like the vampires they are. Or you can use them as stepping-stones toward change. Are you striving to be the best version of yourself? If the answer's yes, then you're enough, exactly as you are."

If only she knew who I really am—or who I *am not*.

"You can tell me, whatever it is," Grandma urges. "I'll probably forget by tomorrow. Because, you know. Hashtag old."

There was a time when the person I told everything to was my sister—but that feels like a lifetime ago and, for just an instant, as I bask in Grandma's warm smile, I consider spilling my guts. About Harlee. About wizard school. About *failing* wizard school.

But I know that would only make things worse. She wouldn't believe me, and even if she did, I would get into even more trouble and . . .

I don't say anything. Instead, I simply turn my gaze back to the pier, back to my long-lost sister, and feel more alone than ever.

Meet my sister, force of nature

I'm eight years old, sitting on the school steps on a June afternoon, waiting to be picked up, tears sneaking over my freckles. Between my shoes is a pile of shredded paper.

"Cara?"

I look up to see Su hovering over me.

She sits down beside me on the steps. "I'm not late, am I?"

Of course not. Su is *never* late. Even at the age of twelve, she's ultra-responsible.

"Where's Mom?" I sniffle. "She's supposed to get me today."

"Mrs. Hong went into labor. So you're stuck with me." She puts an arm around me, draws me in to lean on her shoulder. "What's with all the paper?"

"Nothing."

Su reaches down and starts gathering the shreds.

"I said it's nothing—just leave it!"

"To Dad," she reads as she inspects one of the larger

scraps, "from your Supernova."

"Please don't—"

"A Father's Day card?" Su marvels as she continues collecting the pieces. "Why did you rip it up?"

"I didn't," I say, doing my best to stifle the tears. "Lisa Wendleson did. She said I couldn't make a Father's Day card because I don't have a . . . a . . ."

So much for stifling the tears.

Su cradles me, which I know is mostly to comfort me, but also to disguise the fact that she's crying, too. She cries about Dad way more than she lets on. I've heard her late at night when I get up to use the bathroom. My sister's nickname is "Tsunami" because she's such a force to be reckoned with, but on nights like those, I always think it's because of her tsunami of tears.

"We have a dad, Cara," Su says eventually, once she's composed herself. "You understand that, right? He's just not with us anymore." She looks at me, sweeps a strand of hair out of my eyes, then lifts my chin. "Personally, I think he will love this card. We'll put it on the mantelpiece. He'll see it."

"No, he won't!" I cry, leaping to my feet. "It's ruined. And the next time I see Lisa, I'm going to punch her!"

"Cara!" Su chastises. "Resorting to violence is *not* the answer."

"I don't care!" I shout as I storm away, down the street.

Su eventually catches up with me. She takes my hand

in hers as we head home. She doesn't say anything more, but that Sunday, on Father's Day, I wake up and walk into the living room to see my card perched on the mantelpiece, painstakingly taped together, piece by piece.

CHAPTER 18

They Never Let Poor Cara Join in Any Wizard Games

ONCE FAMILY DAY IS OVER, Dragonsong's students are back to fretting about the suspension of spellcasting. Everyone is especially disgruntled about the watered-down Wizard Games scheduled for the upcoming weekend—that is, everyone except me. I'm still determined that Gusto and I should get to participate, so on Monday, I visit the Spellography classroom to appeal to Professor Vitrix. He's been chosen as the officiator of this year's Games, and he'll be the key to letting us join.

When I enter the chamber, it's to find Vitrix ensconced at his desk, conferring with a student. It's Georgia, of all people, hovering over him with a clipboard in hand, so I immediately try to beat a retreat.

Something mewls, freezing me in my tracks. I turn back to see Vitrix's familiar, an elegant lynx, smirking at me with golden eyes from his perch on the windowsill.

"Can I help you?" Vitrix wonders.

I swallow; might as well do this thing. "I was hoping I could ask you a question," I say, tentatively stepping forward. "About the, uh, Games."

Vitrix frowns. I've never spoken to him in person, but Yuna warned me that he can be extremely haughty—which he now demonstrates by raising his chin and scanning my sludge-gray uniform. His lynx begins nonchalantly licking a paw.

"You are a MOP," Vitrix announces, as if this is news to me.

His nostrils flare, like he's just caught a whiff of something atrocious. He must be old, but his alabaster (that's a Mom word) skin is wrinkle-free and he has long golden hair (not blond, but actually gold-colored, like the metal), which he now swishes aside, as if to show it off. Georgia mimics him by flicking back her own perfect chestnut hair. (Despite the ban, I bet she's enhanced it with a straightening spell—something I haven't been able to master. The last time I tried, my hair looked like I had danced with a lightning bolt.)

"I'm, uh, Cara Moone," I tell the professor.

"So?" Vitrix asks.

Georgia snickers; I can feel my stupid freckles begin to glow.

"Well, I was just wondering, uh, since the Games aren't going to require the use of the Field this year—I thought Gusto and I could participate."

Vitrix shifts ever so slightly in his seat, like he's wearing a robe of thorns and the merest gesture might slice him open. "Gusto?"

"He's also in the spell sweeping program and—"

"Tell me—Miss Moone, is it?—would we invite a mermaid to a footrace?"

Georgia doesn't snicker this time—she peals with laughter. Her hedgehog pokes his head out from her pocket and leers at me. Vitrix's lynx grins ear to ear. My freckles turn to fireworks.

"Perhaps I should say 'carp,'" Vitrix continues with a condescending sneer. "Given the way you are gaping at me."

"A *carp*?" I mumble, twisting my hands nervously together.

"Seems appropriate," Vitrix says pensively. "They are bottom feeders."

"Personally, Professor, I think there is a great deal of value in sticking to tradition," Georgia pipes up.

"Indeed, Miss Dirk," Vitrix says, turning away from me. "Now, what were we discussing before the rude interruption? Ah, yes—the team names for the proper wizarding students participating in this year's Games."

I slink out, feeling Georgia's smirk following me the entire way. The good news? I'm halfway down the stairs before the tears come.

The rain is teasing the tall windowpanes on Saturday evening as I hunker down in a quiet corner on the second floor of the library. My classmates are in for a damp one at this year's annual Wizard Games—like I care. I've decided to protest my exclusion by not spectating—unlike Gusto, who's gone to cheer on Yuna's team. Zuki has opted to stick with me and curl up at my feet, probably more out of his disdain for getting his precious tails wet than any political stance. It's certainly not because he prefers my company. I've been giving him the wart, punishment for him hanging out with Harlee during Family Day. Unfortunately, Zuki doesn't seem to understand the silent treatment—he's been prattling on, oblivious to my lack of responses.

"You're missing the Games," Miss Epigraph says as she meanders over to my table. She has a book perched on her shoulder like a pet bird; it even coos in her ear. "Don't you want to see who wins?"

"Harlee Wu's team will win," I respond, without even looking up from the tome I've dragged over from the section on magical creatures. It's called *Bestia Obscura*—I've decided to take another crack at squix research.

"Very well," Miss Epigraph declares, her bird-book offering a sad chirp. "If you need me, I'll be refiling the section on magical mischief. It's all out of order again."

She might be telling a joke, but before I can scan her expression for any clues, she floats away.

"Find anything?" Zuki asks, hopping onto the bench alongside me.

I would prefer to keep ignoring him, but it's hard to stick to that when you're as lacking in the popularity department as I am. "No," I relent. "There doesn't seem to be anything . . . *scientific* written about squixes. It's all hearsay and old wizards' tales."

"You can't be the first one to ever find a squix egg," Zuki says.

"Obvs," I tell him. "But seems wizards always just destroy them and kill the mothers. There's this assumption that squixes eat magic, but there's no reported cases of it, at least that I can find. I mean, how would anyone know that they eat magic if they always just kill them straight away?"

"Well, Mama Squix did lay her egg at the site of a major Magical Occurrence," Zuki says. "That fits what the stories say. Right?"

"Not really. It wasn't regular spell dust at the train wreck. It was the toxic black slime stuff."

A muted cheer comes from outside and I glance up, despite myself.

"Sounds like the tournament is heating up," Zuki observes. "You sure you don't want to go out there?"

An image of everyone cheering for Harlee as she receives a giant golden trophy flashes through my mind. "Yep. I'm sure."

I lug the book back to the magical creature section, Zuki at my heels. "We need to go back to the restricted chamber," I tell the fox over my shoulder. "I bet there's something there on squixes."

"No way," Zuki says. "The books in there are terrifying. Besides—OW!"

"What is it?!" I cry, whirling around.

"Don't you hear it?" Zuki asks, crouching low and using his tails to cover his ears.

"No. Hear what?"

He doesn't answer. Instead, he starts to salivate. Next, he

jumps to his feet and begins spinning in circles, swatting himself with his own tails.

I drop to my knees to try to corral him, but all I get is a face full of fur. "What's happening?!"

Zuki is yipping and yowling now, but even over his cacophony, I finally hear it. A faint whine, like the high-pitched call of a teakettle. It's as if the noise is coming from inside my own head, and I press my hands to my throbbing temples to try to quell it. I feel a slight pain, the kind you experience when the pressure changes inside an airplane.

Miss Epigraph flies over. She's clearly unaffected—other than being extremely spooked, which I can tell because of the faint scent of must exuding from her (normally she has a new book sort of smell). "Cara, what is it?"

"I don't know! Zuki just started freaking out and—"

A sound of smashing glass comes from the center of the library. Miss Epigraph and I glance at each other in surprise—then she whisks away. Even though I feel slightly woozy and Zuki is still spinning round and round like a washing machine on a supersonic spin cycle, I stagger after Miss Epigraph.

I've just made it out of the magical creature section when it's like a switch goes off in my head; the whistling sound stops, and I instantly feel better. I charge down to the main level and find Miss Epigraph in the rotunda, gaping at the display case of Riva Dragonsong's relics. The glass has been shattered and everything inside is gone. Her gemstone, her wand, her spell book . . . all gone.

Spider-leg chills scamper down my spine. It wasn't so long ago that I toyed with the idea of breaking into this very display, so that I could steal Riva's possessions and wield forbidden magic. I didn't have the guts—but *someone* did.

Tears, thick as sap, are dribbling down Miss Epigraph's cheeks. "Who would do such a thing?"

That's when I notice the black slime. It's trickling down from a narrow slit suspended in the air near the display case. The floor trembles beneath my feet.

I don't say it out loud, but it's pretty obvious who's responsible for this magical robbery: Harlee.

It *has* to be.

CHAPTER 19

And the Winner of This Year's Wizard Games Is . . . No One

I RACE OUT OF THE library—I have to fetch my spell sweeping gear to clean up the slime, but, more importantly, I want to see if I can catch Harlee.

I nearly plow right into her, charging from the opposite direction.

She skids to a halt. "Did you hear that? It came from the library—didn't it? Who's in there?"

I should be the one interrogating *her*, but Harlee has the sort of voice that compels you to answer. It's probably sorcery. "Just Zuki. And Miss Epigraph, of cour—"

"Did you do something?" Harlee asks accusingly. "Experiment with something you shouldn't have?"

"What? Because I'm a MOP?"

"Because you're a novice wizard," she says. "Maybe you—"

"Me?" I cry. "What did *you* do?!"

Harlee suddenly slumps against the wall and slides to the floor with her eyes closed. It's only now that I notice the beads of sweat rolling down the sides of her forehead. It's not how I'm used to seeing her, and I have to admit that it's strange that she was running *toward* the scene of the crime instead of away from it. Still, Harlee's clever. Maybe this is all part of the ploy.

"What do you think I did?" she murmurs after a moment, her eyes still shut.

"*Someone* robbed the library," I tell her, watching her carefully.

Harlee's eyes fly open. "What did they take?"

"Riva's stuff. Like you don't—"

"Come on; I want to see," she says, climbing ponderously to her feet.

"Actually," I say, "I have to get my gear. The place needs purging. There's a mess in there."

"There's a mess everywhere," Harlee says, gesturing to the nearby window.

One glance outside makes me rush through the nearest door and into the school's main courtyard, where the tournament is being held. Correction: *was* being held. Because it turns out that *everyone* experienced that wave of nausea and confusion.

The courtyard looks like a battlefield—*after* the battle is over, and in this case it's clear that the losing side was Dragonsong Academy. I'm not sure who the victor was, but it's pretty evident that no one will be awarded a trophy for this year's Games.

Students and teachers are slowly picking themselves up off the ground, groaning and mumbling, rubbing their foreheads or the backs of their necks. Familiars are still wandering, fluttering, or slithering in circles, bumping into things, like someone slipped mugroot ale into their feed bowls. The rain is still misting, but the courtyard lights are blazing brightly, revealing a scene of misery. Everything has been trampled; there's not a table, a signpost, or a chair left standing. Even some of the windows in the surrounding buildings have been shattered. I spot Gusto nearby, tending to Yuna, who has one of her knee-high socks rolled down. It looks like a familiar nipped her because a trickle of blood is leaking from her shin.

"All the familiars went hysterical," Harlee says, appearing behind me.

I flash her a suspicious glare. "And you don't happen to have one, do you? *Interesting.*"

"What? A familiar?" Harlee says. "Yeah, I don't do helpful magical pets. Like I said, they went berserk. Everyone else collapsed to the ground in agony."

"So why are *you* okay?" I wonder.

She shakes her head in confusion. "Do I look okay?"

She doesn't, but she definitely seems in better shape than the rest of the school. Yes, she's covered in perspiration and her face is flushed, but she still managed to stagger inside—unless she was there all along. I have half a mind to demand she empty her pockets, to see if Riva's relics are tucked somewhere within her crimson robes. But if they are, that means she somehow managed to impair the entire school with a spell. If she was willing to do that, what is she going to do to *me*? My gaze wanders back to the courtyard. There are plenty of experienced wizards about, but none of them seem in any condition to come to my aid if push comes to spell.

The ground trembles again, and a piercing howl sounds from the library—the telltale call of a rupture in the Field.

"I really have to go," I tell her, speeding off.

I make quick work of the toxic spell slime in the library. What takes a lot longer is the cleanup of the school grounds. Miss Terse handles the brunt of the work, but everyone helps out. Not only is there physical damage to repair—windows, torn turf, dislodged cobblestones, trampled hedges—there's also the other type of mess. And, no, I don't mean the spell dust kind. I mean the sort caused by—as Harlee called them—"helpful magical pets." Let's just say, I wish certain familiars wore diapers.

At least that aspect of the disaster can be addressed with a shovel. More worrying are the injuries, because Yuna was only one of many who were bitten, pecked, or scratched by a freaked-out familiar. Most of the wounds aren't serious, but it quickly becomes clear that everyone has become a little too reliant on magical mending. That sort of spellcasting is currently suspended, of course, which means everyone is left to heal the old-fashioned way. It makes for a lot of grumpy patients in Dragonsong's infirmary.

The entire school is unnerved by the robbery, and even though the administration plods forward with a "normal" schedule, it's all anyone can talk about.

"Why would someone want to steal Riva Dragonsong's stuff anyway?" Gusto wonders as we're settling into our desks for Beastology class on Tuesday evening. "What's the motive?"

He's directing the question toward Yuna, sitting next to him, but she doesn't reply. Instead, she's pensively stroking Agi as she stares at the large metal birdcage that is a permanent fixture on Master Tandrot's desk. The cage is empty—or at least it appears to be. Sometimes, I get the sense that something *is* in there and it's just invisible to the human eye. Or at least to the remedial wizard eye.

As for Tandrot himself, he's slumbering in his chair. He can somehow wake up at the exact minute class is supposed to start. I always thought this was a spell, but it's apparently something he can just do, since magic is now banned.

"You could sell talismans on the dark market," one of our classmates, Mya Vuong, suggests from two rows behind Gusto. She has a horned rat snake looped around her neck and it offers a hiss to emphasize her point. I think her familiar is extremely cool—it's bright green and looks like it has a unicorn horn on its nose—but the hiss makes Gusto grimace (he has a thing about snakes).

"Risky," says Caleb Garcia, who's sitting next to Mya. "Get caught, and it's straight to Krakatau Keep."

"It still doesn't make sense," Josh says, tapping a finger on his desk. "I mean, Riva's talismans are pretty to look at it, but so what?"

"Whoever stole them isn't going to look at them," I announce. "They're going to use them."

"That's perverted!" Josh exclaims. "That wouldn't even work."

"Yes, it would," I say, and now I realize the entire classroom (except for Tandrot, who's still sleeping) is staring at me with rapt attention. "It's forbidden, but it's possible."

Yuna finally snaps to attention. "You're talking about occuli," she declares.

"Huh?" Gusto asks.

"Occuli," Yuna repeats, holding me in her gaze. "Cara . . . how do you know about them?"

"I read," I snap. "How do *you* know about them?"

"My grandfather's library," she replies, narrowing her eyes at me. "He's a member of the Low Council and he has all sorts of books on arcane subjects. But where did *you* find a book that mentions them?"

There go my freckles. But I decide to keep my mouth shut.

Yuna shakes her head. "Riva Dragonsong's talismans would be the perfect candidate for someone who . . ."

I frown at her. "For someone who *what*?"

Yuna turns her gaze back toward Tandrot's birdcage. "Never mind."

It's her dismissiveness that sends me over the edge—the spell that cracks my cauldron. "No, Yuna," I growl, rising to my feet. "Say what you were going to say."

She sighs and glances back in my direction. "For someone who wants . . . *more*."

"More?" Gusto parrots. "What do you mean, *more*?"

I feel a surge of guilt and shame—it's like Yuna has the ability to see right through me, like she knows I contemplated stealing Riva's relics. Or maybe, I realize as a crack forms across my heart, she thinks I actually did it. But that just evokes another emotion in me: rage.

"She means magic," I tell Gusto, even though I'm glaring at my roommate. "She means someone who doesn't have enough of it. Someone who isn't a real wizard."

"I never said you weren't a real wizard!" Yuna cries.

"What, then? Someone who comes from a Bliss family?"

"Hey!" Caleb cries. "*My* family is Bliss."

I throw a sidelong glare at him, sitting there with his ferret familiar clinging to his shoulder. He might come from Bliss parents, but he's on a proper wizard track—in other words, completely unhelpful to my argument. I turn my ire back on Yuna. "You think *I* robbed the library?"

"N-no!" Yuna says in a fluster. "It's just that you said you've been reading up on occuli. And you're always so . . . look, did you mess with my potions kit?"

"No!" I retort, even as another wave of guilt engulfs me. I collapse back in my chair, silently berating myself. I was able to replace Yuna's vial of manticore venom after "procuring" some from the Apothecarial Arts lab, but knowing her, she has her kit organized in a particular way that I didn't get quite right. Dratch!

"I didn't take Riva's stuff," I huff, crossing my arms. "But do you know who was lurking around the library that night? *Harlee.*"

Yuna groans. "Seriously, Cara? This? Again?"

"Think about it," I say. "She casts a spell on the school and—"

"No wizard has that kind of power," Mya interrupts. "It's unheard of."

"No, it's not," I counter, thinking of the wizard fairy tales I read while hunkering down in my room after the Locker Incident. "There are creatures whose voices can lure or trick wizards. And how about the story of Theradune the Betrayer? He had this flute—they called it the Wizard Whistle—that allowed him to stupefy and murder his brothers."

"That's a fairy tale," Yuna scoffs.

"Oh yeah? The preface to Ysabella Arkin's Third Edition says that the tales are based on historical—"

"Now you're just showing off," Gusto interjects.

I guess he doesn't like me upstaging his beloved Yuna. Before I can continue, though, I feel something nudge my leg—Zuki has turned up. He's been conspicuously absent since the robbery—like many of the familiars at Dragonsong, he's been struggling with the aftereffects of what happened at the Games.

"What is it?" I ask irritably.

"We've been summoned," the fox announces, his eyes flitting between me and Gusto.

"Class is about to start," Gusto protests. He only gets three classes with Yuna, and he's loath to miss them.

Zuki flicks his tails. "I'm just the messenger."

I release a dramatic sigh as I stand up and begin collecting my books. "What does Quibble want now?"

"*Master* Quibble," Zuki corrects me. "And he's not the one doing the summoning. It's Headwizard Singh."

What's a wizard without a wand?

I've said it before, and I'll say it again: there are all kinds of wizarding activities that can be accomplished without accessing the Field. Take me for example: I'm raising a squix egg, I've figured out how to neutralize toxic spell slime, I've researched occuli—but do these things earn me any credit?

Nope.

Because no self-respecting wizard relies solely on brewing invisijuice or persuading a dragon to give her adversary an extra-strength suntan. You want to be considered a real wizard? Then you've got to master connecting with the Field.

Which is why, as far as Yuna and my other classmates are concerned, I'll always be less than—just a remedial wizard. These last few weeks, I thought Yuna and I were getting some of our roommate magic back, becoming friends again. But then she goes and suggests to the world that I'm the library thief. Okay, yes, I *considered* it, but I didn't go through with it. And, yes, I did technically steal from Yuna, but that's different—it was for a good reason, and I replaced what I took.

But do I get any benefit of the doubt?

Of course not.

Because to Yuna and everyone else, I'll always just be a miserable MOP.

CHAPTER 20

A Little Witch Crystal Can Tell You a Lot

YOU COULD SAY MY BEST friend at Dragonsong Academy is detention (because that's who I spend most of my time with—get it?). Still, I've never been called directly to Headwizard Singh's office, which means that whatever's happening is serious. As Zuki, Gusto, and I wind our way up the staircase in the administration tower, my mind contorts like a wizard yoga basilisk pose. What if Headwizard Singh shares the same suspicions about the robbery as Yuna? What if she thinks I'm somehow responsible?

"Wizard school was fun while it lasted," I mutter.

"Just try to be positive for once," Gusto says.

"What? I'm positive. You don't think I'm positive?"

"Sure," Zuki agrees. "You're positive that everyone's against you. Positive that—"

"Yeah, yeah," I cut him off.

We arrive at an antechamber, where we're greeted by Mr. Cavendish, Singh's assistant. He tells us to sit, then, as if out of force of habit, reaches to tap his summoning mirror, only to find himself contemplating a blank spot on the wall because that sort of magic has been suspended—or at least limited to emergencies. With a sigh, he notifies Headwizard Singh the old-fashioned way, by knocking on the door. He then places a crystal horn against the oaken wood. It's like the old glass-against-the-wall trick because when Singh speaks, her voice is clear and crisp.

"We're not quite ready for them," she announces.

The glass is certainly witch crystal, with its own innate magical properties, which means it doesn't draw on the Field. I guess breaking out the witch crystal is preferable to wiring up an intercom or local web network—the idea of something that can be bugged or hacked makes the average wizard's skin itch.

Mr. Cavendish returns to his desk. "We're waiting for one more, anyway."

"I thought Master Quibble was already in there," Zuki says.

"This is our entire crew, then," I tell Mr. Cavendish.

He stares longingly—again—at the empty space on his wall left behind by his confiscated mirror, then casts his eyes to a perch in one corner of the office, where an ancient-looking bat is hanging upside down. It's his familiar, and based on the way it's trembling, it's still recovering from the Wizard Games incident. Mr. Cavendish releases another woeful sigh. "My job used to be a lot easier," he mutters, standing up. "I'll be back."

After he heads down the stairs, I turn to Zuki and Gusto. "What's going on?"

"A representative from the High Council arrived early this morning," Zuki says. "Kanika Mwangi. She's a head honcho! A top dog, the main event, the—"

"And now she's in there with Quibble," I murmur.

"*Master* Quibble," Gusto corrects me. "Cara, what are you cooking up?"

I blink at him innocently. "What do you mean?"

"You have that look."

"I just think we should listen in on what they're saying. It obviously involves us."

Before he can object, I snatch up the crystal horn that Mr. Cavendish conveniently left unattended on his desk. I mean, he's practically begging us to eavesdrop. I put the horn to the heavy oaken door and, with Zuki nestling beside me, begin spying. Gusto remains seated, arms crossed in protest, like he's not listening. Which, of course, he is.

". . . these incidents are escalating, becoming increasingly prevalent," comes the crackling voice of someone who must be Mwangi. "At first, minor magic seemed to cause no harm to the Field—only the most powerful spells seemed to inflict pain. But now? Even the simplest spell splits the Field open. We are worried it may never recover."

That's all it takes to intrigue Gusto. He leaves his seat and joins us at the door.

"Can the Field . . . *die*?" I ask him. "Does that mean no one will be able to use magic? Like, ever?"

Gusto's eyebrows knit together. "Just keep listening."

"Sure, now you want to—"

"Shhh!" he warns.

"Thankfully, we believe we have discovered the source of the problem," Mwangi continues. "I'm afraid you will find this upsetting, Trick."

Quibble finds *a lot* of things upsetting, so her statement doesn't really surprise me. I can imagine him harassing his chin hair—unless he's trying to show better decorum in front of a member of the High Council. But I'm pretty sure the only way he's going to avoid that chin hair is by sitting on his hands.

"There is a name being whispered on the wind," Mwangi says. "Cipher."

"Cipher Mourn?" Quibble chokes out. "He's alive?"

I glance at Gusto and Zuki. "Who's Cipher Mourn?"

Gusto shakes his head. Zuki doesn't respond at all, but he does seem to turn whiter than usual.

"We are not sure if Mourn himself is alive," Mwangi says. "Yet, whether from the grave or some secret den, your old adversary continues to cast his shadow. Cipher is now the name of a cult, one started in Mourn's name."

"A cult with what purpose?" Singh asks.

"To wield magic," Mwangi replies. "By using *occuli.*"

Gusto whistles out loud, and now it's my turn to give a warning hush.

"Occuli?" Singh gasps. "Any sensible wizard—"

"These cultists are not wizards," Mwangi interjects. "They're Blisses."

"Blisses with occuli?" Gusto blurts. "I didn't even know what an occuli was until today!"

"This is bad," Zuki moans.

"Gotta keep listening," I say, turning my ear back to the door.

"Your crew discovered one of the earliest incidents of the malignant residue, right here in the school's auditorium," Mwangi says. "This points to a possible connection between Cipher and Dragonsong. Perhaps Cipher has an ally here, someone who aided in the theft of Riva Dragonsong's relics."

I can feel Gusto's gaze drilling into me. "For Merlin's sake, Gusto. It wasn't me. *Okay?*"

"It's just—I mean, you've been reading up on occuli."

"So? Since when did reading become a crime?" I demand.

But I'm not the only one who's been provoked. "Our students are submitted to rigorous screening and ethical testing," Singh declares, her voice so sharp you could use it as a razor. "They would never be tempted by such foolery."

"Perhaps," Mwangi concedes. "Still, we are certain that Cipher is building a cell in this region by recruiting Bliss youth."

"This is all very elucidating," Quibble says slowly. "But why are you telling *me?*"

I have to admit, I have the same thought. Quibble *might* have once been headwizard, but now? He's running a MOP crew.

"We are installing an agent to patrol Bliss schools, to lure any recruiter into the open and hopefully expose the larger cell," Mwangi explains. "Inevitably, our agent will be required to perform magic. We need a crew on hand to provide immediate sweeping, especially given the present instability of the Field. The crew best suited for this mission, Trick, is yours."

"A real job!" Gusto whispers excitedly.

I grant him a faint smile—part of me is thinking that the last time we went on a "real" job, we nearly got eaten. But I decide not to bring it up, since I'll probably be accused of being negative.

"Find another crew," Master Quibble says flatly from inside Singh's office. I can hear him stand up, push his chair aside. "This mission is too dangerous. Caradine Moone is on my crew! I won't take her into danger."

My cheeks burn hot. Does he really think I'm that useless? I'm the one who discovered the toxic slime in the first place— and figured out how to neutralize it!

"The crew needs to blend into a Bliss school setting," Mwangi says calmly. "Which means your students, Trick. We understand there are demons here for you to deal with, but . . . how do I put this? It's not up for negotiation. Saraya, call in the spell sweepers."

I nearly drop the listening horn in my haste to return it to Mr. Cavendish's desk, but we manage to plant ourselves in our seats just as the imposing headwizard opens her door. She arches an eyebrow at us, as if she suspects we've been misbehaving.

"Mr. Cavendish?" she wonders.

"I think he went to fetch someone," I tell her.

"I see. Please enter."

She guides us into her office, which is large, with shadowy alcoves and flights of steps winding up to other rooms. The space is decorated with mandalas, multi-limbed statues, and countless bookshelves. Everything seems immaculately organized and in pristine condition—which is a little disappointing. You'd think the head of a wizard school would decorate with some cobwebs and clutter, just for a bit of street cred—but nope.

At least there's a giant bird perched in one corner. By giant, I mean a bird that is large enough for a person to ride. This is Zivah, Headwizard Singh's familiar. It's a storm bird, which is like a phoenix, but instead of being reborn in fire, it's resurrected in the clouds of a lightning storm (sounds tricky!). The bird cocks her head inquisitively as we enter, then promptly goes to sleep.

Master Quibble says nothing; he doesn't even glance in my direction. He simply stands there, gripping the back of his chair and staring at the floor. The scar across his face is burning red. I can't tell whether it's from anger or dismay. Maybe it's a bit of both.

Singh introduces us to Madame Mwangi. Her skin is a deep brown, her hair Zuki-white, and she's clutching a staff. She also has some sort of wildcat with a long and ringed bushy tail draped over her shoulder.

"Would you like to tell them about the mission?" Singh asks.

"Oh, they know," Mwangi says, her eyes twinkling.

Singh shakes her head in disappointment. "Caradine Moone! What exactly did you—"

"What is your question, child?" Mwangi asks, gesturing at me as she speaks. My freckles begin popping like kernels on a hot pan. Her cat familiar seems to chuckle.

"Uh . . ."

"I can hear it, this question," Mwangi prompts. "It dances on the tip of your tongue."

"Okay, well—I get how our crew can blend in. But what about the wizard leading the mission? How's an adult going to pass as a teenager? Will they pretend to be a teacher? Because I don't think Bliss high schoolers will—"

I'm cut off by a loud knock on the door.

"Ah," Mwangi says. "Impeccable timing. Our mission leader has arrived. Saraya, please let in our young champion."

Young champion? My internal alarm bells begin blaring. "Oh no," I murmur as I reach out and grip Gusto's wrist.

"What?" he wonders.

"I should have known," I say with a sigh.

"Enter," Singh beckons.

The door swings open, but I don't even look. Some things are so predictable.

CHAPTER 21

There Are No Safety Demonstrations When You Fly Dragon Air

THE MOONLIGHT IS JUST BRIGHT enough for me to catch my brooding reflection in the goldfish pond. I'm sitting on my favorite bench, near the same pond where Harlee translocated me all those weeks ago. So much has happened since then—the entire magical world has been flipped upside down.

And so has mine.

Here I am, about to go on a top secret mission to help save the Field, the secret society of wizards, and possibly the world (okay, maybe that's a bit overdramatic)—but there's just one problem.

A *giant* problem.

Harlee is leading our mission. She's going to be my boss. Which is bad enough—but the worst part? She's probably the one responsible for this entire situation. Mwangi mentioned a Cipher "ally"—if Harlee didn't rob the library directly, she was probably in on it. She's the one who's been working with the bad guys all along—she *has* to be.

But no one's going to listen to me. Which means my crew

and I are headed into the jaws of danger led by the person who's responsible for keeping the teeth sharp.

I feel something stir within my robes, and I reach into my pocket to soothe Nova. I've decided to bring her along. I don't exactly have a choice—I can't leave her behind to starve or hatch without me.

"I'll look after you," I assure her.

"Cara?" a voice calls from the shadows. "Who are you talking to?"

Startled, I quickly pull my hand out of my pocket and glance up to see Yuna lingering nearby.

"*Not you*," I retort.

It's been a few hours since we fought in Beastology class, but the pain of it still feels raw. Yuna wasn't in our room when I hastily packed my bag for the mission, and I sure didn't bother leaving a goodbye note.

"I thought I missed you," she says. "Is it true?"

"What?" I ask, avoiding eye contact.

"Rumor is you're going on a secret mission with Harlee Wu." The mention of Harlee must cause me to visibly scowl, because she adds, "It *is* true. Lucky you."

Now I definitely look at her. "How do you figure?"

"Seriously, Cara? This is it! *The* moment. The prophecy—don't roll your eyes! Think about it. The Field's in jeopardy. Harlee Wu's off to save it—and you're going to be a part of it. This is your chance."

I open wide, stick my finger inside my mouth, and make

a theatrical gagging sound.

"Be nice for once," Yuna mutters.

"*You* be nice. I thought we were friends."

"We *are* friends. You're the one who won't talk to me half the time. You're the one who shuts me out."

I stand up, roll my shoulders. "You're the one who accused me of robbing the library."

"No, I didn't!"

"You *thought* it."

"Then I *thought* about it some more, *and didn't accuse you.*" She crosses her arms and draws in a deep breath. "You really don't see how lucky you are, do you?"

"To sweep up after Harlee?! To watch you and everyone else become wizards?"

"*You're* a wizard!" Yuna cries in exasperation.

"Don't you get it?" I growl, my worst insecurities stirred into a frenzy. "I can't be a *real* wizard. I just don't have enough magic in my blood!" I flash back to Professor Vitrix's cruel words. "You might as well ask a mermaid to win a footrace."

Yuna shakes her head in disappointment. "Has it ever occurred to you that a mermaid can still race? Just in a different way. She could be faster than anyone."

"But she wouldn't be the best runner. She can't even run."

"But she's still fast, in the right situation."

I exhale. It's really annoying to argue with Yuna. She thinks she's so clever—and the worst part? She is.

"If you ask me, spell sweeping *is* wizardry," Yuna declares, gesturing passionately. "It's important. Maybe more now than ever before."

"Easy for you to say," I mutter.

Yuna shakes her head at me, her face clouding over with what I can only interpret as dismay. "Actually, Cara, it's rarely easy saying anything to you." She fidgets with a strand of her silver hair. "Look, I'm really sorry for what happened in class. For upsetting you. Can you forgive me?"

I glower at her, one part of my brain contemplating if I should admit stealing her manticore venom. But I really don't want to explain the reason I took it in the first place. So, instead, I simply nod.

She rushes over and embraces me. I can't remember the last time we hugged, but we used to do it all the time. I've missed it more than I care to admit.

"Good luck," she says as we pull apart.

"Thanks," I say—not even sarcastically, but genuinely.

Then she leaves. I should, too, but instead I slump back onto the bench. That's when I hear a soft hum and lift my chin to see Miss Terse shuffling along the far side of the pond, her broom sashaying across the cobblestones. She reminds me of that old woman I saw when I was a little kid, the one I naively thought flew away on her broomstick. Of course, she was probably nothing more than a pathetic old woman, sweeping a sidewalk.

It's easy for Yuna to spout philosophies about wizardry. I'm glad we made up, but she's never going to understand what it's like to be me. Not really. All I know is that there's no way I can end up like that old woman on the street—or Miss Terse.

Zuki eventually fetches me and I begrudgingly follow the fox to Singh's tower. Surprisingly, we don't stop at the headwizard's office, but continue trekking up the tower's twisting steps. I don't really see the point of climbing to the top of the school when we'll just have to head back down to the docks afterward, but maybe this is Harlee's first official order: annoy Cara Moone as much as possible.

Then we reach the top and step out the door, onto a long flat roof, and my negativity instantly evaporates.

Standing before me is the most beautiful creature I've ever seen.

It's a dragon. Not one of those horned beasts that lumber around mounds of gold and snort smoke from their nostrils. This one has a beautiful, sleek body that sparkles with rainbow colors in the moonlight. Its golden eyes shine with intelligence. Its long, diaphanous wings are spotted like a butterfly's.

I'm sure my heart stops for a moment. Because, let me reiterate—it's the most gorgeous creature I've ever encountered (and let's keep in mind I hang with a snow-white fox with three luxurious tails).

"So nice of you to join us, Caradine," Singh says, prompting me to take a few dazed steps toward her, the rest of the crew, and the dragon itself.

I dare to brush my fingers across the creature's iridescent scales; they're soft, and ripple at my touch. Then I peer up to see that there's some sort of box attached to the back of the dragon—a compartment for passengers—and it sinks in.

Holy dratch. I'm going to fly on a dragon.

"Are you ready?" Singh asks, and I'm just about to respond when I realize that she's addressing Harlee.

"Ready," my nemesis replies. "But not happy." She gestures to the front of the dragon, where Master Quibble and Gusto are stroking its chin (Zuki looks extremely jealous). "Trick should stay here. They all should. I can do this on my own."

Of course Harlee wants to go without us. She wants all the glory for herself—or, more likely, to cavort unchecked with her Cipher buddies.

"Are you telling me you're going to do your own sweeping?" I interject, partly because I want them to remember that I'm standing right there.

"I'll take Zuki, then," Harlee informs Singh, without even glancing in my direction. "Not Trick."

Singh doesn't waver. "You need him."

"*Need?*" Harlee growls. "Why? So I can worry about him losing it the moment things get messy? Look what happened last time."

My skin prickles. She's clearly referring to whatever happened between Master Quibble and this Cipher Mourn guy all those years ago, and I'm dying to know more.

"Trick is going, Harlee," Singh declares. "And his entire crew. You must protect them."

I cough extra loudly. Like Harlee's going to protect us if she's part of the Cipher plot. Maybe no one will believe me about Harlee robbing the library or using an occuli, but *I* believe me. Which means that maybe Yuna is right—this *is* my chance. If my crew is going to remain safe—if the Field is to remain safe—then it's down to me to protect it, because I'm the only one who really knows what's going on. I'll single-handedly thwart Cipher's diabolical plans and, for once, I'll be the star of the school. Then they'll *have* to transfer me into a proper wizarding program.

"There's nothing else to say, then," Harlee tells Singh. "I will do as I'm told. *As always.*"

We climb into the dragon carriage, which is cramped, with hard wooden benches and porthole windows. Once we're all packed in, a new face appears at the door.

"Captain Szarka at your service," she greets us as she hangs a small portable light on a hook in the ceiling. "And Dörgés, of course. She'll do most of the heavy lifting." She pauses to chuckle at her own (cringey) joke.

She returns to her seat outside, at the base of Dörgés's neck. Master Quibble stares out the nearest window. He doesn't seem well. I wonder if he hates flying—or just the fact that he's going on this mission. With me.

Dörgés charges across the runway-roof, then lifts into the air. My stomach goes the opposite direction. I cling to Zuki and turn my head toward the window—if I throw up on his tails, he'll *never* forgive me.

Once we level off, Harlee pulls out her sketchbook, and her pencil begins dancing across the page. I lean over Zuki, trying to catch a surreptitious peek at what she's drawing—or, if I'm being honest, to see if I can tell if it's an occuli.

"Hey, watch the tails," the fox warns me.

Harlee lifts her eyes in a glare. "Just ask, why don't you?"

She flashes me the page to reveal a drawing—an *exquisite* drawing—of a girl rising through the clouds, eyes closed as if in meditation, a halo of light encircling her head. So, on top of everything else, Harlee is a fabulous artist.

Figures. But I can't help offering some criticism because— well, it's me. "Is that supposed to be an angel? Maybe you should add wings."

Harlee shakes her head. "Maybe you should mind your own business."

"Pfft," I mutter. "I'm just trying to help. How is she sup- posed to fly without wings?"

"It's gorgeous," Gusto interjects in a tone that sounds like Mom trying to soothe a spat between me and Su.

"All kinds of things can fly that don't have wings," Harlee says curtly.

"Oh, really?" I retort, though it takes me a moment because Dörgés lurches again. "Like what?"

"Helicopters," she says. "Squirrels. *Unicorn underwear.*"

I walked right into her trap. There go my freckles; they could light up the sky.

It's going to be a long, long mission.

That is, if we survive the dragon flight.

Ways of wizardly transport
(none of them involve brooms)

These are some of the methods wizards use to get around:

<u>All the normal Bliss ways</u>
I should point out, though, that wizards are loath to buy bus, subway, train, or plane fares; I think it's because they could sneak onto any of these vehicles with a mere blink of their eyes, but there's a moral conundrum that comes with doing that, the kind wizards don't want to contemplate too deeply.

<u>Vehicles fueled by dragon methane</u>
This fuel is environmentally friendly, but we can't share it with the rest of the world because it's a pretty limited resource—plus, how do you explain gas made from dragon poop?

<u>Dragons themselves</u>
Something I've clearly romanticized.

Various other magical creatures
I will not make the same mistake as I did with dragons.

Translocation
Currently prohibited, of course.

Our feet
There's the whole tradition of the wandering wizard (walking stick mandatory, long white beard and pointy hat optional).

What's *not* on the list? BROOMS.

Yes, I'm bringing it up again because I know how people think. They can listen to the most renowned expert on a subject—and then have everything they've learned instantly overwritten by the latest post on their Instagram feed. I can't count the number of times I've seen some Halloween GIF of a witch soaring across the night sky on her broomstick, her silhouette cast against the pale of a full moon. Looks so cool, right?

Wrong. It would be *freezing*.

Just think about all the impracticalities of broom travel. Razor-sharp wind. Ice-cold rain. Chafing in all the worst places. And if there's anyone out there who insists on thinking that you can simply solve all those problems by shouting, "Magic!" then you really haven't been paying attention.

CHAPTER 22

Welcome to Wizard Town

THE FLIGHT IS TURBULENT, BUT at least it's short. I really don't get why there aren't seat belts on dragon carriages. Maybe it's because wizards pride themselves on stiff constitutions—or maybe it's because they're accustomed to clamping themselves down with spells. By the time we disembark, Gusto, Zuki, and I are all feeling wobbly.

Harlee, of course, is completely unfazed. She pats Dörgés's side, calls a thank-you to Captain Szarka, then turns to Master Quibble. "You know this place better than anyone. Lead the way."

"And 'this place' is where exactly?" I ask, shouldering my bag.

We're inside some sort of hangar, with no view of the outside. As Dörgés was descending, I did manage to catch a glimpse of city lights, though mostly I was concentrating on not dying. I'm guessing we're not at Sea-Tac International Airport.

Quibble draws in a deep breath and exhales—as if he's finally decided to accept his fate. "We're in the Wizard Quarter," he says, turning to guide us across the hangar. "Hidden within the heart of Seattle."

The prospect of finally visiting Seattle's secret magical neighborhood helps me forget about my queasy stomach. I've learned a bit about wizard quarters in my Secret Geography class and now, at last, I get to experience one for myself. According to Professor Hart, keeping wizard quarters hidden utilizes a lot less magic than you'd guess. Mostly, it's underground levels, ordinary doors (there's nothing intriguing about a door labeled "Electrical Room") and a Wi-Fi dead zone—actually, *no* electronic signals will work in wizard quarters. Even a drone can't fly overhead without unceremoniously crashing. Then there's the belief that if any Blisses *do* inadvertently enter a wizard quarter, they won't notice what's right in front of their very eyes.

I don't really buy it—yes, Blisses are labeled as ignorant, but I'm not sure how anyone could be *that* oblivious. It only takes *me* about fifteen seconds of wandering through Seattle's Wizard Quarter to realize how different it is from a normal urban neighborhood.

First of all, there are no cars, buses, or taxis, which means there isn't the regular cacophony that comes with traffic. As for the people, they're dressed in eccentric clothing—capes, robes, and a variety of hats and headdresses. The accessories they don't have? Phones. Which means no one is meandering along staring at their screens (though I do see a guy face-plant into a tree because he's distracted by stargazing). The thing that really catches my eye is the variety of familiars. Everywhere I look, I see a raven perched on a shoulder or a hare trailing behind her master. At one point, we spot a peacock with its feathers on full display.

"Gorgeous," Gusto says admiringly.

"What's so special about it?" Zuki yips. "It only has one tail! I have three. That thing is just a glorified chicken."

"Jealous much?" I wonder. Once Zuki starts on his tails, he can go on for hours, so in an attempt to change the subject, I add, "This place is kind of like Pioneer Square. All stone and red brick. And nothing's higher than three stories."

"They may not be higher, but they are lower," Quibble says. "Some of these places run deep."

"You would know," Harlee mutters.

I'm not sure what she means by that remark, but the Q-Man lets it slide, and we keep moving. All the stores are still open, well after midnight, but that's no surprise—wizards like to stay up late. I make a mental note to try to visit a few of the shops during my free time—that is, if I get any free time. Since I'm on a supersecret prophesied mission to save the world, it's doubtful.

We pass by a food cart with the words *Sticky Stuff* emblazoned on the side, and I can't resist pausing to take a closer look.

"Just keep moving," Gusto advises.

I scowl at him. It's easy for him to have such a casual response to everything—this clearly isn't his first visit to a street full of cool wizard stuff. But I'm not about to miss out because this is just another mundane day at the market for the rest of my crew.

I turn my back on Gusto and take a closer look at the *Sticky Stuff* cart.

Big mistake.

The vendor isn't selling whimsical magic candy, but stuff—stuff that is still *moving*—impaled on sticks. It's possible this is the first time I've felt sorry for a dragon slug or an infernopede. I scurry back to the crew.

"Told you," Gusto says.

I know Gusto's not gloating (he's not the type), but I still feel embarrassed. And out of place. If I don't fit in at Dragonsong, I definitely don't fit in here.

"Don't worry about it," Gusto consoles me. "One time, my mom coaxed me into eating a sky-wriggler and I threw up blue for two blocks."

I give him a nod of appreciation as we round a bend and arrive at what appears to be the hotel district. We pass by a few decrepit establishments that seem like they're in disguise as haunted mansions and eventually arrive at a place called the Drowsy Druid.

The clerk is persnickety (with an even more persnickety rat on his shoulder) and wants to haggle over our reservation until he seems to recognize Master Quibble—then he quickly hands over our keys (actual metal keys, like something used to open a dungeon door) and we head up to our rooms on the third floor. Thankfully, we all get separate rooms—as the clerk passed out our room keys, I had a moment of panic, thinking I'd have to room with Gusto, which would be awkward, or with Harlee, which would be worse. My room is smaller than the dorm I share with Yuna and, of course, there's no window bench with a beautiful ocean view.

"I bet Harlee has a suite with a view of the entire quarter," I complain to Nova as I take her out of my pocket and place her under my pillow.

I've just started unpacking my things when I hear Harlee and Quibble arguing in the hallway. We haven't even been here for five minutes. I poke my head out to see what's going on. Across from me, Gusto's door also opens a crack, and we exchange a quizzical glance.

"I said we're staying here," Harlee tells Quibble. "The crew needs rest. We all do."

"Kazuki and I have old friends to visit," Quibble argues. I notice that he's not wearing any of his spell sweeping gear.

Harlee crosses her arms. "Friends. Right. Where? Which one of your old drinking holes is so important for you to visit?"

I'm not exactly a Q-Man fan, but Harlee's tone seems extremely harsh. She might be our leader, but she's still basically a kid and he's one of our teachers.

"I'm just going to poke into a few corners," Quibble says. "See what I can turn up."

"To Morgana's hearth with that," Harlee retorts. "The Council already conducted its investigation here. We need to concentrate on *our* mission: the Bliss schools."

Quibble doesn't say anything; he just fiddles with his chin hair.

"Well?" Harlee snaps eventually, and I'm kind of glad that I'm not the only one irritated by the Q-Man's ponderous nature.

"The Council knows how to stir the cauldron well enough," he finally says. "But they don't know enough to scrape their spoon along the bottom to see what kind of crud sticks to it."

"And you do?" Harlee snipes.

Quibble offers her a faint smile—at which Harlee thrusts a finger into his face. She's so tall, she doesn't even have to look up to do it, but it's jarring to witness, and I feel the sudden need to come to his defense.

"Leave him alone!" I blurt. "Master Quibble knows what he's doing," I add, even though I'm not sure he does.

Harlee whirls on me, and I can see the passion—or maybe it's magic—rising in her cheeks. Her glare is so intense that it actually prompts me to take two steps backward.

"Harlee," Zuki says softly. He wraps himself around her ankles, like a house cat. He's purring like one, too.

Her gaze drops down to the fox and I'm saved from incineration by eyeball—at least for the moment. "I'm not a little kid anymore, Spooky," she says. "The Council put *me* in charge."

"Being in charge means making decisions," Quibble says calmly. "And right now, you can decide to either trust the oldest and most experienced member of your crew, or treat me like a broken old man. Which will it be?"

Harlee shakes her head, all the wind sucked out of her cape. "Keep him out of the pubs," she tells Zuki with a tone of resignation. Then she shuffles to her room and clicks the door shut.

Gusto exhales, and so do I. Quibble and Harlee obviously have some issues to work out, but it's not anything I want to dwell on right now—I've got my own agenda.

"I'm coming with you, Master Quibble," I announce.

"Definitely not," he says.

I march up to him. "Look, Master. You know I'm just going to end up following you. The only way I'm staying here is if you perform some magic spell to lock me in my room—and I'd like to take this moment to remind you that drawing on the Field is currently forbidden."

He nods slowly, and contemplates the stairs (there are no elevators in a wizard hotel), as if he's anxious to get going. For him, that glance is the equivalent of a little kid impatiently jumping up and down while waiting for his mom to dig a treat out of her purse.

"Very well," he says at last. "Augusto, you can join us. Help Caradine stay out of trouble. But bring your gear, scrubs. We might need it."

"Thank you," I breathe.

I may not be a wizard, I may not even feel worthy of being in their town—but that's not going to stop me from making the most of it.

The "magical" monikers of wizard shops

A few things stand out to me as we traipse through Seattle's magic town. One, there are no malls or plazas, just individual stores lining the streets. Two, wizards like old-fashioned services. You want a new iPhone? Good luck. You want the elbows of your sleeves patched? You've come to the right place. Finally, the shop names—well, let's just say wizard humor is an acquired taste. Just take the following:

The Mermaid's Boots
A cobbler (which, you probably don't know, makes and repairs shoes).

Lady Godiva's Wardrobe
This is a clothing store. The name is funny, I guess, because Lady Godiva is famous for . . . well, you can look it up.

Gorgon Optometry & Eyewear

There's a sign in the front window that says: *Our prices will petrify you.*

Moon to Morn

As far as I can tell, this is the wizard's version of 7-Eleven. I bet they don't sell Slurpees. Or maybe they do, and they have disgusting flavors like infernopede or spider venom.

Hansel & Gretel Bakery

Uh, the thing Hansel and Gretel are most famous for baking is A PERSON. (If you happen to consider a wizard a person, which I do. Some people will be tempted to shout, "But she was a witch!" but let me say here that they are the same thing. "Witch" is just a name coopted by Blisses and used to cast magical women in a bad light. Sexist *and* successful, based on their depictions in numerous fairy tales. No matter what, she was still a person, which still makes the name of the bakery gross.)

Under the Cover of Darkness

A bookstore specializing in arcane magic—in other words, a shop that screams "Cara Moone." (I mean, it literally screamed *something* that sounded eerily like my name as we sauntered past. The Wizard Quarter is so cool.)

The Nightshade
A restaurant. But you definitely don't want nightshade in your sauce, because—well, imagine me making the gesture of my hand cutting across my throat.

The Slubbering Spell
A pub. I suppose after a few mugroot ales, magic gets sloppy.

The Orgulous Ogre
Another pub. I don't know what *orgulous* means, but I'm guessing it's not the type of adjective you usually use to describe ogres.

The Witching Hour
I can glean no hint as to what this shop sells; the sign features a broken hourglass. If I had to guess? A pub. Because Master Quibble sure leads us past a lot of them. Which makes me wonder (begrudgingly) if Harlee has a right to worry about what he's up to.

CHAPTER 23

Master Quibble Scrapes Bottom

WE TRAIPSE THROUGH A SEEDY section of the Quarter and eventually arrive at a dilapidated building with a faded sign that reads: *The Two-Eyed Cyclops ~ Fine Antiques ~ Cosimo Balthasar, Purveyor.* I can only imagine what qualifies as an antique in a wizard's estimation. The entire wizarding world seems to be mostly composed of them. (Reminder: Yuna uses a *phonograph* to play her music.)

"Cosimo is from a Bliss family, with plenty of connections to that world," Quibble tells us as he pauses in front of the door. "If anyone knows about the dark market, it's him. Don't touch anything and let me do the talking."

Just before we enter, I take another glance at the "two-eyed" cyclops on the sign. It has the customary one eye above its snout; the second eye is the one it's squeezing in its hairy fist. There's even goopy eye juice dripping between the beast's fingers. In other words, the sign is appropriately gruesome, so I feel like this shop has promise.

We enter, and I'm not disappointed.

It's like Halloween barfed inside. Scanning the dimly lit space, I spot tilting stacks of grimoires, wooden crates wearing cobweb veils, and tall gilded mirrors lazily half-clothed by dusty curtains. There's even an Egyptian sarcophagus standing in one corner, its lid slightly ajar, as if the mummified pharaoh once dwelling within it squeezed out for a stroll. A stench of must and decay clings to the air.

"You could get lost in here," Gusto murmurs.

I nod. "Maybe that's where the smell comes from—customers who didn't make it out."

There's a definite warehouse vibe to the place—the only aisles are those haphazardly created by the clutter of artifacts. I'm drawn down one of these aisles and find myself in front of a mannequin wearing a suit of what I recognize from my history books as wizard armor. At the mannequin's base is a weathered box, and I kneel to read some words crudely carved into the ancient wood: *For the Hunting of Wizards*. I lift the lid to find padded compartments containing a tarnished flintlock pistol, an assortment of bullets, and various vials of colored liquids. There is also a set of gruesome tools: scissors, forceps, a scalpel, and a glass syringe. I like my spooky stuff, but this is way more than I bargained for.

"Yikes!" Zuki cries as he and Gusto sidle up next to me. "You don't think those scissors are for cutting tails, do you?"

I'm relieved that he's freaking out—it allows me to shift the focus away from my own heebie-jeebies. I scratch his chin to soothe him, then run a finger along a conspicuously empty compartment, about the size of a marker pen, in the very center of the box. "What went here?"

"Don't know and don't *want* to know," Gusto says. "Come on, let's find Master Quibble."

We catch up to him at a counter at the back of the labyrinthine store. He taps an ancient bell and a halfhearted *ding* sounds. Next to the bell is a skull with spider legs reaching out of one eye socket like a clutch of fingers. I'm not sure about the spider, but the skull looks real—I can see each and every crooked tooth. It's normally the kind of thing that would impress me, but I'm still shaken by that wizard-hunting kit. The sooner we get out of here, the better.

We hear Cosimo before we see him—grunts and groans and a weary "I'm comin'" emanate from the shadows behind the counter before the man himself shuffles into view. He's robust, with a stained shirt that appears to be losing an argument with his belly. As soon as Cosimo sees our master, he stops short, extracts a hankie from his pocket, and wipes it across his forehead. Cosimo's a white guy, but his face is flushing red as a phoenix.

"Been a long time, Trick," he says with a grimace. He leans over the counter, eyes darting back and forth between Gusto and me, like he's trying to figure out if he should be worried about us. But the brooms slung across our shoulders seem to set him at ease.

"What can I do you for?" Cosimo wonders. He has a giant nose, mapped with veins that seem to pulse, as if in alarm.

"Someone is selling talismans to Blisses," Quibble replies with uncharacteristic bluntness.

Cosimo rubs his hand against the back of his neck. He's just wiped his brow, but he's still sweating. "It ain't me, Trick. I run a clean shop."

I feel Gusto tugging my sleeve; he's gaping upward, into the low-hanging rafters, where an enormous purple-black snake is coiled around a beam. It has an intelligent gleam in its eyes and its blue tongue flickers with menace. Cosimo's familiar, I surmise.

Master Quibble runs a slow and deliberate finger across the surface of the counter, leaving a visible trail in the dust accumulated there. But he doesn't say anything; he leaves Cosimo to sweat—which, of course, he does. Profusely.

"Look, Trick, I already been hassled by them others what the Council sent round."

"You haven't been hassled by *me*," Master Quibble declares.

There's a commanding timbre in the Q-Man's tone that I'm not accustomed to. He lifts his finger and stares at the film of dust on its tip. He stares for a long time. The only sound is the tick of some clock or device sequestered in the nether regions of the shop. "You show them the tomb, Mo?"

"The tomb?"

Master Quibble finally lifts his gaze from his finger. "Yes, you know. *The tomb.* The secret cellar you access through the sarcophagus."

I turn my eyes back toward the mummy's coffin. It's a *secret doorway?*

"Everything down there is clean. I swear, Trick. Go take a peek."

The spider—ugh, I guess it *is* real—scuttles out of the skull and makes a dash across the counter, as if it wants to avoid the interrogation. Master Quibble has one hand on the counter, and the hairy little beast is scampering straight toward it. I watch, horrified, as the bug closes the gap—Master Quibble doesn't even flinch.

The spider never reaches his hand. Before that can happen, the snake shoots down, snatches the spider in its jaws, then recoils to its beam, all in one fluid motion. I watch in disgusted fascination as the last of the bug's twitching legs slip into its mouth.

Gusto audibly groans—but Master Quibble still hasn't blinked. He just continues staring at Cosimo.

"There are no talismans in here," the flustered shop owner insists. "Not that I know of, anyway."

That's a hedge if I've ever heard one—the telltale sign of someone trying to cover his tracks, just in case his lie gets caught. I know from experience. The thing is, if you want to be a good liar, you have to know when to stop talking.

Cosimo doesn't. "I don't sell talismans, Trick."

Master Quibble lifts his hand from the counter and strokes his chin hair. "What about your brother?"

"Brother?" Cosimo asks slowly. "What brother?"

Master Quibble slams his fist down so suddenly that it causes everyone to jump—me included. I'm not accustomed to that kind of outburst from our master. It's possible that I have a newfound respect for him.

"You forget that night in the Dragon, Mo?" he demands.

"You don't go there anymore, do you?" Cosimo says. "I heard you quit drinkin'."

"You told me about Dante that night. Your twin brother. Your *Bliss* brother."

"Oh," Cosimo rasps quietly. "*That* brother. Can't help havin' relations, Trick."

I watch a smile curl across Master Quibble's face—he smiles so rarely that it's kind of creepy. "What about telling him about us, Mo?" Master Quibble muses. "Telling him about wizards? Can you help *that*? Where's Dante now? Still wandering around, passing himself off as one of our kind? Did you let the Council know about that little secret?"

Gusto and I stare wide-eyed at each other. I'll admit I thought Master Quibble was bluffing when he told Harlee he could dig up information the Council hadn't found. But a Bliss pretending to be a wizard? Master Quibble is definitely onto something.

Cosimo's shirt is so soaked with sweat, it's like he took a shower in it. "I don't know where Dante is, Trick. I swear. Disappeared, long time ago. Told you about him in confidence, Trick. I thought you were too . . ."

"Drunk to remember?" Master Quibble finishes for him. "Well, I do remember. And I've been asking myself, 'How does a Bliss pass himself off as a wizard?' I can only think of one way: he uses occuli."

I swallow. That's exactly what I've thought of doing. What I *think* Harlee's doing.

"Maybe he even starts sharing them with his friends," Master Quibble continues. "His Bliss friends. Next thing you know, we're here. Field is bleeding black and magic has been suspended."

"That doesn't . . . I don't—it's nothin' to do with me!" Cosimo sputters.

Master Quibble finally slides his fist off the counter. "Our world's in danger of collapsing. You better figure out which side you're on, Mo."

"Is it true?" Cosimo presses. "You quit drinkin'?"

"That's my business."

"You won't be goin' by the old haunts, then," Cosimo says, wiping his brow again. "Don't take kids to those kind of places."

Master Quibble peers down at us, as if he's just remembering that we're there. Then his gaze flits back to Cosimo. "We'll leave you to your business, Mo. Looks like it's thriving."

It doesn't, of course—we're the only ones in the shop. We wander back outside, where an autumn gust has picked up, and Cosimo's sign creaks in the wind. The way it's swaying makes it look like the cyclops is brandishing its fistful of eyeball at us.

"What next?" Gusto wonders as he pulls out a stick of witch's delight and begins nervously gnawing on it.

Master Quibble strokes his chin hair. "I think it's time to get a drink."

CHAPTER 24

There's No Dancing at the
Dancing Dragon

WE DON'T HEAD ACROSS TOWN, but *down*town, which means descending into the subterranean levels of the Quarter. Seattle is famous for its underground tunnels. One summer, my family and I did the tour, but we didn't see anything like this—I guess the tunnel complex is a little vaster than what they mention on the Bliss brochures. Once we're down below, Master Quibble leads us along a meandering street, then through a zigzagging alley, down a flight of stairs, through another alley, and to a ramshackle building that looks like it's begging to be condemned. Remnants of faded plaster cling indifferently to the brick walls, and the windows are boarded over. There's not even a sign out front.

"What is this place?" I ask.

"The Dancing Dragon," Quibble replies. "One of my old drinking holes."

"Emphasis on the word 'hole,'" I quip.

"Oh, it's a hole, all right," Zuki adds. "A pit of squalor. A ditch of despair. A chasm of—"

"Uh, Master?" Gusto speaks up. "Harlee was pretty adamant about—"

"Did you notice how many times Cosimo asked me about visiting my old haunts?" Quibble interrupts. "Why do you think that is?"

"Because he's worried about your liver?" I suggest.

The Q-Man offers me a faint smile. "Because that's where we'll find his brother. Come on—we've scraped the bottom of the cauldron; time to gaze upon the grunge on the edge of our spoon."

"We can go inside?" I ask in surprise. In Bliss Seattle, they'd never let a kid into a bar. (I mean, I don't think they would. I've never tried!)

"Stay close," Quibble advises.

He leans against the front door and after a few tries heaves it open; it's so tight, it makes me wonder how often anyone ever visits the Dancing Dragon. Or maybe, I reconsider, they just rarely leave.

It's dark and hazy inside, with a low ceiling and many shadowy nooks and side booths—in other words, old-fashioned. But it's not cool and retro, just old and dingy with the faint stench of mold. It's clearly the type of place where people come to hide. Or possibly die.

Patrons are slumped over tables or entrenched in corners, mugs in hand. A fireplace flickers meekly in the far corner; for some reason, the flames are green. There is an old phonograph on the counter, emitting a haunting tune that weaves its way through the hazy air like a spell.

Master Quibble takes a stool at the bar and beckons us to the seats at his left. My stool is so high that my feet don't touch the floor. I feel way more out of place here than I ever did wandering through the outside sections of the Quarter.

The barkeep lumbers over. She has three vicious scars running diagonally from her chin to her right cheek, raised, puffy and shiny. Something clearly raked its claws across her; I wonder if it was one of the patrons.

"Trick Quibble," she says quietly. "Last time I saw you, Singh had to carry you out with a spell. What will it be—the usual?"

Quibble raises a deferential hand. "I'm off the spirits, Haddie. I'll take anise and soda."

"This ain't the Ogre," the barkeep—Haddie, I guess—grumbles. "You want somethin' fancy, stick your neck in there. Ginger beer is the tamest I got."

"Ginger beer it is," Quibble concedes. "Three of them."

Haddie eyes Gusto and me, as if she's sizing us up or considering kicking us out. But, once again, I think the sight of our brooms saves us—spell sweepers are known for solving problems, not causing them. As for Master Quibble, he obviously has some sort of reputation—everyone seems just a little wary of him. Haddie bustles behind the bar, then plunks down three grimy mugs filled with frothing golden liquid.

"What's with the fox?" she asks, which makes me suddenly realize Zuki has left my side. I crane my neck and spot him sniffing around the corners of the tavern.

"Hunting vermin," Master Quibble says over the moan of the music.

"I don't want trouble, Trick," Haddie warns, throwing the bar rag over her shoulder. "Best you leave. Hate to see somethin' happen. 'Specially with kids here."

"What is that supposed to mean?" I mouth to Gusto.

Wide-eyed, he shakes his head.

"We'll leave once our drinks are finished," Master Quibble says.

He settles in over his mug, one hand gripping the handle, the other pestering his chin hair. It seems like he's lost in thought, but I know when he's in that sort of mood, and this isn't it. I catch a flicker in his expression; he may look like he's distracted by drink, but his eyes are scanning the Dragon.

I follow his lead, skimming the tavern as inconspicuously as possible. Master Quibble said that Dante was Cosimo's twin brother, so I automatically search for someone who looks just like him. But it's near impossible to identify anyone, partially because it's so shadowy and partially because most everyone is wearing heavy cloaks with hoods.

I hear a hiss and peer down to see a snake twisting right past my stool. Even though my feet are already off the ground, I instinctively curl my knees. I'm not as freaked out by snakes as Gusto is, but this one is huge and black—and I've seen it before.

"Master, that's . . ."

He nods. "Cosimo sent his familiar to warn Dante. Won't be long now."

Gusto has turned ashen. I grab on to his sleeve to save him from cracking open his skull in case he faints, and watch as the serpent writhes across the floor. It soon pauses in front of what appears to be an empty table in a nearby alcove. Then it rears upward, long neck undulating as its tongue flickers. I watch as a shape detaches from the shadows and leans forward into the faint light. The figure is wearing a hooded robe, but if that's Dante, then his twin got all the seconds at dinnertime. This guy's a skeleton.

Master Quibble is on his feet. "Dante Balthasar," he announces.

The guy doesn't reply—he just springs from his seat and bolts toward the back of the tavern.

"Out the front door!" Quibble commands as he goes in pursuit. "Run round the back and cut him off!"

Gusto is still staring, freaked out by the snake, so I yank him off his stool. I have to slam my shoulder into the front door to thrust it open, and then tumble out awkwardly, nearly crashing headlong into someone coming the other way.

Harlee. Why am I always colliding into her? It's like the universe wants us to literally butt heads.

Her face twists into a snarl. "What the—"

"No time!" I gasp, pushing past her.

Gusto and I race around the corner and into the alley to

see Dante trying to slip out of one of the Dragon's back windows, his cloak snagged on something. It takes me a moment to realize the something is Zuki's teeth. With a feverish kick, Dante breaks free—Zuki squeals—and crashes clumsily to the ground. He's up in an instant and charging straight toward me. His hood has fallen down, revealing a pale and sunken face, but my eyes are more focused on what's in his fist.

A wand.

Not his, if he's a Bliss—which means the wand is definitely an occuli. He fires a blast at me as he charges forward; I hear the cobblestones crackle at my feet, feel a prickle in my toes, and am vaguely aware of Gusto screaming at me to watch out.

But there's no way I'm letting Dante escape. I unsling my broom and swing it with every ounce of my non-magical strength. I don't bother aiming for Dante's midsection—I go right for his ankles to send him sprawling across the cobblestones. With a satisfying clatter, he smashes into a collection of garbage cans on the far side of the alley.

"Ta-da!" I sing, twirling my broom.

"Uh, Cara?" Gusto says. "Your boots are—"

"Just what the dratch is happening?" Harlee demands.

Thankfully, Master Quibble and Zuki choose that moment to slide out of the window where Dante made his escape.

"He stepped on my tails!" Zuki moans, trotting up to me. "My beautiful tails! Are they smudged?"

"You'll live," I tell him. "Probably."

"Probably? What do you mean prob—"

"They look better than my feet," I tell him, which is an educated guess based on the smoke curling up from the toes of my blackened boots. But nothing feels burnt or broken. Just tingly.

"You drunkard!" Harlee yells at Master Quibble as he approaches. In her crimson robes, she really stands out against the gloomy grays of this forgotten corner of the Quarter. "How could you bring *them* here?" she rails. "They're kids."

"Kids?!" I snap. "We're nearly the same age!"

"Yeah?" Harlee jeers. "Do you want to talk about your unicorn under—"

"You followed us," Master Quibble (thankfully) interjects with an accusing tone as he marches across the alley to where Dante is still slumped on the ground.

"I didn't follow you," Harlee contends, stomping after him. "I just came to the place where I hoped you wouldn't be. I hate being right."

I roll my eyes—I doubt it. As Gusto, Zuki, and I join them in front of Dante, I notice the satchel lying near the fallen man. It's flipped open and disgorging items across the cobblestones: wands, rings, amulets. Quite the haul.

Kneeling, I prod a wand, the one that Dante attacked me with. It's bound at the hilt with leather and its wooden shaft is embedded with beads of glass. It's not Riva Dragonsong's, which means it was stolen from somewhere—*someone*—else, along with the other talismans.

I tentatively pick up the wand. There's no shiver of magic, no sudden surge of power, but that's no surprise. It takes more than simple touch to coax magic from an occuli (or from the Field, for that matter); it requires focus and intention. I turn the wand over in my hands, contemplating its power. Or, if I'm being completely honest, *coveting* it.

It's one thing to hang out in the Dragonsong Library and *think* about forbidden magic, but now here I am, deep in the Wizard Quarter, on a dangerous mission being led by a girl who's probably out to betray us, and the key to surviving . . .

Well, I might be holding it in my hand.

CHAPTER 25

The Book Is Always Better

ALL I NEED TO DO is slip the wand into my robe while everyone's distracted. What's the harm of using it when I really need to? What would be so bad about one flick of the wrist? One zap? The Field could probably take it—and so could I. I mean, if Harlee *is* using an occuli, she shows absolutely zero side effects. Maybe if you have *some* magic, you can handle it . . .

"Cara," Gusto says fretfully. "You have that look in your eye."

I don't respond, just keep fingering the wand.

"Cara," Zuki adds. "*Look at him.*"

I follow the fox's swishing tails to see Dante rising woozily to his feet. The would-be wizard is a pale photocopy of his brother, gaunt and bleached of life, with swollen black bags beneath his eyes. He's not just knocking on death's door; he's pretty much marched through to the other side.

I exhale. Maybe this is how my sister's vaping habit started— you just try it a couple of times and then . . .

Gusto slowly takes the wand from my hand and I watch

haplessly as he stuffs it back in the satchel, along with the other magical items. He hands the bag to Harlee, who begins shaking it in Dante's face.

"Where did you get this stuff?" she demands.

"None of your business, child."

"Child?!" she explodes (I guess she really doesn't like the taste of her own potion). "Give me answers! Now, *Cipher*!"

"I'm not one of Storm's crew," Dante retorts. "Just someone who profits from his lust for magic."

Master Quibble steps around Harlee and stares Dante in the eye. "Cipher Storm? Is that the leader of their cell?"

Dante's eyes dart. I know that look—he's let something slip, and now he's mentally kicking himself. "I've never met him; just his underlings," he says as he reaches into a pocket and pulls out a tarnished coin.

I squint at it; for some reason, it seems familiar.

"Are you trying to bribe us?" Harlee asks incredulously.

Dante throws his head back and laughs, revealing a mouthful of rotting, brown teeth. "This is no ordinary coin." He closes his hand around it and brandishes his fist at us—and that's when an image from the wizard fairy-tale book flashes into my memory.

"That's Eurybia's Torch!" I shriek.

The crew stares at me.

"A talisman forged by the dark wizard Eurybia!" I explain in a panic. "It could incinerate an entire village!"

Harlee thrusts the satchel of occuli into my arms and raises her wrists to counterattack. The hot glow of wizardry begins to burn on her cheeks, then tangles of light lash out from her fingertips—but only for an instant, because Master Quibble slaps her arms down.

"No!" he cries as Harlee's magic extinguishes. "Everyone! Out of the way!"

Clutching the satchel of occuli, I stumble backward, watching in horror as beams of light begin to radiate from Dante's clenched fist. A smug smile takes shape on his withered face—he's going to blast us with everything he has.

Except there's one problem: what Dante *has* is nothing. There's no magic in his blood. He was able to fire the wand at me, and he's obviously handled other occuli, but the price for using something as powerful as Eurybia's Torch?

He can't pay it.

Dante's smile turns to a scream as his hand ignites into a giant ball of white fire. Even as he frantically shakes his wrist, trying to extinguish the flames, the fire winnows up his arms, then across his chest, savaging him. He collapses to the ground, writhing and howling. As the blaze consumes him, black slime begins oozing from his every orifice—his mouth, his nostrils, his ears, even the corners of his eyes. It's like the animated picture in the *Forbidden Magic* book, but worse, because the picture didn't have sound or smell or heat—and it didn't cause the ground to quake.

There's a final burst of fire—then Dante's gone. All that's left behind is a burbling, smoking pool of black tar, the occuli coin sitting on top in smug defiance. A giant, jagged rip hangs over Dante's remains—another wound in the field. The reek of rot fills the alley.

Gusto leans over and begins throwing up; I don't blame him. I drop the satchel of occuli to the ground because, yep, I'm good—no more temptation to use forbidden magic here.

I hear other murmurings and turn to see a small audience of wizards gathered in the alley, drawn out of the tavern by the commotion.

"Constables will be arriving soon," Master Quibble announces. "They'll want to know what happened here."

This prompts a few worried glances; clearly, some of these wizards aren't keen to be seen by the authorities. They scurry away.

"Come on, Augusto," Master Quibble says, helping my queasy partner to his feet. "Let's go fetch you another ginger beer to settle your stomach. Caradine and Kazuki, handle the cleanup. Save the coin and talismans for the constables."

As the Q-Man guides Gusto away, another rumble reverberates through the alley, so violent that I nearly lose my footing and stagger into Harlee.

"Easy now," she says.

"You take it easy," I retort in embarrassment as I turn to confront the angry mouth-thingy dangling in front of me.

It's the biggest I've seen yet. The Field's wounds are getting worse, thanks to Dante's vicious spellcasting—and Harlee's. She tried to use magic here, too, I remind myself. Which means she's *still* been involved in every single case of toxic slime I've encountered. I mean, yes, she only did it to counterattack Dante, which wouldn't make sense if she were on his side, but she could still be using her own occuli. Sure, it doesn't explain why she doesn't look like death warmed over, but I'm not about to abandon my suspicions yet.

"Cara?" Zuki says, as there's yet another quake. "We better hop to it!"

I nod, lower my goggles, and begin misting the slime with Moone Brew. "I'll spray, you sweep up the neutralized dust."

Harlee leans over me, grimacing as I work. "So, this is what's happening with the Field now? All the time?"

I give her a glance. I definitely shouldn't poke the hydra, but I can't resist. "Yeah, like you don't know."

"What's that supposed to mean?"

I keep squirting my Moone Brew.

"I think you should tell me," Harlee says. "I'm your leader."

I whirl on her and push up my goggles. "Master Quibble is my leader."

Harlee frowns. "And right now, I'm *his* leader."

"You're the leader of this *one* mission. Not the boss of him. Tell her, Zuki."

"What?" the fox asks, his gaze flitting between me and Harlee. "Uh . . . yeah. Well, you know me. I'm not much for talk. Strong, silent type—that's me. Quiet! Shy. Introverted and—"

"Okay, then shut up," I say, still facing Harlee. "I know about you," I tell her, gesturing to what's remaining of Dante. "Every time you twitch your pretty little fingers, this dratch happens."

Harlee blinks at me. "What are you talking about? It's been happening all over the place."

"Yeah, but it started with *you*."

"Wh-what?"

"You know," Zuki intervenes, "maybe we should talk about this later. Maybe—"

"Every time I've had to deal with one of these messes, you've been involved!" I declare. "It's like you're tossing some sort of magical grenade into the Field."

Harlee takes a step back, contemplating me. She must be thinking hard because I can see her temples pulsing. "Every time you've purged this kind of mess was after one of *my* spells? Are you sure?"

"Are magic foxes annoying?"

She stares at me, perplexed.

"Yes, I'm sure!" I reply in exasperation. "The first time was in the auditorium after you pulled your little stunt—"

"Little?" she asks, the hurt plain in her tone.

I roll my eyes. "What were you still doing there that day? You told Professor Plume you forgot something. But that was a lie."

Harlee fidgets. "Why do you think that?"

"Cara's a lying expert," Zuki explains, which means getting my fiercest scowl.

"It *was* a lie," Harlee admits. "I just needed a moment to myself. I zoned out in the basement, waiting for everyone else to clear out."

Likely story, but I decide to keep going. "Then there was my locker. You blew it open and it gushed toxic gunk. And—you were on the field trip to the train wreck, weren't you? Did you cast a spell?"

Her lips twist.

"It *was* you!" I cry. "I knew it."

"It was only something small," Harlee confesses. "*Really* small. I needed Steve Winsome to stop ogling me. He's such a creep and I—"

"It still left spell dust," I tell her. "And it's worse when you use an . . ."

"Use a what?" she wonders.

I scratch the back of my neck. I don't have the guts to outright accuse her of wielding an occuli. I'm still not sure I'm right and, besides, Master Quibble is back inside with Gusto—it's not like Zuki can do much to protect me if Harlee decides to blast me into oblivion.

Though, as I watch her begin to pace, temples throbbing, I wonder if she's going to do that anyway. She makes me think of a volcano about to blow. The last time she erupted it was bad news for my locker—and me.

But she doesn't erupt, not this time. She simply stops and looks at me again. "I'm not the only one involved in all your examples," she says.

Of course she wants to shuffle the blame. "Oh yeah? Who else, then?"

She draws in a deep breath. "You."

I open my mouth to respond, but nothing comes out. Because the truth is that it's something that hadn't even occurred to me. I mean, I'm just a spell sweeper. What effect would I have on the Field?

"My magic might be a grenade," Harlee says, "but maybe you're the one pulling the pin."

Worst toothpaste ever

Here's the thing when it comes to spellcasting: going back to my toothpaste analogy of the Field, the tube is *not* bottomless. You take something out, something needs to go back *in*. And that something comes from the wizard herself—you're essentially returning a bit of your essence to the Field.

If you try to overdo it? Try to cast a spell that demands more life-force than you can afford? Well, I refer you to Exhibit A: the pile of goo formerly known as Dante Balthazar.

But at least if you're a wizard, what you're returning to the Field is *magical* life-force (even if you die in the process of spellcasting). If you're a Bliss, like Dante, you're paying with *talentless* essence—basically, you're stuffing the equivalent of cavities into the toothpaste tube. Or, to think of it another way, *anti-magic*.

Which explains why wounds are appearing at Magical

Occurrence sites, spewing black slime. The Field is like a body trying to expel an infection.

Which, I guess, makes me like a nurse.

Unless I'm part of the disease.

Yep, Harlee's gotten into my head. Big-time.

CHAPTER 26

There's Nothing Cuter than a Baby Squix

AFTER THE PURGE, HARLEE LEADS the crew back to the Drowsy Druid, except for Master Quibble, who stays behind to explain the situation to the constables.

My brain continues to churn. How can I be responsible for what's happening with the Field? My innate magic is meager, and the only occuli I've ever touched is the one Dante used when he tried to fry me.

Then I remember something Su once told me: the best defense is a good offense. This could be Harlee's approach. Maybe she's gaslighting me, deflecting suspicions from herself by trying to accuse me of being involved. . . .

"Cara, are you okay?" Gusto asks me as we arrive at the Druid. "You've been, uh, unusually quiet."

"Just exhausted." My mind feels like a magic fox chasing all nine of its tails, each of them a different theory. By the time I stagger back into my room, there are only a few hours left until dawn. I don't even kick off my boots, I just collapse onto my bed. I left Nova nestled beneath the pillows, but now I reel the egg into my arms and cradle her against my chest. She coos my addled mind to sleep.

I awake to the strange feeling of something moist against my cheek.

"Huh?" Groggily, I lift my head, but it's pitch-dark in the room and I can't see a thing. I can sense that it's morning, though, so I fumble across my bed to the window and throw up the blackout blinds.

I hear a vibrant chirp and turn to find a mess on my bed: scattered shell fragments and hardened strands of blood and yolk.

"Nova?" I cry, half in excitement, half in a panic because I'm terrified that I've squished her in the night.

I carefully run my hands over the bed cover, searching, and at last find her hidden beneath a fold in the blanket.

She's the most adorable thing I've ever seen, tiny and rose-colored, flecked with purple spots. Her eyes are huge and round, and her legs are nothing more than tiny feelers that tickle my flesh when I scoop her up in my palms. Like her mama, she is covered with near-invisible bristles, which suddenly shimmer with color when I hold her close. At first, I think it's a warning, but her chirp is so sweet and delightful that I decide the color is an expression of happiness.

There's a knock on my door and I hear Gusto call my name. "Uh, coming!" I respond.

I tuck Nova into my pocket before opening the door a crack

to see Gusto staring at me earnestly, Zuki hovering behind.

"What?" I ask impatiently.

"Harlee wants us on the move in fifteen. Did you even showe—uh, what's on your cheek?"

I reach up to touch my face and a fragment of eggshell falls away.

Zuki pushes his way into my room. "It happened, didn't it? The squix hatched."

"Hey," I growl. "It's called privacy."

I crane my neck into the hallway to check if anyone is around, but the coast is clear. I quickly tug Gusto into the room and close the door.

"Look," I whisper, lifting Nova out of my pocket.

"Lemme see!" Zuki begs, so I kneel to the floor, Nova cupped in my hands.

"Whoa," Gusto murmurs. "It's so small and fuzzy."

"And cute," I add.

"Well, I've seen cuter," Zuki argues. "I mean, its tail is so tiny. And it only has one of them."

Gusto runs his hand through his thick black hair. "You can't keep it, Cara."

"Why not? I can't just set her loose! She's a baby."

"You should turn it over," Gusto says fretfully. "There's got to be someone here who—"

"No way!"

"It's forbidden," Gusto persists, sitting on the edge of my bed. "How is keeping it any different than using an occuli?"

"Uh, an occuli is a tool of dark magic," I inform him. "Nova isn't a thing. She's a she."

"How do you know she's a she?" Zuki wonders.

"Just a feeling," I say. "I can't abandon her. She's an orphan."

"Look!" Gusto cries, pointing at my arm. "What's it doing?"

Nova is inching up my sleeve like a caterpillar. She stops at one of the folds, sniffing.

Gusto leans down for a closer inspection. "It's licking your robe—look, there's black gunk there."

A long thin tongue—it looks like a thread of silk—is zipping out of Nova's mouth. Despite how tiny she is, she's making quick work of the crust of black on my sleeve.

"Must have splattered on me when Dante turned to goo," I muse.

Gusto starts wringing his hands. "It's eating toxic slime? This can't be good!"

"She's getting rid of it—that's good," I argue.

"But—"

"Just get out of my room," I say in exasperation, shoving Gusto toward the door. "And keep your mouth shut. Okay?"

Gusto shakes his head. "I'm worried, Cara."

"You're always worried," I tell him. "You want something *real* to worry about? Try Harlee."

Gusto groans.

"I think she's involved in this somehow. This dark magic. This Cipher cult."

"No way," Zuki protests.

"Come on, Cara," Gusto says. "You really need to let go of this thing you have with her."

"Thing?" I cry.

"Don't you think it's possible that you're . . . projecting?" he wonders.

"Ooh, big word," I snap. "Did you learn that from Yuna?"

Gusto lets that one slide. "All I'm saying is—are you sure you're not putting all your issues with your sister onto Harlee?"

"Leave Su out of this," I growl. "What does she have to do with anything?"

"Well, you know," Zuki chimes in, "you have the same complaints about both of them: they're pretty, they're talented, they're—"

"This is the most ridiculous thing I've ever heard," I say.

"Honestly, Cara," Gusto says, "sometimes I can't figure out if you're jealous of her, if you want to be her, or if you just wish she was your friend."

"Who are you talking about now?" I demand. "Harlee or Su?"

Gusto sighs in exasperation. "See what I mean?"

I sneer at him. "Ha, ha. You'll see soon enough, because—"

"What's going on in there?" a voice sounds from the hallway.

Speak of the wizard. I thrust a warning finger to my lips and pluck Nova off my sleeve—but before I can stick her in my pocket, Harlee flings open the door. I hide Nova in my fist.

"Well?" Harlee demands. Gone are her crimson robes with their flared sleeves and flowing train. Instead, she's wearing a hoodie and jeans, like any normal Bliss teenager. She still looks cool; I guess she can pull off any kind of look. "What are you kids arguing about?"

"Nothing," I say, feeling a shiver of worry that she's onto Nova. But I'm saved from offering further explanation because at that moment Master Quibble comes trudging up the stairs and everyone rushes out to meet him. I make sure to go last, taking time to slip Nova into my pocket.

"Turns out, Cosimo skipped town after we left," the Q-Man explains as he tiredly kneels and lets Zuki lick his hand. "Constables will comb his shop, but I doubt he's left behind any clues that will help us."

"So last night was all for nothing," Harlee contends, crossing her arms.

Master Quibble strokes his chin hair. "I wouldn't say that. Dante did give us a name before his untimely demise. *Cipher Storm*. Something you can use when you're undercover."

Harlee rolls her eyes. "Yeah, maybe I'll just stand in the middle of the school hallways and call out, 'Hey, Cipher Storm here? Anyone know a Cipher Storm?'"

"Don't be so annoying," I speak up. "It's better than noth—"

Master Quibble waves a placating palm in my direction. "You're tired, Harlee. Like all of us. But don't discount the grains of sand. That's how we build a bridge. That's how we cross the sea."

"Save your wizardly wisdom for your drinking buddies," Harlee tells him.

Master Quibble sighs. "Harlee—"

"Whatever," she says, pivoting toward me. "As for you, you have ten minutes to shower and meet us in the lobby."

She storms off, leaving the rest of us lingering there uncomfortably. Harlee definitely hates me, but compared to the way she treats Master Quibble? It's like I'm her BFF.

Operation Occuli:
Daily Schedule

After a few days, we settle into a pretty consistent routine. Let me just say this mission is lacking some excitement.

6:30 a.m.
Wake up. Which is obscene—how do Bliss students get up so early?

6:31 a.m.
Shower, eat breakfast, play with Nova, plot ways to prove Harlee is responsible for the potential doom of wizardkind.

7:30 a.m.
Climb into the clunker of a van provided to us by the Council and drive to the next high school on the top secret list Harlee keeps hidden in her pocket.

8:30 a.m.
Harlee starts school, pretending she's a Bliss student. If it's

her first day, then Master Quibble goes with her to register her for classes, playing the role of her father. Harlee and the Q-Man don't look anything alike, but maybe he tells the schools that he's her stepfather or something. I bet it drives Harlee bonkers.

8:31 a.m.–4:00 p.m.
While Harlee struts the halls of the Bliss school, the rest of us sit in the van, parked a couple of blocks away from the school, waiting.

If Master Quibble isn't around (like going for a walk or fetching our lunch), I take Nova from my pocket and feed or play with her. It stresses Gusto out, but it's not like I'm going to leave her alone at the Drowsy Druid. She's always hungry! At first, I really flew through my manticore venom, but experimentation has taught me that she'll eat anything that most wizards consider harmful. This is one of the great things about staying in the Wizard Quarter; it has a variety of stores that offer exactly the sorts of ingredients I need, and every couple of nights, I sneak out after midnight and go shopping.

I wish we could hang out in the Wizard Quarter when Harlee's at school, but we have to be on call in case something happens and she needs to cast a spell that requires sweeping. Throughout the day, Zuki shapeshifts into dog form and trots over to the school to check in with Harlee. If she requires our services, we'll jump into action—though all of this is theoretical because, so far, we have done NOTHING. Harlee hasn't needed to cast a single spell. (Either that, or she has and she's lying about it because she's a leading member of the Cipher cult, duping us all. I mean, isn't it sort of interesting how she isn't making any headway in her investigation?)

4:00 p.m.

Drive back to the Druid while Harlee gives us a debriefing, which usually consists of the single terse sentence "I found out nothing." (Once again, she's probably lying.) After three or four days like this, we move on to the next school— which feels too quick, if you ask me. But, big surprise—no one ever does.

5:00 p.m.

Dinner in the Wizard Quarter, usually at a place called the Cranky Cauldron.

7:00 p.m.

Free time. We often hang out in the games room and play wizard's billiards (try to say *that* three times in a row), which requires a level of skill (and possibly magic) I don't currently possess.

10:00 p.m. onward

In our rooms. There is no actual sleeping curfew—it's against a wizard's nature to tell someone when they should sleep. Which is good because, as mentioned, I often need to sneak out and procure something poisonous for Nova to devour.

And then? Wash, rinse, repeat.

CHAPTER 27

I'll Give Bliss School a Miss, Thanks

"ANYTHING TO REPORT?" MASTER QUIBBLE asks hopefully as Harlee slides into the front seat.

It's the end of another day on Operation Occuli (that's my name for it, but I'm considering changing it to Operation Boring, which is actually more descriptive). Harlee's on the third or fourth school on her infiltration list (I've lost count) and she's still turned up nothing.

Harlee grunts at Master Quibble. Two weeks in, and her attitude toward him still hasn't softened.

"Maybe it's time we move on to the next school," he suggests as he starts the van.

"I need more time here," she says brusquely.

"Oh?" Master Quibble asks, pulling into the street. "What did you discover?"

"Stuff."

Master Quibble sighs. "Harlee, you need to tell us. What if—"

★ 255 ★

"You suddenly disappear for another three years?" Harlee finishes for him.

"*AWK*ward," I mutter under my breath, which causes Gusto to frown. The truth is, I like it when Master Quibble and Harlee snipe at each other—it's a refreshing change of pace for there to be conflict that doesn't involve me.

"I can accept your anger with me, Harlee," he tells her. "What I can't accept is you not following mission protocol. The Council—"

"Fine," she snaps. "I'll tell you. Because I *have* to." She takes a breath before announcing, "I found out about a party. Halloween night."

"Seems pretty normal for the Bliss world," I contribute from the back seat.

"Yeah, except this . . ." Her gaze flits to the back seat, as if she's debating whether a ragtag crew of MOPs is worthy of hearing what she has to say.

"What is it?" Master Quibble prompts.

"They're calling it 'A Storm Event,'" she reveals.

"A storm event? What does . . ." I nearly rocket out of my seat, wrapping both hands around Harlee's head rest. "As in *Cipher Storm*!"

"Personal space, please!" she warns.

"Okay—but admit it!" I say as I sit back down. "It was a good thing we found Dante. He gave us that name."

"Caradine," Quibble chastises. "We're all on the same team."

I slump back into my seat, mimicking his lecturing tone

under my breath, which makes Zuki snicker.

"So, now what?" Gusto asks, raking a hand through his hair.

"There's this senior named Ford," Harlee replies. "If you want to get invited to this party, it's through him. Only those deemed 'worthy' get to go."

"Is that different from any other party in high school?" I wonder.

"Yeah," Harlee says impatiently, "because I'm pretty sure this is a party to officially initiate new cult members. Ford must be the recruiter Mwangi told us about, working under Storm. This is our chance to nail a whole lot of Cipher cronies."

Or to walk right into a trap, part of me thinks.

"Maybe we can crash the party," Gusto suggests.

"The location is secret," Harlee informs us. "Getting invited—like, as an initiate—is the only way to find out where it is."

"Have you met this Ford fellow?" Quibble asks.

"No, just seen him around," Harlee replies. "Looks like a real creep."

"Duh," I say. "If he's a part of Cipher."

"And what about Storm himself?" the Q-Man asks. We arrive at a stoplight, which gives him the opportunity to look intently at Harlee. "Do you know who he is? Have you seen him?"

Harlee shakes her head. "Probably keeps a low profile. Gets Ford to do the dirty work."

"You need to convince Ford that you'd be a good recruit,"

Quibble advises. "Get invited to this party."

"Thanks, like I don't know that," Harlee snaps, turning to stare out the side window.

"Halloween is in two days," Gusto adds. "We don't have much time."

"Yes, you're all being extremely helpful," Harlee grumbles.

"Pretend you're into him," I recommend, despite the fact that a large part of me is convinced she's in on the whole thing.

"Right—because that's not suspicious at all," Harlee says. "I said he's creepy, not stupid. Besides, rumor has it that he has a girlfriend at some other school."

"We'll discuss it more tonight—after updating the Council with this new intel," Master Quibble says as the light turns and we continue rumbling forward in our dilapidated ride. "We'll formulate a plan."

"I don't need your help," Harlee insists. "I got this."

"I bet you do," I mutter.

"What's that supposed to mean?" Harlee asks, her head snapping toward me.

I shrink beneath her intimidating glare. "Go, Team Harlee?"

She shakes her head in bewilderment, then turns back around. "This mission can't end soon enough."

For once, she and I are in agreement.

"Do we have to listen to the weather report a kajillion times a day?" I complain as I lounge in the back of the van, using Zuki as a pillow. It's the next day, and we've all got the midafternoon grouches as we wait for Harlee to finish her last class.

"The weather can tell us a lot," Quibble replies as he tunes the ancient radio in our van. It doesn't even have a digital display, just one with a needle that migrates along a row of numbers. "As I've said many times before, scrubs, if the Bliss news reports something unusual, then—"

There's a knock on the side of the van, so thunderous that I jump from my seat and nearly bang my head on the ceiling.

"Hurry up!" Harlee's voice hisses from outside. "It's me."

Gusto double-checks to make sure that Zuki is in dog form in case anyone's watching from the street, then slides open the side door to reveal Harlee in an extremely frantic state.

"What is it?" Quibble asks fretfully.

"Need a cleanup," Harlee says breathlessly. "Now."

"What happened?" I ask.

"I'll explain on the way. Come on."

Gusto and I clamber out of the van, knapsacks over our shoulders. I cast a longing look back at my broom inside the van. I really wish I could take it, but it's far too conspicuous; we're stuck with using smaller-sized whisks.

"I better come, too," Zuki says, his single dog tail twitching in excitement.

"Just stay here," Harlee tells him over her shoulder as she speeds down the street. "Need to be discreet." Then she glances at Gusto and me and adds, "*Hurry.*"

"Now can you tell us what's going on?" Gusto asks as we race along.

"Thought I could break into Ford's locker," Harlee pants. "Wanted to steal his phone, find out information about the party. But it wasn't there."

"Wait a minute, you already did the breaking-in part?" I ask. "With magic? You should have called us *before* you cast the spell."

"I was trying to do it before the period ended. Didn't think it would cause that much of a mess, but the locker is leaking like an oil spill."

We arrive at the school, and Harlee slows to a walk. "This way," she says, leading us around the back. It's an older building, made of brick, but it's otherwise lacking charm.

"Doors are locked during school hours," Harlee explains as she guides us to a low window. "I left this open so we can get in and out."

"Why did you think the phone would be in his locker anyway?" I ask as Gusto squeezes through the window.

"It's an official rule—no devices in the classrooms," she replies.

"Right," I scoff. "You actually think Blisses follow *that* rule? They'd rather give up oxygen."

"I get it—I screwed up," Harlee says. "Okay?"

Harlee admitting to making a mistake is universe-shifting, but I don't have time to relish the moment because she's already forcing me through the window. I drop down beside Gusto and then Harlee follows.

"C'mon," she urges. "You have to clean up quickly, before they let out for the day."

It's quiet inside the school, and very institutional—in other words, plain and bereft of art or cool architectural elements like we have at Dragonsong.

"How do you survive here?" Gusto wonders, glancing about. "It's very . . ."

He can't quite bring himself to say something negative, so I decide to swoop in for him. "Soul-sucking," I offer, feeling a newfound appreciation for everything about Dragonsong— even Quibble's office. At least he's usually got a three-tailed fox roaming around in there. This place? It looks like the most exciting thing that might happen here is an impromptu math quiz. "Welcome to Boring High," I add.

Harlee shakes her head in irritation. "Just keep your voices d—"

She's cut short because the entire building suddenly quivers. Then it growls. Next, it rumbles so viciously that Gusto and I stagger and collapse to the floor—which is now buckling beneath us like a sheet of cheap tin. It's as if the building took my soul-sucking comment to heart, but of course, the quaking is a result of Harlee's ill-advised spellcasting. It's not the school that's angry—it's the Field in pain.

"Congratulations," I tell Harlee as the lights flicker. "You just made Boring High exciting. And *deadly*."

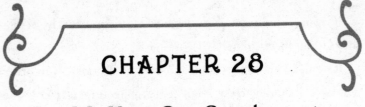

CHAPTER 28

Can We Have One Cataclysm at a Time, Please?

AN ALARM BELL SOUNDS AND a fevered announcement blares over the PA system, urging everyone to drop and cover; the school thinks an earthquake is happening. Harlee, who has somehow managed not to lose her feet, yanks me to mine and begins pushing me down the hallway. Gusto scrambles after us.

We reach the slime before the locker is even in sight, burbling down a wide staircase, like a lava flow with a score to settle.

Harlee gasps. "Dratch! It's made it this far?"

"Gotta get to the source," I say, slipping on my goggles. "Gusto—"

"I'll start here," he interrupts, neutralizer already in hand. "Go ahead."

I scurry up the stairs, keeping to the edge to avoid the goo. The building is still quaking, the alarm still ringing. I stumble around a corner, and don't have to guess which one is the spell-compromised locker—there's only one with its door flung open, vomiting slime. I charge ahead, hopscotching over the winding river of residue to reach the row of lockers. On the outside, they look nothing like Dragonsong's (they're plain, boring metal) but the inside of Ford's is all too familiar because of the rift suspended there. This one seems extra nasty, belching a warning at me as I approach, causing textbooks, binders, and a black duffel bag to fly out.

I quickly begin squirting the laceration with Moone Brew, and the rumble reduces to a tremble. Inside my pocket, I feel Nova going berserk; she can smell the toxic magic and wants to sink her snout into it.

"Not right now," I tell her.

"What?" Harlee says, looming behind me.

"Uh—nothing," I reply as I keep dousing the slit. "What kind of spell did you perform, anyway?"

"Just a finger flutter," she says. "You know, to unlock the combination."

"If that's true, then the Field is definitely getting worse."

"What do mean, if it's true?" Harlee demands. "And do you need to wear those goggles? We need to be inconspicuous."

"Oh, sorry, would it be better if I wander around blind because I got sprayed by poisonous spell gunk?" I retort. "Would that be inconspicuous enough for you?"

"I'm just saying—"

Suddenly, a tongue of black—an actual tongue—shoots out of the rift and wraps itself around her sleeve. She shrieks in a very un-Harlee-like way, then raises the opposite hand to attack.

"NO!" I cry. "You'll make it worse."

I fire my Moone Brew at the rope of slime, causing it to hiss and rip asunder. Once she's free, Harlee leaps back and begins frantically tugging off her sweater. I will admit, I enjoy seeing her thrown out of cool mode and into this moment of frenzy, but I've got a job to do, so I turn back to the rift. It's really fighting back—something I haven't seen before.

As I continue squirting, I glance over my shoulder at Harlee. The way stuff is gushing out of the locker, she has to have used an occuli, not just some simple "finger flutter." Of course, if she *is* working with Cipher, why would she have to break into the locker in the first place?

I shake my head, trying to clear my thoughts so that I can focus on the task at hand. My conspiracy theories are starting to drive *me* nuts.

The wound finally seals, the quake stops altogether, and the alarm bell cuts off. No one appears in the hallway, though. They're waiting for aftershocks, I comprehend, which is good because it gives me more time. I turn my attention to the remaining residue and it's only then that I realize that Nova has squeezed out of my pocket and is snuffling along the bottom shelf of the locker, sucking up the toxic gunk. She's getting bigger and harder to control. But she's making quick work of the slime, so I let her continue and turn my attention to the residue that's winding across the floor. Harlee has retreated to a nearby bench and is staring in disgust at her sweater, which she has unceremoniously dumped onto the floor—which is good, because it means she's too preoccupied to notice Nova rooting around in the locker.

I keep spraying the trail of toxic residue until there's nothing left but swirls of gray dust. Gusto pokes his head around the corner and wipes his brow.

"It's a lot harder to sweep up with these tiny brooms," he complains.

"Just be quick about it," Harlee orders from her bench. "Once they release the Blisses, it's going to be chaos in these hallways."

"Keep working from that end," I call to Gusto. "I got this side."

He nods and disappears back around the corner. I turn to see Harlee stuffing her sweater in the nearest garbage can.

"What are you doing?!" I cry. "You can't just throw away toxic slime. Here." I snatch the sweater away from her and fling it into the bottom of Ford's locker, conveniently covering up Nova. "I'll deal with it," I tell Harlee—or Nova will, I add to myself.

I begin sweeping up the dust around the locker and Harlee wanders up behind me again. "Maybe I should take another look for that phone."

"No!" I squeal, pushing her back. "I told you, it won't be in here." The sweater is jiggling around at the bottom of the locker, a telltale sign that my baby squix is licking it clean.

"Well, we have to stuff everything back inside," Harlee says, stooping to collect some of the things that have flown out of the locker. "Have to make it look like nothing happened. What's this?"

She's picked up a notebook and some things have slid out—a photo and an ornate black comb (I guess guys can like nice things, too). Harlee holds up the photo for me to see. "Must be Ford's girlfriend. Dratch, she's totally out of his league."

I lift the goggles to the top of my head and peer at the photo—my stomach immediately twists into a knot. The girl in the picture is slim, pretty, and . . . *I know her.*

"I th-thought this was Ford's locker," I stammer.

"It *is.* Why?"

I snatch the photo from her and flip it over. It reads: *For Bradford.*

"Bradford . . . ," I murmur.

"What's going on with you?" Harlee says. "Let's put everything back and get out of here. Like, *now.*"

But I just stand there, dumbfounded.

Ford. Bradford. Brad.

They're one and the same. My sister's boyfriend. A Cipher cultist. He's gotten Su mixed up in way more than vaping. He's gotten her mixed up in dark magic. He's going to initiate her into his insidious circle. *Tomorrow.*

I collapse against the next locker and slide down to the floor. How can Brad be a villain? I mean, his name is *Brad.* Or Ford, or Bradford—or whatever. None of those names exactly instill terror.

I guess that's why they have Cipher nicknames.

Harlee leans over me. "I don't know what's gotten into you, kid, but unless you want to compromise all our hard work, we need to fly."

I nod, fumble to my feet, and grab Harlee's sweater from the bottom of Brad's locker, keeping it in a bundle to conceal Nova, who's still nestled inside. Harlee hastily shoves everything back in Brad's locker and slams it shut.

We meet up with Gusto just as the doors open and swarms of students begin spilling into the hallways. They're all talking a mile a minute, checking their phones (which, of course, aren't stored in their lockers), and making frantic calls to their parents to tell them about the "earthquake." But the cataclysmic event they've experienced is nothing compared to the one that has just sent a shock through my system.

As soon as we reach the van, I sink into the back seat, still clutching Harlee's sweater. It's only now that I have the where-withal to wriggle my fingers into the bundle, locate Nova, and maneuver her quietly into the pocket of my hoodie. Satiated by her feast of black slime, she's already sound asleep. This is despite the blare of sirens that is growing louder by the second—Bliss emergency services are headed to the school in response to the quake.

"What happened?" Master Quibble asks nervously. "Are those sirens about us?"

"Everything's all right," Harlee assures him. "Not sure why *she's* freaking out."

That snaps me out of my emotional tailspin. "I'm not freaking out." Which, of course, is a complete lie.

"*Something* happened," Gusto says. "What is it, Cara?"

I draw in a deep breath and close my eyes. I don't know how to tell them about Su—I'm not even sure if I *want* to tell them, especially Harlee. But my mind is spinning, and my defenses are down. "I've met him," I finally say.

"Who?" Quibble asks.

"Ford," I murmur. "I mean, Brad. Whatever you want to call him. He's my sister's boyfriend."

"Your sister is mixed up in all this?!" Harlee exclaims, whipping around to lean over her seat.

"Not on purpose!" I cry, my eyes flying open. "She would never . . . she's—you don't know Su. She's *perfect*. An angel." Well, she used to be, I add silently, and now I find myself clinging to that version of her like it's a life preserver. It's only half-inflated, at best.

Quibble is working his chin hair, hard. "You're sure about this, Caradine? Your sister is dating this boy?"

I stare at the ceiling, nodding. The image of Brad at our dinner table plays in my mind, curling his arm around Su, seducing her, controlling her. I fight the urge to throw up.

Quibble runs his hand fretfully over his bald head. "The Council suspected there was a link between Cipher and Dragonsong. Now we know—"

"There's no connection!" I insist. "Su doesn't know the truth about Dragonsong. She thinks it's an artsy school for losers."

"I'm not a loser," Zuki declares. "I'm a winner! A champion, a—"

"Her boyfriend knows the truth," Harlee interrupts. "*He's* the connection. He's using your sister to get at us. At least now we have a way into the party."

"How do you figure that?" I wonder.

"Your sister's obviously going," Harlee says. "Text her. Get her to tell you where the party is."

"I'm not going to do that! Besides—"

"They don't exactly have that kind of relationship," Zuki pipes up.

I swat him. My dysfunctional relationship with Su is *my* business.

"Which school does your sister go to?" Harlee asks. "We can pick her up, brew us a tongue-loosening draft, then go eradicate us a Cipher cell."

"You're not doing that to my sister!" I screech. "If you—"

"We need to cool down," Quibble intervenes. "Think everything through."

"I'm the leader here," Harlee says. "And I say we—"

"And I'm the one with a driver's license," Quibble cuts her off. "We're going back to the Quarter. You want to launch a formal complaint with the Council? Go ahead. While you're at it, you can propose force-feeding a Bliss truth serum."

Harlee goes to say something, but the words die in her throat. He's got her there—there's no way the Council will approve of her plan.

At least I hope not.

And if they do? Well, I'm not going to let anyone hurt my sister. She's in trouble, and I need to save her.

Like she's saved me, a kajillion times.

Meet my sister, maker of magic

I'm in fourth grade, still in Bliss school, sitting across from Principal Rathbone in her office.

Su and Grandma are escorted in by the school secretary.

"What is it this time?" Su asks as I slouch in my seat, clutching my planner to my chest.

Rathbone flashes a disingenuous smile at my sister. "Is your mother coming?"

"She's delivering a baby," Su says, taking the chair next to me.

"Oh, I see." Rathbone leans forward and steeples her fingers. "It's best if one of Cara's guardians is present."

"I'm present," Su says. "So's our grandmother."

With a discerning gaze, Rathbone scans Grandma, who has a giant and garish rose braided into her gray hair. "Is she suited to . . ."

"No problem," Grandma says, eyes dancing. "Some days I'm so befuddled I can't remember who I am. Last week I thought I was Joan of Arc. Today, though? I'm ninety-seven percent lucid."

"She's joking," Su tells Rathbone. "About the Joan of Arc thing. Not about being lucid. Which she is. Why did you drag my little sister in here?"

Rathbone frowns. "She gave Marcus Smith a black eye. That type of behavior is completely unacceptable and, I'm afraid, means automatic suspension."

Su turns to me. "You punched someone?"

"I didn't touch him!" I protest, which is the truth. I mean, I *wished* for him to have a black eye, and he did get one, but my fist was definitely not involved.

Su nods. She's only thirteen, but you would never know it by the way she carries herself. "Any witnesses?"

"It was obviously Cara," Rathbone says.

Su arches an eyebrow. "Obviously? It's Marcus's word against Cara's."

Rathbone plasters another smile on her face. "Marcus is a top student, with no history of this sort of behavior. Your sister, on the other hand, is continually—"

"He drew on my planner!" I blurt.

"This?" Su says, wresting the folder out of my arms. On the cover is my name scribbled in giant letters, but missing the *E* on the end of *Moone*. Below is a cartoon of me with my pants dropped and my butt sticking out. Get it? Cara *Moon*. "Did you show this to your teacher?" Su asks me.

"He told me to just wipe it off. But it's permanent marker."

Su rises calmly to her feet. I almost feel sorry for Rathbone—she knows "Su-short-for-Tsunami" well enough from my sister's own days at her school, but I'm tempted to intervene and scream: *Red alert!*

"What I find really distressing," Su states, "is that someone drew this image of Cara on her binder—it's nearly *pornographic*—and the teacher—what's his name, Cara? Mr. Edgemont?—did absolutely nothing about it. I'm also extremely dismayed that you, Principal Rathbone, don't have the least bit of concern about this behavior from a male student against my sister. I know you're fretting that my mother isn't here, so I will make sure to inform her of this incident and that my sister was subjected to this depraved bullying. Maybe she can take it up with the school board."

Grandma chuckles. Su barely paused to breathe during her oration.

"Th-there is no need to blow this out of proportion," Rathbone stammers.

"Agreed," Su says. "We'll be leaving. I volunteer at a nursing home and my shift starts in fifteen minutes."

That was the end of the incident. Marcus didn't get in trouble, but neither did I.

My sister used to have a magic all her own. Now? She's

got herself wrapped up with a guy who has his own magic, too—but it's the worst kind. Which is why I need to break Brad's spell on her. If I save her, I'll get her back. She'll be the old Su. The one who used to love me.

CHAPTER 29

It's (Not) the Most Wonderful Time of the Year

WIZARDS *ADORE* HALLOWEEN. FORGET CHRISTMAS, Lunar New Year, or any other holiday that comes to mind—for wizards, Halloween is the most wonderful time of the year. You might assume it's because of all the spooky stuff on display, or the unabashed celebration of all things eerie, or even the junk food—and you wouldn't be wrong. But, if you ask me, most wizards love Halloween because they can parade around in their robes with impunity—everyone just assumes they're in costume.

"It's like hiding in broad daylight," Yuna once told me.

But I'm *not* feeling it this Halloween.

Yes, I can wear my wizardly Dragonsong clothes on any Bliss street today, but it's irrelevant. I'm stuck in my room at the Druid, waiting for news about the correspondence between Harlee and the Council, which is taking forever, because they're only exchanging messages via ravens and owls. Turns out Brad's high school canceled classes for the day (due to the "earthquake"), depriving Harlee of any final opportunity to ingratiate herself with him and get an invite to the party. Instead, she's decided to pursue permission from the Council to enact her Kidnap Cara's Sister & Make Her Drink a Truth Potion plan.

I pace the floor, losing my mind. I consider texting Su (I'd have to leave the Quarter to get a signal), but what would I say? Then I consider calling Mom to tell her outright that Su's in trouble, but same thing—what would I tell her? "Hey, Mom, remember Su's boyfriend? Did you know he's dabbling in dark magic that makes you explode into black goo if you take it too far?"

"I can't just sit here and do nothing," I finally announce to Nova as she snores away on my pillow. "I need to find Su."

I strap on my gear—belt, broom, everything—it'll be easy to pretend I'm dressed as a witch or a ghostbuster or something. Then I stuff Nova and my phone into the pockets of my robe, button them shut, and open the window to sneak out, like I've done a dozen times before. It's only early afternoon, but I can't risk being seen by any of the crew. Once I'm free of the Quarter, I'll Google the quickest way to reach Su's school by transit, and just hope that she's there instead of playing hooky with Cipher Brad.

I have the window halfway up when the door to my room bursts open.

"What do you think you're doing?" Harlee demands, storming inside.

I guiltily step away from the window. "Knock much?"

Harlee crosses the floor to stand between me and the window. "Just so you know, the Council won't let us take your sister. No Bliss-napping. No potions."

"Did they say anything about *saving* her?"

"I'm working on it."

"*Working on it?* That's not good enough. She's my sister. Maybe you don't know what it's like, coming from a wizard family, but—"

"How about we don't talk about my family," Harlee warns.

"Fine—how about we talk about how wizards like you are used to pushing people around, getting your way, without worrying about the consequences for us poor Blisses."

"You're not a Bliss," Harlee snaps.

"My sister is. But that doesn't mean she doesn't count. You think you're better than everyone else. But you're not. Especially her."

"You don't know what I think," Harlee retorts. "What did I do to make you hate me so much?"

"Uh, how about what you did to my locker?"

"You're the one who got in *my* face," Harlee argues.

"Right, how dare I mess with the Chosen One," I taunt.

Harlee swells with anger. "You think you know me—*and my family*—but all you've got is this gossip you pick up in the hallways. It's garbage."

I open my mouth to say something, but she just keeps going.

"You think wizards are at the top of the world order, don't

you?" Harlee says, pacing back and forth in front of me. "You have it all backward, kid. We're at the bottom."

I laugh. "Are you joking?"

"Don't you get it?" Harlee says in exasperation. "We're the ones who stay hidden in the shadows. The Blisses are the ones who get to strut around and live their lives however they want. They have the power."

"But we're—I mean, wizards have *power*," I argue. "Actual power. That's why we get chosen for wizard school."

"Chosen?!" Harlee spits. "They spirit us away from home. They literally hide us on an island."

"You make it sound like a prison," I scoff.

"It feels that way," Harlee says, slumping down on my bed and staring past me, out the window. "Sometimes. A lot of the time." Her temple is pulsing, like it does when she's deep in thought. "That's the way it has to be, so we don't hurt them while we're learning how to control . . . *it*. I get that. What I don't get is you thinking it's so great, like it's some sort of privilege."

"But . . . it *is*," I sputter. I can't even believe I'm having this conversation. It's like she expects me to feel sorry for her—*her*, Harlee Wu, the Queen of Dragonsong. "You can do anything. You can snap your fingers and—"

"Snap my fingers and what? You know what I can't do? Snap my fingers and be normal. Be safe." She shakes her head, still staring out the window. "Did *you* choose to be the way you are?"

"Of course not."

"But *they're* choosing," Harlee says, passionately gesturing into the air. "The Cipher cultists. We've got this delicate balance happening. Everyone does their job and it's okay. It's safe. But they're ruining it. They could hurt themselves, other Blisses, and *us*. All their messing around will reveal us to the Bliss world—and then what? We're back to being burned at the stake."

The creepy wizard-hunting kit in Cosimo's shop flashes into my mind. But it was an antique. "They don't do that kind of thing anymore, not these d—"

"You know what I mean," Harlee interrupts. "Burning us at the stake would be merciful compared to what they'd actually do. Locking us in some laboratory and sticking us with needles. And what if the Field collapses? What does that mean for us? What if we stop . . ."

She's worked up, and not just with anger. I can't even begin to decipher what exactly is burbling beneath the surface. Part of me suspects she's had a major blowout with Master Quibble and now she's in this emotional free fall. It's not the Harlee Wu I'm used to seeing, not the Harlee Wu I know and loathe.

"Stop what?" I urge.

"What if we need the Field?" Harlee continues. "Not just to perform magic. But to *survive*?"

"You mean, without the Field you think wizards could *die*?!" I gasp. "Don't you think that's a little over the top?"

She doesn't respond, which makes me wonder if she knows

something I don't. She *is* mission leader—quite possibly, the Council has revealed top secret details about the situation to her.

I shake my head—it's too much to absorb at the moment. "Honestly?" I tell her. "Right now, I just want to help my sister."

Harlee sighs. Then she rises, brushes past me, and saunters to the half-open window. I wait for her to slam it shut, but instead she shoves it all the way open, then turns to me with a heaviness in her eyes. "I really hope she's worth it."

I stand on the platform, waiting for the next train to arrive. I finally work up the nerve to text Su, and decide to keep it simple: *Where are you? Need to talk. It's urgent!!!* Then I stare at my phone, willing a quick reply—but nothing comes. Not a surprise; I can't remember the last time we exchanged texts.

At least Harlee has given me this chance to find Su. After listening to her rant in my room . . . well, it's possible I've misjudged her. Maybe she's not a calculating Cipher agent. Maybe she's just a girl who got mixed up with occuli. The thing is, it's hard to change your mind about someone after hating on them for so long. So, yes, it's possible that sending me after Su is her gift to me, her treat. But it could also be a trick—it *is* Halloween, after all.

The station is busy, with pirates, clowns, and any number of witches coming and going. It's nearly a miracle that I notice the white dog amid this colorful cast of characters, but there it is, snuffling around a nearby garbage can. It's wearing a collar, but has no leash, which makes me wonder where the owner is—until I realize that it's Zuki in disguise.

I roll my eyes. Zuki's the worst. He can shapeshift into any kind of dog and he still goes for something white and cute with a ridiculous poofy tail. I guess you can shapeshift your physical form, but not your vanity.

I make my way over to a less busy end of the platform, then watch from the corner of my eye as Zuki "subtly" meanders in my direction. When he's close enough, I kneel under the pretense of tying my boot.

"I know it's you," I tell him.

He doesn't respond, just preens his tail—which is very magical-fox-like, but not very doglike.

"I just wanted you to know I'm not falling for it."

More preening.

"And I'm definitely not going to say anything to you," I continue. "People will think I'm weird talking to a dog."

"But you're talking to me right n—"

"Aha!" I cry, thrusting my finger in his snout.

"I mean, um: *woof.*"

"Why are you following me?" I demand. "Did Harlee send you?"

Zuki twitches his tail, then frowns—he clearly finds it dissatisfying to wag a single short tail. I notice the fancy gemstone dangling from his collar. Big surprise. He went for the bling.

"Maybe I'm just worried about you," he offers.

"Are you?"

"Well, actually, it's Nova I'm most concerned about," Zuki says. "She's just a baby and you're taking her right into enemy territory, the heart of danger, the—"

"All I'm doing is going to Su's high school," I say. "To pull her *out* of danger. Sorry to disappoint you. You can slink back to Harlee now."

"I'm sticking with you, Cara."

"Suit yourself," I tell him as the train approaches. "Just keep it together. Okay?"

He barks in response, and I scoop him up and hop aboard the train.

"Your puppy's cute," the nearest Bliss says to me. He's dressed like Batman, complete with fake padded muscles. "Cool costume, by the way—especially the broom. What are you supposed to be?"

I shrug. "You know. A witch."

"You don't look like a typical witch," Batman says appraisingly.

"Uh . . . yeah, I'm from this anime. You probably don't know it. It's obscure."

Batman looks like he's about to say something, but then his phone dings and he turns away to attend to his ever-so-important texts. Bliss technology sure makes it easy to throw them off your scent.

I wish I could say the same for Zuki. Because, yes, part of me is glad he's here, but another part of me can't help suspecting that Harlee sent him after me for some diabolical reason.

Like I said, it's hard to change your mind about someone.

CHAPTER 30

Things That Cipher Doesn't Worry About—Like Lung Cancer

I'VE ONLY BEEN TO SU'S school a couple of times to see her in debate competitions, so I don't really know my way around. By default, I head for the front door and arrive just as it begins disgorging students at the final bell. My Bliss elementary school was always awash in Halloween decorations at this time of year—but not this place. As I enter, there's not a cardboard bat or jack-o'-lantern to be found, and no one's in costume, which catches me off guard until I come to the conclusion that Bliss high schoolers think they're too cool to dress up for Halloween.

I should stand out like a broken wand, except that everyone's too entranced by their phones to notice me. I scoop up Zuki, so he doesn't get trampled, then check to see if Su's replied to my text. She hasn't.

"Have to find her the old-fashioned way," I mutter.

I wander the hallways, mustering the courage to ask a few people if they know Su, but only get strange glances until two girls in identical goth costumes stop short at my question. I guess some of the kids here *did* decide to dress up.

"What do you want with Moone?" one of the girls asks as they circle me, backing me against a row of lockers.

"Uh, she's my sister."

"Ah," says the second girl. "You're *Little* Moone."

The girls glance around conspiratorially, and that's when I realize that they're not just *dressed* the same—they're identical twins. Some sort of secret language seems to pass between them, and they escort me down the hall, past loitering students, and stop in front of what looks like your basic janitorial closet door. My inner alarm bells begin blaring, but before I can do anything, they open the door and shove me onto a long stairwell.

I stumble down the steps to arrive in a dank room where boilers and industrial-sized pipes rattle against the walls. In addition to a very particular—well, let's just call it a "bouquet," the ancient underbelly of the school features the requisite shadowy corners and flickering lights. Zuki whines and burrows his head into the crook of my elbow.

I turn to confront the twins. Clearly, they're not dressed for Halloween. They're dressed for being members of Cipher. They're wearing identical chokers with jet-black stones around their necks. Upstairs, I assumed it was costume jewelry, but now I know better. They're *occuli*.

I'm in trouble. Big trouble.

"Moone's not at school today," Twin Number One informs me, blocking me from the stairwell. "She's preparing for her big night. *Initiation* night."

I consider attacking them and making a run for it. It wouldn't be the first time my broom took out a Bliss with delusions of grandeur. But there *are* two of them. I glance down at Zuki; he's got his head burrowed even deeper into the folds of my robes. I so knew he wasn't going to be helpful.

"Don't try anything," Twin Number One warns. "We can defend ourselves." She fingers her choker to make her point.

I exhale. Brad's clearly told them I go to wizard school. What he hasn't told them—what he couldn't, because he doesn't know—is that I'm a wizard fail. Whatever these girls think I might do to them . . . I can't.

Twin Number Two takes out her phone and begins texting someone. She gets an instant reply, and smiles. Then she lights a cigarette and takes a long drag before passing it to her sister. She lights another one for herself.

"Do you mind? That's disgusting," I tell them, waving away the smoke. I'm tempted to launch into one of Mom's health lectures, but quickly realize it would be pointless—if you've decided to mess around with dark magic, you're probably not overly concerned about pumping carcinogens into your lungs.

"We'll take your broom and your belt, Little Moone," Twin Number One says.

"*And* your phone," Twin Number Two adds.

The phone I don't care about—Su's clearly not going to text me back—but it's hard to part with my gear. At least Nova remains safely hidden in my pocket. They force me farther into the dark recesses of the basement and we arrive at what appears to be a dead end, where old pieces of plywood and lumber are stacked. The twins shove me behind the pile and I discover a yawning hole in the cement wall.

"Yeah, I'm not going through there," I declare.

I feel something hot and searing against the back of my head, causing me to scream and jump forward. They burned me with a cigarette, I realize—I can even smell the burnt hair.

"Behave, Little Moone," Twin Number Two chides me as she and her sister follow me.

Twin Number One switches on a flashlight to reveal that we are in a long, dark tunnel. We begin trekking down it, with the flashlight and the glow of the twins' cigarettes our only sources of light. Zuki's fur doesn't glow in dog form. Besides, he's mostly curled up into a ball in my arms, whimpering—even though I'm the one who got burned by an evil twin's nicotine stick.

We arrive at a set of stairs carved crudely into the rock. This isn't your average basement tunnel—this is something different, like a secret route to the Cipher base.

Yep, I'm in huge trouble.

I'm forced down the stairs, into another dark passage. We keep going and, eventually, I smell the fetid odor of sewer water. We must carry on for another fifteen minutes before our path ramps down into muck. The tunnel is large enough for a train to go barreling through—or, I guess, a boat. The twins have long since finished their cigarettes, but now they light up again, causing me to instinctively flinch. They titter at my nervousness, but before I can even scowl in their direction, I notice a movement along the wall. A figure separates from the shadows and strides up to us.

It's Brad. He looks like a walking cadaver, thinner than when I first met him, but it's definitely him. He has heavy black bags under his eyes, but there's nothing tired about his demeanor. "Not the Moone sister I was expecting to see tonight," he declares, eyes glinting.

"I know who you are," I spit. "I know *what* you are."

"I could say the same to you," he replies in contempt. "*Wizard Girl.*"

I sneer at him. "Cipher Brad."

"It's Cipher Bane, actually," he informs me humorlessly. "I see you've already met Cipher Vex and Cipher Jade. I trust they took good care of you?"

"Yeah, I love secondhand smoke. Where's my sister?"

"Don't worry about her. She's preparing—it's her big night."

"No, it's not!" I growl. "She's not the sheep you think she is."

Brad—I just can't bring myself to call him Cipher Bane—gives me a vague, indecipherable smile. "On that, we agree."

"Do you think you could do *something*?" I snap at Zuki. "Anything? Like, maybe shapeshift into something threatening?"

"Oh, yeah, sure," he says.

He leaps out of my arms, swishes his tail, and in an instant is standing in front of me in . . . his normal magical fox form.

I give him a dramatic sigh. "I was actually thinking of something more like a wolf. A big, ugly, scary wolf."

Zuki stares at me like I'm out of my mind. "Ugly?!"

"Perhaps I was wrong to worry about your magic," Brad says in a chiding tone. "How pitiful you are."

He's right—I *am* pitiful. How am I supposed to save Su? I'm so remedial that I can't even intimidate a henchman named Brad.

"Let me reveal some of *my* magic," Brad announces. He extends a skeletal hand to flaunt the large gemstone perched on his index finger. It's green with a splash of yellow, and in the very center is a black slit, giving it the appearance of a reptilian eye.

My jaw drops. I've mooned over that stone countless times in the school library. It's Riva Dragonsong's—the stone that famously allowed her to commune with dragons.

"Give that back!" I cry. "It belongs to Dragonsong! Thief!"

Brad's thin mouth curls into another strange smile. "Technically, it was Cipher Storm who stole it."

"So what?" I growl. "It's still stolen and you—"

"Your kind is so arrogant," Brad interrupts. "We steal and you label it an egregious crime. You, Wizard Girl? You steal and it's simply your right."

"Except I haven't stolen anything," I retort.

One eyebrow arches on his ghostly forehead. "Oh? What about your sister's hairpin?"

"My sister's . . . ? I didn't steal it. I *borrowed* it. That's what sisters do! It was just a hairpin. And she got it back."

"As if you didn't know what it was when you took it!" Brad

accuses me. "That hairpin was my gift to her. I didn't even get a chance to show her what it did before you stole it."

"What are you talking about?!" I cry. "It's a hairpin."

"Oh boy," Zuki murmurs. "Cara? I think your sister's hairpin is an occuli."

I gape at the fox, incredulous, then turn back to Brad and keep gaping. "But it's just a . . ."

I trail off. My studies have taught me that *anything* can be a talisman. Except the hairpin isn't a talisman—not now. It's been perverted into an occuli.

And I used it.

Not wittingly, not really—but I had that hairpin, back when all this started. It was with me when I first saw the black rift in the auditorium. It was in my locker when Harlee cast her spell on it. It was at the train wreck site. What did the *Forbidden Magic* book say? That even the *presence* of occuli during a spell-cast can cause problems. All these weeks, I've been thinking it was Harlee with an occuli. But it was *me*.

"Holy dratch," I murmur.

"Yes," Brad gloats, "it's a lot to digest, isn't it?"

That snaps me back to anger. "Do you have any idea what your occuli have done to the Field? We can't perform *any* spell-casting now—not even pure magic—without making it bleed."

Brad snorts. "*Pure* magic? So elite, so—"

"That fancy comb in your locker," I interrupt in sudden realization. "It was an occuli, too."

"I suppose I should be upset that you broke into my locker,"

Brad says. "But thievery is your kind's second nature."

I shake my head. "You're so ignorant."

"The ignorant one is you," Brad claims. "You will see, Wizard Girl. It's time for you to learn the truth about your secret society."

He traces his finger around Riva's stone, causing it to sing, which in turn sets the tunnel—and the Field—quaking. A few seconds later, an enormous serpentine creature emerges from the water. It's an amphibious dragon, grotesque and leering, all blackened scales and twisted spikes. It's radiating heat, steam wafting from its scales and smoke from its nostrils. The Cipher sisters force Zuki and me atop the beast's slimy back and climb on behind us. Brad straddles the dragon at the base of its neck, and we're off through the tunnel. There's no carriage or even a saddle; we just have to cling to the edges of the jagged scales. Bacteria-ridden muck sloshes and splashes around us as we plow forward.

My stomach churns with dread. What was I thinking, coming to save my sister? I'm the one in trouble—*again*. Maybe she'll have to be the one to save me.

Except, this time, I'm not sure if she can.

Or will.

CHAPTER 31

Mind: Blown

I DON'T KNOW HOW LONG we travel on the back of the dragon, but it's too long. By the time we come to a stop, my limbs are aching, my boots are splattered with putrid sludge, and my brain is still churning about the overload of information Brad dumped on me.

"I think some of that muck got on my tails!" Zuki whines as we dismount.

I cast my eyes over his fur, which is indeed smeared with a film of lumpy brown scum. "They're fine," I tell him.

We're at the mouth of an ancient drainage pipe, jutting out over a harbor. I recognize it as Elliott Bay, home to the Port of Seattle. I turn to take one last hopeful look at the tunnel behind us. It occurs to me that it must be connected to the Seattle Underground, which is definitely way bigger—and way more populated by dragons—than the tourist literature lets on.

There's a small fishing boat moored below and after we're all on board, Brad starts up the motor and we head out into the bay. It's cold, and there's a mist in the air. I pull my robe tight around me. We weave between several massive container ships and eventually arrive at a derelict freighter that looms over our little boat. The sun is beginning to set, and in the fading light I can see that the freighter is rusty and slightly listing—it's a ghost ship, decommissioned and waiting to be scrapped.

But it's not empty. I can hear harsh electropop music from the speaker system within its corroded innards, which means it still has power. The ship itself is quaking—though not from the music, or even the wind and waves. Its trembling because of toxic spell residue, which is revealed as we pull alongside the battered hull and I spot the telltale rivers of black slime leaking from various cracks and holes. Nova begins going berserk inside my pocket, clawing to get out.

"You've been having too much fun playing with your occuli here," I say to Brad. "Your secret base looks like it's one dark spell away from sinking."

"We don't play games out here, Wizard Girl," he assures me. "Which you will discover soon enough."

"There's something I think I should tell you," Zuki says.

My default is to respond with something snide, but I'm too worried and exhausted to come up with anything clever. Instead, I settle for slumping against the wall. We're on the top deck of the freighter, locked inside a rusted shipping container—the large metal kind that get stacked like giant bricks. It's pitch-black inside—or at least it would be if it weren't for Zuki's fur.

"Uh, Cara?" Zuki prompts, nudging my arm. "I'm talking to you."

I nod wearily and, out of habit, reach into my pocket to check on Nova—but she's gone. Somewhere between disembarking from the motorboat and being tossed into our makeshift prison cell, my baby squix escaped, gnawing a hole right through my robe. She probably couldn't resist the smorgasbord of black goo aboard the Cipher ship—but now she's gone, and I'm wracked with worry.

The ship pitches, causing our prison to rattle and shift. I cling to the sides of the container and Zuki, lacking the ability to find footholds on the metal, leaps into my lap. Eventually, the ship settles, but it's clearly doomed.

I push Zuki off me. I have no idea what time it is, except that it's definitely running out. Brad said all would be divulged at midnight. That can't mean anything good.

"I know you think this is bad," Zuki says. "Catastrophic. Horrendous. Disastr—"

"Really?" I interrupt. "That's what you wanted to tell me?"

"Harlee's coming to rescue us," Zuki announces.

I snap my head toward him. "What?! How do you know? And why didn't you tell me this, like, four hours ago?"

"I thought you would get upset," Zuki says. "You know, because you have issues with Harlee."

"ISSUES?" I screech.

"See?! You *are* upset."

I bang my head against the wall. I'm upset for all kinds of reasons. I'm upset because I lost Nova. I'm upset because I got us captured. I'm upset because my sister is in trouble. And, yes, I'm upset about Harlee. But not because of what she did.

Because of what *I* did.

And blamed her for.

But then something occurs to me, and I whirl toward Zuki. "Harlee *did* send you after me."

"Yes, because—"

"To lead her to Cipher! She pretended to care about my sister! She pretended to care about *me*."

Ranting about Harlee feels like my favorite bench in Dragonsong's garden—safe, comfortable, known. It's way easier to keep hating on her than having to deal with my guilt about her. Besides, this time she actually *did* do something to betray me.

"And . . . and you're a part of it!" I say, shaking my finger at Zuki.

"I'm on *your* side," Zuki says defensively. "I'm in prison, too, you know. And some of the muck from those tunnels got on my tails. I mean, just look at the state of my fur, of my—"

"You're unbelievable," I tell him. But my tirade is done; I'm back to feeling exhausted, and I collapse against the wall. "How exactly is she supposed to find us, anyway?"

"She's tracking me," Zuki replies. "See this gem on my collar? It's a twinning stone. The two halves attract each other, which means she can follow us."

"I don't think she's going to be able to track us through those tunnels and across the bay," I tell him. "I mean, if she could, wouldn't she have gotten here already?"

"Well . . ."

He trails off, and by the twitch of his tails, I can tell that my admittedly less-than-positive logic is making headway in his magical canine brain.

"She's the Chosen One," he finally says, though feebly.

"I sure hope so," I mutter.

For once, I might actually mean it.

"Little Moone, it's almost midnight." The Cipher twins beckon in unison as they fling open the door to our prison. "Time to party!"

They're wearing long black robes with heavy hoods that conceal their faces, but even without their annoying voices, I'd be able to tell it's them because they reek of cigarette smoke. They force me and Zuki out of the container and across the ship, where the wind and rain harass us. The deck is a disaster, peppered with holes and fissures, partly from wear and tear, but mostly from toxic spell slime, which claws across the metal like nasty fingers. We're taken one deck down, where the heavy electropop music surges from the speaker system. Its throbbing beat does little to disguise the rocking and rattling of the ship, but if the tumult bothers the twins, they don't show it.

"All your dark magic is going to sink us," I inform them. "I hope you can swim."

"You'll just have to fly away on your broomstick," one of them teases. "Oh, wait a minute—you can't. We took it!"

I roll my eyes. Seriously? They think my broom is for flying? I imagine them straddling it and trying to jump off the ship— it's a satisfying thought.

We weave through more containers, many of them tipped over, and step through a ruptured bulkhead to arrive at a cargo hold so vast that our footsteps echo. The only illumination comes from candles: there are hundreds of them, perched atop various crates and abandoned cargo, and placed in two lines to create a central aisle—not exactly the best decision on an unstable ship. As we're prodded forward, I begin to discern other things stacked on the crates: wands, tattered tomes, and various other wizardly relics. I'm gazing upon a repository of stolen talismans, I realize. Then I see my broom and belt among the haul. How I'd love to bust open a bottle of Moone Brew on this place—but even if I could reach my belt, I know there's not enough there to neutralize the amount of toxic magic that's seeping through the ship.

We reach the far end of the hold, where the candlelit aisle leads, and I see a makeshift stage and altar, built with a few crates stacked upon wooden pallets. Behind it, painted on the bulkhead, is a garish mural that depicts comic-book-style figures in hooded robes, battling against the Cipher conception of wizards—spellcasters with long white beards, pointy hats, and ornate staffs. Kind of sexist, if you ask me.

"What is this place?" Zuki murmurs.

"The site of their initiation ritual," I tell him.

"No talking," one of the Cipher twins warns.

"Kneel," her sister commands.

When I don't budge, they force me to the cold metal deck. Zuki crouches alongside me, whimpering. The darkwave music continues to pound.

Maybe it's not just an initiation ritual. Maybe it's going to be a sacrifice.

I peer over my shoulder and see people streaming into the hold behind us to kneel in orderly rows. Some are like the Cipher sisters, disciples dressed in long black robes, but others are regular teenagers—the new initiates, I realize, the ones who were deemed worthy of being invited to the party. I scan the throng, but it's too dark to see if Su is among them.

The twins force me to turn back toward the altar just as Brad takes his place in front of it. He's wearing a hooded robe, too, and now he raises his pale hands, as if in some demented prayer.

"Welcome, acolytes of Cipher," he greets the assembly as the music fades to a background hammering. "Tonight is a glorious night. One of celebration and ceremony. Our cell expands; the cult of Cipher grows. Rise! Your queen arrives! All hail Cipher Storm!"

"*Queen?*" I murmur. "Who the . . ."

I crane my neck around, fighting against the restraining grip of the Cipher twins, to see someone new gliding down the aisle toward the altar. She's dressed in a flowing, sumptuous black gown, with long fingerless gloves, and a dark veil disguising her face.

But the veil doesn't matter. I know who it is.

I'd recognize her anywhere.

My sister of many names

The summer before Su started sixth grade, her best friend Amelia got cancer and had to undergo chemotherapy. Su showed up to the first day of school with her head shaved bald. When she was in seventh grade, her friend Evan got suspended for breaking "dress code" by wearing a skirt to school, and Su arrived the next morning in a suit and tie, her hair chopped short. In ninth grade, she decided to protest climate change and descended upon downtown Seattle, leading a wave of six hundred students (the videos went viral).

Yep, my sister really is a force of nature—just check how many TikTok followers she has. If Su sets her mind to something, she's going to do it. And if you get in her way—look out. She'll wash right over you and wipe you away. Which is why she ended up with "Tsunami" for a nickname. I think some kids in her high school genuinely don't know that Su is short for Suzannah.

All these aliases: Su. Suzannah. Tsunami.
Now I can add one more name to the list.

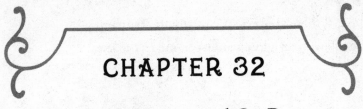

CHAPTER 32

The Truth Hurts—and So Does a Wizard Whistle

IT'S A GOOD THING I'M already on my knees, because I feel so dizzy, I would have collapsed anyway.

"This doesn't make sense," Zuki mumbles. "Dante said Cipher Storm was a *he*!"

"He also exploded into black goo," I say, which isn't really any kind of counterpoint—except, I guess, proof that people make mistakes.

Su sweeps past me and takes the stage, full of poise and elegance. She removes her veil, setting it on the altar to reveal an expression of delight and confidence. She must see me kneeling there, but she doesn't acknowledge me, doesn't give me so much as a glance.

But I can't take my eyes off her. Now that she's in front of me, I can see just how elaborate her gown is, layered with gossamer silk, the bodice enhanced with ornate sculpted metalwork and glistening with black gemstones. Her hair is a nest of braids and buns, adorned with her occuli hairpin. She's the dark queen of midnight, morbid and forbidding, but still glamorous.

The ship shudders, its iron ribs groaning under the strain. The candles flicker; some even tip over and extinguish. No one seems to care. Maybe Cipher actually *likes* the idea of a haunted ship.

Once the tremor subsides, Su's black-painted lips curl into a smile. "Welcome to tonight's momentous occasion," she declares, her gaze panning the crowd.

I sense the audience behind me stir in anticipation. Su lets the moment hang, her eyes shining. She's the same orator I've known my entire life. With her honeyed tongue, she could coax a dragon right out of its scales. Which is why I should have known that it wasn't Brad leading *her* astray.

"I see you," Su proclaims at last. "You are bewildered. Distraught. Misunderstood—by your parents, your school, your peers. How could you *not* be misunderstood? They don't see you for who you truly are."

A murmur of assent rises from the crowd.

"An undercurrent of evil courses through our world," Su continues, lifting her open palms to the air. "They call us Blisses, because they view us as ignorant. Unworthy. Expendable. In their arrogant estimation, only *they* are worthy of wielding magic, a magic that should be everyone's right. They conceal this power from us, deprive us of it, even as they exercise it against us."

"What?!" I blurt out. "That's not tr—"

One of the Cipher twins clamps her hand over my mouth; the other digs her long fingernails into my shoulder. Growling in frustration, I struggle to break loose. Everything Su is saying is so twisted, so demented. But she's got everyone's rapt attention.

"The wizards' magic threatens us all," Su warns. "But a revolution is beginning, and *you* are a part of it. You have been chosen to stand against the tide of evil, to usher in a new era, one in which we bow before them no more."

I finally wrest myself free from the Cipher twins and scramble toward the stage. "This is ridiculous!" I scream. "You don't know what you're talking about, Su! You don't know—"

"It is you who knows so very little, sister," Su interrupts me, ever so calmly.

The twins snatch at me from behind, but Su shoos them away with a backhanded wave. Then she steps to the front of the stage and, finally gazing down at me, unclips something from the metalwork on her dress. Her vape pen? I stare at her, perplexed. So, right in the middle of her ceremony, she's going to take a smoke break? But she just toys with the pen in her fingers.

"Su, you've got it all wrong," I tell her in a pleading voice. "We're not—this isn't . . . I came to help you. To *save* you."

Su breaks into laughter. "As always, sister, I'm the one who's going to save you. *From them.*"

"From them?" I mumble in bewilderment.

"She means us," a voice sounds from across the hold.

It's a voice I know all too well, a voice that's grated on me countless times. Now, though, it causes a whole complicated mess of emotions to boil inside me. I turn to see Harlee striding into the hold, Gusto and Master Quibble flanking her.

"You okay?" Gusto mouths to me as he and the Q-Man come to a stop a few feet away.

I nod, but my attention is focused on Harlee. She marches past me, halting only once she reaches the stage. As usual, she's stealing my spotlight—only, this time, I'm not sure how I feel about it. Yes, she can rescue us—but the only reason she's here is because she set me up, sending me after Su so she could find Cipher. But now it's not just Cipher she's facing. *It's my sister.*

My gaze flits between them, Harlee and Su, the two biggest personalities in my life. Volcano versus Tsunami. *Cataclysmic* is the word that comes to mind.

"Lovely, more magic-makers," Su says, seeming not the least bit perturbed by Harlee's arrival. "You're just in time to witness—"

"Yeah, we don't have time for a villain's monologue," Harlee snaps, raising her hands. The glow of magic swells in her cheeks.

Su just smiles and lifts the vape pen to her lips—and my world explodes with pain as an excruciating needle of sound pierces my brain. It topples our entire crew: Zuki howls, Master Quibble and Gusto scream, and even Harlee shrieks. We're soon all flailing on the deck.

Fighting against the torment, I peer up at Su. The pen is still in her mouth, but she's not sucking on it, I comprehend. She's *blowing* on it. That's when it clicks: my sister doesn't have a vaping habit—she has a Wizard Whistle. That's how she paralyzed the entire school and robbed the library! My classmates dismissed the Whistle as a legend, but it's real. Painfully real.

When Su finally lowers the instrument, it's like a dentist

pulling his syringe out of the pocket of my cheek. I remain in a crumpled heap, my vision swimming. I hear the rest of the crew moan, even Harlee, who audibly gasps, as if she's been drowning and finally broke the surface to draw a long and much-needed breath. When I'm steady enough to glance around, it's to see that the cultists and their initiates have formed an ominous semicircle around us.

"It seems to me you *do* have time for a monologue," Su gloats. "Though I'm not the villain here. *You are.*"

Harlee struggles to her feet, then immediately collapses again. The glare she fires in Su's direction is hot enough to weld metal, but that's the extent of what she can muster. She looks worse than she did the night of the Dragonsong robbery—maybe because she's so close to the Whistle this time. Or maybe it has something to do with Su's intention—before, she just wanted to create a distraction to steal Riva's relics. This time? She wants to hurt us.

I hear Master Quibble groan, notice that he's suffering *almost* as much as Harlee, and the realization strikes me. The more powerful the wizard, the more pain the Whistle inflicts. Any last doubts about Harlee being a magical fraud evaporate—she's the real deal, like everyone always said. I can't even imagine the pain she must be experiencing; I'm just a remedial wizard and I feel like someone tried to clean my ear canals with a razor blade.

The ship rumbles and contorts like it's caught in the grip of a giant fist—the Wizard Whistle is savaging the Field, too. As Zuki whimpers alongside me, I pull myself groggily to my knees and see a fresh rift forming between us and the stage. It's hovering just above the deck, oozing black gunk. This particular wound seems extra virulent; it growls and puckers, which causes everything in the vicinity to ripple and buckle.

There's already a seam in the deck—it's actually a hatch, designed to open up so that the cargo hold below can be accessed—but now the metal is bending and rumpling at my feet. I push Zuki toward Master Quibble, where it seems safer—but I stay put.

"Don't blow the Whistle again," I beg Su. "The Field can't take it. The ship can't take it!"

Su taps the Whistle pensively against her chin. "Oh? *Now* you care about the price of your magic?"

"Magic doesn't do this," I tell her, still wincing from the pain caused by her attack. "Not if you're a wizard. You're destroying the Field, its harmony—"

"Harmony?!" Brad cries, pouncing forward and whipping down his hood. "HARMONY? How dare you speak of harmony? You are destroyers. Murderers. It would be better if your kind didn't exist."

"How can you say that?" I turn to Su for sympathy, but there's none to be found in her expression. "Listen, I don't think you understand—"

"It's you who doesn't understand," Su interrupts. She points past me and I follow her gesture, to where Master Quibble is sprawled, trembling and groaning, with Zuki in his arms. "Do you know how he got his scar?"

"Yes," I retort. "By standing up to your boss."

Su looks momentarily confused. "Oh. You mean Cipher Mourn. Our founder. Our inspiration." She gracefully crouches and leans over the lip of the stage, so close that I can feel her breath. "I met him at the nursing home. You know, where Mom made me volunteer. Mourn's no longer a factor, I'm afraid. But he did tell me the truth about Dad's death—and for that I will be eternally grateful."

"What are you talking about?" I say in exasperation.

Su rises abruptly to full height and points at Master Quibble. "Your beloved master attacked Cipher Mourn. During his storm of negligent magic, a bridge collapsed, cars careened off the road, and people died. *Our father* died."

The world around me trembles—literally and figuratively. "Dad died in a car accident," I tell her. The words come out automatically, by rote, except by the time I finish the sentence, they're at a crawl, riddled with doubt and confusion.

I turn slowly toward Master Quibble.

"N-no!" he sputters. "Those were *his* spells. Too many bystanders to save! I had to act quickly, had to make a choice—"

"Why should you get to choose?!" Su seethes, shaking the Whistle at him. "My dad *died*! But that doesn't matter to you, does it? We're just Blisses, right? Collateral damage."

I gape at Master Quibble. Is *this* why he never looks at me? I thought it was because he hated me, but all this time it's been for another reason. . . .

Guilt.

My heart explodes with a minefield of emotions. Rage, disgust, and sadness all compete for the same tiny bit of territory inside me. It's so overwhelming, I can't even begin to process it; I just turn numb.

"I'm sorry, Caradine," Master Quibble mumbles—and for once he *is* looking at me. "I wish—"

"Wishing isn't good enough!" Brad screams. "How many of us have died by your magic? My parents! Cipher Jade, Cipher Vex—their brother! And—"

"Yeah, yeah, we get it," Harlee says, finally finding enough strength to speak. "Terrible things happened. And now you're using them as excuses to—"

"Spare us your wizardsplaining," Su snaps. "You flaunt moral authority as if it's yours alone to possess. But those days are over."

"No," Harlee spits, rising up. "*You're* over."

She's recuperated just enough strength to counterattack—her hands fly up and magical fire crackles from her fingertips, just like the time when she tried to attack Dante. Except, this time, she's going to attack my sister.

Her fire never lands. Su wails on the Whistle and everything around me dissolves into pain again. The laceration in the Field in front of me moans, the deck ruptures at my feet, and—

Down I go.

CHAPTER 33

That Sinking Feeling You Get When You're—Well, Sinking

I PLUNGE INTO WATER. AT first, I think I've somehow fallen overboard, but after a moment of disorientation and frantic dog-paddling, I realize I've tumbled straight down into the hold. The freighter has clearly been taking on water through the night, which means it's slowly sinking.

When I find my footing on the metal floor, the water comes past my waist.

Okay, maybe not so slowly.

A positive person—like Gusto—would point out that the three feet of water saved me from breaking every bone in my body, but I can't help thinking we're all doomed. Still, I'm alive for now, so I glance around, searching for a way out. It's cauldron-black in the hold, but I spot a dull light in the distance. It's a somber metaphor for my life.

I slosh toward it.

Along the way, I bump into all sorts of containers. Some are wooden and bob in the water, others are the big metal ones—these are too heavy to float, but they shift and slide with the pitch of the ship. If I don't drown, I could get crushed—more crushed than I already feel.

"Master Quibble," I murmur. "Why didn't you tell me?"

How many times have I felt stretched and torn between two disparate worlds—but now, those same worlds are colliding . . .

Correction: they collided a long time ago. Which makes it even worse, because I've been in the dark this entire time. Who else knows the truth about Dad's death? Definitely not Zuki—there is absolutely no way he would be able to keep a secret like that. But Headwizard Singh? The rest of the Dragonsong staff? Even *Su* knew. And she didn't tell me—just chose to keep it to herself and use it against me at the worst possible moment.

What am I going to do about Su?

What am I going to do about *any* of this?

From somewhere above my head, I hear a familiar chirp.

"Nova?"

The baby squix drops onto my shoulder, chirruping excitedly. As I suspected, she's been gorging on toxic spell slime. I can tell by her size and the shimmer of luminescent color she offers me.

"I'm so happy you're here!" I tell her, squeezing her to my cheek.

"Well, that's a first."

I pivot toward the sound of the voice. "Harlee?"

"You weren't talking to me?" she replies, wading up to me.

It makes sense that Harlee fell down here, too—she was sprawled right next to me on the upper deck. But with all this raw emotion seething through me, she's the last person I want to see. I quickly stuff Nova inside the folds of my hood, then throw eye daggers in Harlee's direction.

"You tried to attack my sister," I growl.

"She *did* attack us."

"You can't spellcast on Blisses! Haven't you ever taken an Ethics class?"

Harlee snorts. "Your sister isn't a Bliss. Not anymore."

She's right, I realize. Su isn't ignorant to our existence—which, by definition, means she's not a Bliss. But I'm still not sure how I feel about Harlee trying to attack her, even if it *was* in self-defense.

"Crew's still up there," Harlee says. "We need to get them before—"

Another blast of the Wizard Whistle consumes the ship. With a scream, Harlee collapses and plunges beneath the water. I blindly flail around for her, only to hear her surface on her own, gasping.

A different sound comes from my hood—a gentle purr from Nova. The Whistle clearly doesn't affect her, and that's when I realize that I'm okay, too. At most, I feel only a slight irritation from the Whistle.

Strange.

Harlee clearly hasn't discovered the same immunity, though. After the shrill of the Whistle fades, she lingers next to me. I can sense her presence in the blackness, but she's not moving.

"Harlee? Are you—"

"Just need a minute," she groans.

I've never heard her sound so fragile, so spent. "What are we going to do?" I fret.

"Need to get the crew. Get out of here."

"What about Cipher?"

She draws in a deep, labored breath. "What about them?"

"Are more wizards coming?" I ask. "Isn't that the plan? You followed me here to find the Cipher base!"

"Is that what you think?" Harlee asks incredulously. "I followed you in case you ended up in trouble. *Which you did.*"

She begins churning through the water, across the cavernous hold.

"You really came for me?" I ask, chasing after her. "Like, to save me?"

"Wouldn't be the first time."

"Oh yeah?"

"Uh . . . the auditorium?"

"Well . . ." I mumble, unable to find a snide retort. In the movie of my memory, that incident is called *Harlee Embarrasses Cara* (available in 4D!)—but, reality is, she *did* save me. Though, another part of me argues, she just reacted to me falling. It's not like she made a purposeful decision to come rescue me. . . .

Like now.

Dratch. It really *is* hard to change your mind about someone.

"Aren't you going to get in trouble with the Council?" I ask, hurrying to keep up with her. "For coming to get me? For letting me come in the first place?"

"News flash, kid. We're already in trouble."

"But you still came and—"

"Don't get all sentimental," Harlee declares, bursting the small bubble of whatever was beginning to form inside me. "I don't want to be your BFF. I'm just looking after my crew."

After a long slog, we reach a rupture in the bulkhead and hoist ourselves through to arrive in an engine room. This is where the glow was coming from; an emergency light is flickering on the wall. In its green gleam, I can see just how abysmal Harlee looks. Her cheeks, usually so flush with heat, are sallow and drawn. Her clothes and hair are drenched. I guess I look no better—but I'm *used* to looking no better.

We find a stairwell and clamber up, but when we reach the next level, and the next set of steps, the way is blocked by a mangled bulkhead. At least we're out of the water—though how long that will last, I have no idea.

Harlee pulls a stone from her pocket, the twin to the one on Zuki's collar. The gem seems to tug her fist, and she turns to lead us in a different direction, down a grimy corridor that cuts widthwise across the ship. It's dimly lit by more emergency lights.

A burst of shouts reaches our ears—we're headed the right way. Even though the clamor is muffled, it sounds like all dratch is breaking loose. I pause, shaking my head.

"Quibble should have told me," I murmur. "*Someone* should

have told me." I turn my glare on Harlee. "Did *you* know?"

"About your dad? No." She grabs me by the wrist. "Gotta keep going."

She weaves a path down the corridor, leading me past boxes and crates that have spilled through ruptures in the bulkheads. Strings of toxic magic ooze down the walls. Some of them curl in our direction, snapping and clawing, just like the tongue of slime did in Brad's locker.

"Your sister's wrong, though," Harlee says as she swerves to avoid the aggressive gunk. "Trick was the one who got attacked. Tried to save as many people as he could—but not being able to save people—like your dad—isn't the same as killing them. Not sure Trick sees the difference. I guess that's why he left Dragonsong. Turned to drinking, and—look, I'm not used to defending him, okay? He took off without even a goodbye. I'm just saying he's not the guy your sister is making him out to be."

"Su wouldn't lie about this," I protest. "She's—"

"Poisoned by envy," Harlee interrupts. "They all are. Those kids up there? They're doing this because they want what we have."

"I don't think—"

"You're telling me you've never been jealous of me? Never been tempted to mess around with something dangerous so you can be a little more powerful?"

My freckled cheeks must give me away.

"Yeah, see? But your sister? She doesn't have *any* magic,

nothing. Just anger—fueled by some bitter old man manipulating her. Yeah, you can bet Cipher Mourn's still around, scheming and pulling her strings from behind the scenes, no matter what she says or thinks. She's accusing *us* of being arrogant? She can't see the dragon for the scales."

We reach the stairwell on the opposite side of the ship, which thankfully isn't blocked. Harlee immediately starts climbing, but I hesitate. Once I go up there, I'm going to have to face Su again. I'm going to have to pick a side.

The thing is, I'm just not sure I can.

CHAPTER 34

The Unchosen One

"COME ON," HARLEE URGES, TUGGING my wrist. "We have to keep mo—"

There's another shriek of the Whistle—like last time, I can barely feel its power, but it sends Harlee toppling into me and we both tumble back into the corridor. Harlee thrashes like a dying fish, and there's nothing I can do but helplessly watch. When the Whistle finally ceases, she slowly pulls herself to her hands and knees, breathing heavily. I try to help her up, but she shakes me off.

The ship twists, and more toxic magic leaks through the rents in the bulkheads, clawing at us with slimy fingers. Harlee, sapped of strength, doesn't react, so I throw my arms around her and heave her dead weight into the stairwell. I only make it up a few steps before my strength gives out and I have to deposit her against the wall. At least we're safe for the moment.

I give Harlee a nudge. "Are you okay?"

She nods wearily, but her eyes are still closed. "You know, I really, *really* don't like your sister."

"This isn't her. Trust me, she's . . . it just isn't her."

"Maybe not. Maybe messing with occuli messes with *you*. Turns you vicious." She massages her head. "Or maybe it's a family trait."

"Gee, thanks."

Harlee rises unsteadily to her feet and starts making her way up the steps again, clinging to the handrail. "Low blow. Guess we're alike that way."

"I'm nothing like you!" I protest, chasing after her—though, first, I grab a slat of wood lying on the ground from a broken crate. It feels better to be armed with something, even if it's not my broom.

At the top of the stairs, Harlee consults her stone, then turns right, down another corridor that leads past what look to be crew quarters. There's not much left of them—the bulkheads are riddled with holes and slithering with snakes of deadly goo.

Harlee scowls at the slime, but keeps staggering forward. "We both have trouble controlling our emotions. Both overprotective. Both from Bliss families."

"Your family's not Bliss," I snap.

"What do you know about it?"

Nothing—clearly.

"Told you before," Harlee continues. "Those Dragonsong kids don't know a thing about me. Not a real thing."

"Where are they, then? Your family?"

The ship quakes, tilting so severely that we're sent flying into the nearest wall. The ship tilts the other direction and we go with it. When it stops, we're at a precarious angle, with a tangle of toxic slime hissing at us from above. Harlee instinctively raises a hand to blast the sludge with a spell, but I grab her arm and shake my head.

"I've got the juice," she insists, though her voice lacks conviction.

"Just don't think using magic on this stuff is the best—"

"Fine," she mutters, and wrenches the broken slat of wood out of my hand.

She swings tiredly at the ropes of tar, but they merely wrap around her improvised club and rip it from her hands—though it does give us the chance to scramble past them. The ship is still tilted, so we pretty much have to crawl.

"I hurt them," Harlee suddenly says.

"Huh?"

"My parents. Displayed so young, didn't know what I was doing. Didn't know how to control my powers. That I *could* control them. Burned down our entire house. My parents survived, but . . ." She exhales. "Maybe Cipher is right. Maybe it'd be better if we didn't exist."

I hear it in her voice. She's thought this before.

"Council decided to take me away," she says as we reach a dead end. "At first, wizards told my parents that I needed to go to a special institution." She pauses to slam her shoulder into the bulkhead, but the corroded metal doesn't give. "But I think that got too tricky. They had questions. Wanted me back. I nearly killed them and they still—"

"Of course they wanted you back!" I exclaim. "They're your parents!"

Harlee tries one more shoulder check to the wall, then slumps to her knees, panting and flexing her fingers, as if she's trying to decide if she can summon enough magic to free us. But she's taken multiple hits from the Wizard Whistle—there's not much left in her tank.

"I couldn't go back to them," she says eventually. "How could I conceal *this*?" She waves her hands around, gesturing vaguely at her cheeks. "So, the Council erased me from their memories."

"WHAT?!" I blurt. "They can't do that!"

"They *did* do that."

My mind is bubbling over like a badly brewed potion. So, Dragonsong won't let students cast spells on Blisses, but it's okay for adult wizards to erase their memories? And to take away a kid? Then they turn around and make *us* take an Ethics class?

"It's not so simple," Harlee says, as if she's read my mind. "Being a part of this . . . this . . . *world*. My parents—*I nearly killed them*."

"Not on purpose!" I wring my hands and notice water surging up from below. Though, in reality, it's not rising so much as we're sinking.

"Does that matter?" Harlee asks. "I kill my parents—accidentally, even—then the wizards have to get me anyway. Except then, my parents are *dead*."

"Yeah, but—"

"I hear all the stupid stories at school. All the gossip. Now you know the truth, how I ended up at Dragonsong as a little kid. Trick pretty much raised me—until he didn't."

The ship lurches, and we brace ourselves. I can hear the metal grinding, splitting, surrendering to the sea.

"Now I don't have anyone," Harlee murmurs, shoving the twinning stone into her pocket.

"That's not true!" I exclaim. "You have all of Dragonsong! At least you fit in!"

Harlee snorts, and stares at her hands. "You call this fitting in? Everyone lurking around, pointing at me, pretending like I'm some sort of hero instead of an actual . . . *person?*" She shakes her head at me. "You have no idea how lucky you are."

"Lucky?!" I shriek. "LUCKY?!"

"You're free. Get to do what you want. Not have people watching every little thing you do under the—"

"You're the freaking Chosen One!" I interrupt.

Harlee rolls her eyes. "What a stupid name. No one chooses me, not the actual me. They choose an *idea* of me."

She turns and looks at me, really looks at me, for the first time in the entire conversation. Sweat is pouring from her throbbing temples. I swear there's smoke curling up from her cheeks, like overheated brake pads on a car. It's possible that I'm seeing her, truly, for the very first time, too.

"I'm only confiding in you for one reason," she tells me.

"Why?" I ask quietly, sheepishly.

The next roar that sounds is so thunderous, like the ship

itself is alive—though really, I decide, it's more like one last battle cry before it expires. The lights flicker, then die.

"Because," Harlee tells me in the abject darkness, "I don't think we're going to make it out of here."

The paradox of Cara Moone

A conversation from last year is playing in my mind, over and over again. I'm sitting in Master Quibble's office after failing my sixth grade standardized test. It's my first official day as a MOP. Headwizard Singh is there, too, standing before the massive desk, doing her best to placate the Q-Man.

"Caradine Moone is *not* a good fit for this program," he announces to Singh, as if I'm not even sitting there.

"I disagree," Singh counters. "You should see her in a disaster scenario. She may have saved the Apothecarial Arts lab from exploding."

"It can't work," Quibble insists. "I returned to Dragonsong on the agreement that I would keep a low profile. How can you expect me to deal with this? With *her*?"

I cross my arms. It's not like I want to be here either. I want to be a wizard. A real wizard. But it seems like Singh has already made up her mind that I'm good for little more than a broom.

"Is this a test?" Quibble demands of Singh. "A cruel joke? This can't be simple coincidence."

"No," Singh agrees. "I believe everything is connected."

Quibble draws in a deep breath. "This is wrong."

"And also right," Singh says. "You know as well as I do, Trick, that two seemingly opposing and contrary perspectives can be simultaneously true."

It was, as my sister called it, wizardsplaining—and now I know what that conversation was *really* about. He and Singh were talking about my dad, right in front of me! Instead of having a heart-to-heart with me, instead of telling me the *truth*, they kept it a secret.

That's what wizards do: They play with our lives. They find a kid who's just a little too powerful and take her away from her parents. Find another who isn't powerful enough and give her a broom. Do we get to decide?

Nope.

Maybe Cipher has a point about us. Maybe *my sister* has a point.

My whole life has been all these sides crashing and colliding. Bliss side. Magic side. Wizard side. MOP side. Master Quibble's side. Su's side. Where does it leave me? Everywhere and nowhere, all at once. That's me, Cara Moone—a living, breathing paradox.

Except, this time, it's worse than usual. This time, I'm not just emotionally stuck—I'm literally stuck.

And about to die.

CHAPTER 35

Time to Take Out the Trash

AS I FIGHT THE DESPERATE urge to cling to Harlee, the corridor buckles and bends like a car in a compactor. Everything's bleeding black slime; Nova peers out of my hood and starts taking a nibble.

"Don't worry," I tell Harlee anxiously when she spots the glowing squix. "She's—"

"I know what she is," Harlee says. "I've known you had her since she hatched."

"What?! Why didn't you tell on me? Take her away?"

"Seriously? Didn't we just have a long conversation about kids being taken away?"

"You don't think she's a monster?"

"Do you think *I'm* one?"

I gape at her. I used to, that's for sure.

"Yeah, well, it's about to be one big monster mash in here," Harlee mutters as the walls continue to close in.

But we don't get crushed. Instead, a jagged hole splits open in the corroded bulkhead, providing a narrow exit. Harlee and

I exchange a look of surprise—then promptly dive through and crash clumsily to the deck of the adjoining cargo hold.

We're back where we started: the site of my sister's depraved ceremony. It's taken a beating, like the rest of the ship. Crates and containers are strewn everywhere, cast about by the tumult. A couple of stacks are even on fire—yep, the candles were a bad idea. At least the flames provide us with light.

Then I see my sister, and the weight of everything comes crashing down on me again. She's still on the stage, still clenching her Whistle, but she's got Master Quibble on his knees, one hand wrapped around his throat while she screams in his face. Zuki and Gusto are nearby, floundering in pain, while Brad and the twins guard them. As for the rest of the cultists and initiates, they seem to have scattered—I guess this party was way more than they bargained for.

Harlee gently draws me behind the cover of a crate.

"Gotta sneak up there," she says. "Follow me."

The way the ship is rocking, we don't really have to worry about making noise—what we *do* have to worry about is how we're going to reach the stage, because between it and us are a whole lot of obstacles. Toppled crates. Cavernous holes in the deck. Rivers of black slime. That's when I realize that the lesion in the Field near the front of Su's stage is not the only one—multiple wounds are hovering in the air. With all the magic being cast, it's like someone has taken a sword and repeatedly stabbed the Field in its belly.

It would be simpler to cross a minefield, but Harlee seems

undaunted. She plows forward on hands and knees, using the crates as cover. I follow her, even though my heart is pounding. As we go, tendrils of slime snarl and burble toward us.

"Keep moving," Harlee urges over her shoulder.

As we near the stage, I spot what's left of the stolen talismans, scattered everywhere: wands, amulets, and . . . my broom. Without even thinking, I reach out and snatch it—which catches Su's attention.

"Sister!" she calls over the din. "How nice of you to return."

She wails on the Whistle, causing another round of torment for my crew. But I'm still okay, for some reason. Even Gusto, a MOP like me, seems in pain. Harlee's clinging to the nearest crate, like she's trying to hold on for dear life; I can see the agony in her eyes.

"Get her," she breathes at me between clenched teeth. "Stop this."

I stare at her in bewilderment. I don't know how to *get* Su. I don't even know if I *want* to get her.

"*Please*," Harlee begs.

Maybe it's the compelling tone of her voice. Maybe it's the fact that we just nearly got crushed together. Whatever it is, I find myself rising to my feet and turning to face my sister.

Su lowers the Whistle in surprise, then narrows her eyes at me; she can't figure out why her magic isn't affecting me (join the club). But I realize now that it's affecting *her*. Every time she blows on the Whistle, it sucks life from her, draining her. Even in the time it's taken me to crawl back up here, she's become paler, weaker, the bags beneath her eyes darker. That's why she can't simply blow on the Whistle until we all explode—that would destroy her, too.

Just like Dante. My stomach heaves at the thought.

"Su, that Whistle, it's killing you," I tell her as I carefully tread forward. "Don't use it again. *Please.* It's not worth it."

"The right thing is always worth it," she says, tightening her grip on Master Quibble.

Then, despite my warning, she blows the Whistle again. There are more howls from my crew, more reverberations from the ruptures in the Field. A new gash opens up to my left, spewing slime.

I ignore it and just keep picking my way toward the stage.

Su ceases the shrill, and glares at me.

"Don't worry about her," Brad speaks up. He jerks his chin at Master Quibble. "She can watch us end him."

"What?!" I yelp, freezing in my tracks. "No—don't! Please. That won't solve anything. It won't—"

"Whose side are you on?" Su spits. She squeezes Master Quibble's neck so tightly that his eyes bulge.

There's that word again: *side.* "Su, don't do this," I beg as my emotions swirl. "You're . . . you're breaking my heart."

"Your heart is easily broken," Su snaps. "You're too soft. Weak. Always getting bullied. And it's always me who swoops in and saves you, the one who cleans up your messes. Look what you've done! To us. To Dad. To *me*." She clucks her tongue. "*Your* heart is broken? You barely knew him, but Dad was *everything* to me. And you took him from me."

"Me?! I didn't—"

"Your kind. *Traitor.*"

Her words rip through me. Tears are streaming from my eyes—but her eyes? They are vacant of emotion. Then, as if to add injury to insult, she plays the Whistle again, causing Master Quibble to spasm so violently that he twists out of her grasp and crashes to the floor. I'm so close to the Whistle now that its virulent power causes my ears to burn and my knees to tremble.

Then I hear Nova chirp at me, soothing me.

Nova.

My baby squix is a devourer of dark magic—somehow, I realize, she's been mitigating the power of the Whistle, protecting me from it. If I had been just a regular wizard, a normal student at Dragonsong, I would have destroyed Nova. But I didn't. Because . . .

I'm *not* a regular wizard.

Now I know which side to choose.

My side.

Maybe I'm not one thing or the other. It's like Singh said: *two seemingly opposing and contrary perspectives can be simultaneously true.* I can live in the wizards' world and still be a part of the Bliss one. I can be angry at Master Quibble for having a role in my dad's death, for not even telling me about it, and still understand that it broke him—that he needs healing, too.

I can be a mermaid and still win the race.

"Come closer, I dare you," Su warns, taking a break from the

Whistle. "You think you're somebody, just because they chose you for their special school. *I'm* the somebody in this family, Cara. Not you. ME!"

Her eyes are black, like cauldrons burned dry, and it makes me shiver. This is not the sister I've known most of my life. She raised me like a second mother, stood up for me, held me in her arms—and that's when it strikes me. The words she's uttering aren't hers. They're coming from the Whistle. Its dark magic is coursing through her veins like poison—and I need to cut her off from the supply, need to *purge* her, just like the site of any other Magical Occurrence.

Gripping my broom in both hands, I charge across the last bit of distance between us. My resolve catches her off guard, but for only a second. She blasts the Whistle again, but I ignore it. I dodge the rupture in the Field and its attacking tentacles of slime. I leap over the yawning hole in the floor, the one I fell through before, and land in front of Su, just as she slumps to her knees. She's weakened to the point of fainting. The hand clenching the Whistle drops to her side as she draws in sharp, wheezing breaths.

She stares at me in confusion. "This magic should work on a wizard."

"Here's the thing, Su," I tell her. "I'm not much of a wizard." I draw in a deep breath. "But I'm one heck of a spell sweeper."

I swing my broom, batting the Whistle out of her hand. It rattles away, out of her reach. From the corner of my eye, I see Brad and the twins scatter to find it. As for Su, she collapses to the floor, her energy spent. Crying out for her, I drop my broom, fly to her side, and cradle her head in my lap.

"Cipher Bane?" she moans.

Brad glances vaguely toward the sound of her voice, then turns back to the hunt for the Wizard Whistle. Yep, he's definitely the worst boyfriend ever. What does catch his attention is Master Quibble rising unsteadily to his feet. Brad rushes back on the stage to intercept him, but Quibble doesn't try to flee.

"Sweepers!" he cries. "Evacuate! Get out of here!" When Zuki starts to protest, he adds, "NOW! That's an order! Get to safety and stay there!"

Zuki and Gusto stumble away, but I stay right where I am, with Su. I was never good at following instructions anyway. I watch as Master Quibble staggers across the stage. Even though he's clearly in distress, he's moving *toward* Brad—not to harm him, I realize; if anything, it looks he's going to put his hand on his shoulder. Like he's going to *comfort* him.

Brad simply sneers, then stoops over Su to snatch the hairpin from her hair.

"Master!" I shout as Brad advances on him. "Watch out! That's an occu—"

Brad plunges the hairpin into Master Quibble's chest. I see his eyes flash wide in shock. There's no blood, no magical fire—just a loud cracking noise as he turns to stone. The transformation erases his vivid red scar, leaving behind a monotone gray. What does remain is the confused expression on his face.

Brad whirls around, brandishing the hairpin at me. "You're next, Wizard Girl."

I clutch Su close, like a shield. Despite all that's happened, I still believe that she will always save me.

Su's eyes flicker toward me, weak and morose, and instead, she murmurs, "You could have joined us, sister. Now you will join your master."

Then her body goes limp and heavy in my arms. Brad looms over me, ready to drive the hairpin into my chest. The twins are here now, too, their expressions shining with delight to witness my demise. Nova shrieks and burrows into the folds of my hood. I squeeze my eyes shut and wait for the stab of magic.

"CARA!"

Harlee bursts from the rubble, hands splayed like claws. Her cloak billows in the tumult of the rupturing ship—somehow, after everything, she still looks heroic.

Maybe she *is* the Chosen One.

Harlee's fingertips light up like fireworks and searing strings of lightning crackle across the hold, casting crates and wreckage aside before ensnaring Brad and the twins. I hear them screech—but I don't see what happens next, because Harlee's spellcasting is one more blow than the ship can take. Metal splits, the lacerations in the Field roar, and the deck violently tilts.

My broom clunks against my head. I reach out and desperately grab it—then, as I slide away, I throw my other arm around my sister—or what's left of her.

I've got you

There's a memory I cling to, of that time in the hospital when Dad died: Su holding me, stroking my hair, assuring me that she will look after me. This goes on for hours; every time I make a peep, she just pulls me in tighter and whispers in my ear, "I've got you, Cara. I've got you."

CHAPTER 36

Biggest Purge Ever

I SHOOT THROUGH A HOLE in the bulkhead and drop down the sheer slope of the hull, hanging on to Su. I can just vaguely make out the raging water below. I hear the hiss of snapping slime but skid right past it to smash into one of the crates floating amid the roiling waves. We nearly slip off, I nearly drop my broom, but I manage to dig my toes into the wood. I can hear Nova shrieking over the roar of the world. We're surrounded by giant slabs of metal, jutting out of the water like teeth—but they won't be there for long. Everything is going down.

The freezing waves slosh over our inadequate raft. I manage to sling my broom over my back, then hold Su close, my mind spiraling. Everything's upside down. My sister, the one I always counted on, was happy to let her scumbag boyfriend kill me, while the person I spent so long hating leapt to my rescue.

I had Harlee wrong. In so many ways. Everyone says she's the one who's going to save the world—but one thing I know for sure is this: she saved *me*. So many times.

My makeshift boat bumps and bashes into the bones of the

ship, like it's determined for us to go down with it. I scramble to keep myself and Su afloat, but our crate is sinking. I hear someone shouting my name and turn to see a small skiff approaching us, piloted by a boy and a glowing fox. They look dreadful, but at least they're alive. Gusto stretches out, grabs the broom strapped across my back, and manages to pull us in. Working together, we lift Su's limp body onto the skiff; then I follow, collapsing to the bottom in a clumsy heap.

"Are you okay?" Gusto asks.

"Harlee," I gasp.

"I think she's still on the ship," Zuki says. He's shivering, but not from the cold, I realize. It's from the torture of the Wizard Whistle. "Don't worry—she's with Master Quibble."

He doesn't know. But I don't have the heart to tell him, not right now.

"Have to get Harlee," I tell him as I start to undo his collar.

"Master Quibble ordered us to get to safety," Gusto says. "Harlee knows how to look after herself."

"But she shouldn't have to," I growl.

"We can't go back there!" Gusto cries. "Cara, just this once, don't leap before you look. It's too dangerous."

"Look after Su," I tell them as I rise shakily to my feet. "Promise me."

"Harlee's a *wizard*," Gusto says. "We're just—"

"PROMISE ME!" I roar. Clutching Zuki's collar—and the twinning stone—I leap from the skiff and onto the side of the nearest chunk of sinking wreckage.

Honestly, I don't know if Harlee Wu is the Chosen One.

But I choose this.

I choose her.

It's a mystery how I have any strength left, but maybe I'm running on pure adrenaline—just like Harlee was when she saved me from Su.

Following the pulsing pull of the twinning stone, I pounce from one piece of debris to the next. There's toxic sludge everywhere, still swelling and oozing around me, but I don't let it slow me down, and eventually I reach the largest remaining section of the ship, pointing straight up to the sky like a knife blade. I scale it, finding handholds and footholds in the ruptured, uneven hull. One wrong move and down I go—and it doesn't help that some of the metal is so rusted and damaged by magic that it peels away at my touch. Nova offers me a squeak of encouragement from my shoulder. At least if I die, I won't be alone.

Concentrating on the twinning stone, I reach the lip of the hull and pull myself around it like it's a tight corner, only to discover that all that's left of the decks are serrated stumps. Wedged between one of them and an inner girder is the statue of Master Quibble. Harlee has her arms wrapped around him, like a little kid clinging to her father. She's soaking wet, drenched by the waves pounding through the fissures of the sinking hull fragment, and I can see faint and feeble zaps of light sparking from her hands. She must be trying to save Quibble—maybe by turning him to flesh, maybe by levitating him. I don't know for sure, but what *is* clear is that she can't do it. Her batteries are finally exhausted. There's nothing left to draw from.

Nova chirrups again, spurring me forward. I climb to Harlee, grab hold of her arm, and try to tug her away.

"I won't leave him!" she growls.

I exhale. She harbors all this rage toward him. All this disappointment. But on the other side she still has this unfathomable love. How can you let go of that?

You can't.

I *know.*

So I don't try to pry her from him. I let her cling to him, and I cling to her, and the slice of ship descends into the crashing and colliding waves. As we're sucked down, Harlee tries to keep holding on to Master Quibble—fiercely—but the sea wrenches his monolithic dead weight from her arms, and he disappears into the depths.

Which leaves just the two of us holding each other in the frigid water, with Nova chittering in my ear. It's so cold I think I'm going to pass out. What keeps my senses alert is the storm around us, rumbling and raging as we bob in the sea. You'd think it was a hurricane, but I know these aren't the forces of nature savaging us. These are the forces of magic—*infected* magic. The various lesions in the Field have stretched together to form the mother of all wounds, hovering above the sea and puking poison.

Tentacles of slime whip toward us and everything spins amid the turbulent whirl of waves—not just us, not just the remnants of the Cipher ship, but other vessels in the vicinity, too. Ensnared by the gunk, they bash together like toys in a tub—except plastic ships don't explode or burst into flames like these ones do. There's fire, there's water. It's pretty much the end of the world.

One of the whips of toxic sludge wraps around me and Harlee, two or three coils thick. As the tentacles squeeze the air out of me, I glare into the toxic purple void showing through the rift. I've seen it so many times before, but never like this, so massive, so mighty. The infected interior churns, an ulcer on the stomach of the Field.

Nova leaps onto my head, squeaking frantically. She's trying to tell me something, but I don't understand what. Then, suddenly, she hurls herself from my shoulder and plunges into the water, straight *toward* the ulcer.

I try to scream for her, but nothing comes out. The coils have completely robbed me of breath and now I watch in a daze as Nova reaches the rupture. A web of slime entangles her, but she simply eats her way through it. She lunges at the rift, clings to its edge—then I lose sight of her.

She's gone.

I can't even comprehend what she's done. *Why* she's done it. I don't have to dwell on it long, though—the ulcer suddenly morphs, twisting and twitching like a pair of lips puckering at the taste of something repulsive. Next, there's a thunderous roar, and an invisible wave of energy reverberates across the sea, rocking us even more.

The coils of slime release us, falling lifelessly into the sea, the rupture seals shut, and the world—in an instant—is calm.

"Wh-what happened?" Harlee gasps, blinking in bewilderment, as we hug each other in the water.

"Don't know," I say slowly—though I have a sneaking suspicion that I might. Nova sacrificed herself. She fed *herself* to the wound. And by doing so, she somehow closed it.

"Dratch," Harlee murmurs weakly. "We might live. Go figure."

"Don't worry," I say between chattering teeth. "We could still freeze to death."

We kick our legs, trying to stay afloat as we cling together, but I soon realize that Harlee's movements are weakening. I'm losing her. I try to pull her tighter and kick for the both of us. I glance around, hoping for some sign of Gusto and Zuki in their boat, but I don't even know if they're still around, or still alive. There's flotsam everywhere—busted pieces of ship, crates and containers, all kinds of junk that was aboard the various freighters that were ripped apart in the cataclysm of magic. I head toward a wooden pallet, to see if I can at least lug Harlee onto it, but I can't reach it before it bobs away.

I hear sirens sound from the shore and see lights flare to life, both in the sky and on the surface of the water. It's the Coast Guard and other Bliss emergency responders, I realize, coming toward us in their boats and helicopters.

"How do you think we're going to explain this?" I ask Harlee. Her head collapses onto my shoulder.

"Come on, stay with me," I grunt. "You can't die on me. You're Harlee Wu!"

She doesn't respond, and I have to keep furiously kicking to keep us afloat. I spot a pulsing light heading across the surface toward me and I blink at its brilliance. It's not until I hear the familiar chirp that I realize that it's—Nova?

She's the size of a barrel.

"What happened to you?" I murmur in bewilderment.

She floats alongside me and kisses my nose with her snout.

"How did you get out of there?" I ask. "Actually, how did you close the rupture? How did you do anything?"

Her only response is another chirp, but that's when it occurs to me. She didn't feed the rupture. It fed *her*—based on her size, a lot. Like an algae eater in a fish tank, like a leech on a wound, she absorbed the toxicity, neutralized it—and, in the process, closed the biggest, meanest mouth-thingy I've ever seen.

"You make a great spell sweeper," I tell her.

She chirrups again, then dives beneath the surface of the water, swimming away to continue feasting on the pools of slime still floating all around. I soon lose sight of her and I realize she's gone—this time, for good. She's literally outgrown me, and now I'm all alone.

Harlee emits a moan.

Not quite alone, I guess. I pull Harlee close and we bob like two lost souls in the wreckage of the night.

"Don't worry," I murmur. "I've got you."

CHAPTER 37

Things Get Real

I HEAR ZIVAH BEFORE I see her. Headwizard Singh's massive storm bird caws, then descends from the sky, appearing out of the clouds like a gust of magic. She's never looked so beautiful. Maybe I think this because her plumage is darker than when I last saw her, black as ink and highlighted by lightning streaks—or maybe it's because she's coming to rescue us.

Headwizard Singh is straddling her back and, as Zivah flutters next to us, she reaches down, grabs me by the broom still strapped to my back, and with unexpected strength pulls both me and Harlee up alongside her. She throws a heavy cloak around our shivering bodies, and I melt into warmth. I can feel myself disappearing into slumber, but I fight it.

Struggling out of the comforting folds of the cloak, I glare at Singh. "Why didn't you tell me about—"

"Your dad," she finishes for me. "It wasn't my decision. It came from the High Council, but I should have . . ." She exhales; like I've always said, apologizing does not come naturally to wizards. "We need to talk about it, Caradine. But right now—"

A new explosion rocks us from below, prompting me to lean over and peer at the scene.

It's not good. Ships are sinking, flames are funneling out of wreckage, and emergency crews are swarming to the area. I can hear the wail of sirens and the frantic shouts of rescuers. If this kind of disaster doesn't put the magical world in jeopardy, then I don't know what will. If the Bliss world discovers us, what happens next? Maybe all Harlee's fears will become reality.

"Got to go back down there," I tell Singh. "Gusto and Zuki are there. With my sister. And she's not in good shape."

"Neither are *you*. Time to rest; time to let others clean up for once."

"But—"

"We've got people on the scene," Singh assures me. "This is not the first magical disaster we've had to deal with."

"But it's *my* crew. *My* sister. And Master Quibble—" I can't bring myself to say it. That he's gone. "Just drop me down there. I have a job to finish."

"No," she says firmly.

"Stop underestimating me!" I erupt. "You don't think I can do this, but I can! I know about all sorts of magic. I know potions. I know about creatures. I may not have a 'real' talisman, but I have my broom and I can—"

"You are the one underestimating *me*," Singh interrupts sternly. "Because I know all this about you, Caradine Moone. Why do you think we made you a spell sweeper? Do you think just anybody can do it?"

Another reversal on a night of reversals—a perspective that is the exact opposite of my own. As I stare down at the disaster below us, I feel that familiar yearning burble to the surface: *I want to be a real wizard.*

"Yes, and you're a spell sweeper," Singh tells me, reading my mind. "Look around you, Caradine. This is as real as it gets."

CHAPTER 38

No More Sweeping Things under the Rug

IT'S A TRANQUIL MID-NOVEMBER AFTERNOON, and I'm sitting in the garden next to Riva Dragonsong's statue, Zuki curled at my feet. Other than us, the only people here are Gusto and Yuna, parked on the other side of the pond, sharing a bench and a stick of witch's delight. It's quiet and cold, but at least it's not raining—which, in the Pacific Northwest, always counts as a victory.

The bell chimes, signaling the start of the school day, and students pour into the garden, crossing to their various destinations. Everyone comes to a screeching halt, though, when Harlee appears. I catch a slight grimace on her face as she's swarmed—but, hey, that's life when you're the queen of the school. She can now *officially* add "Chosen One" to the title because the entire student body is convinced that she fulfilled the prophecy when she "single-handedly" stopped Cipher and healed the Field. (We actually don't know if the Field is permanently restored. The wizards are studying the situation, but wizards are slow, which means, out of caution, magic is still suspended. We're living in a new sort of normal now.)

Zuki tugs on the hem of my cloak. "I thought you were going to swing by the Vault to call home. To check on Su."

I shrug. "I'll have to do it later."

Su's in a Bliss hospital, still recovering. I've seen her once, though she wasn't conscious then. As far as Mom and Grandma know, Su got herself entangled with the wrong crowd and was spirited away to a boat party that went horribly wrong. It's basically the truth—except for the very minor detail of, you know, her wielding *dark magic*.

I have no idea how my sister feels about me now. Or, truthfully, how I feel about her. Yes, she was poisoned, but is it completely gone from her system? Is she back to her old self? I don't even know if she remembers anything from that night— or *anything* to do with Cipher. Wizards—*apparently!*—have the power to erase memories, and they might have erased hers. But they haven't erased *mine*, which means I won't ever be able to expunge that image of Su staring at me with her empty, burnt-cauldron eyes.

I asked Headwizard Singh if they wiped Su's mind, but her answers were extremely cryptic and evasive. The conversation about my dad was better, though not much. Let's just say that there were a lot of paradoxes, and a lot of wizardsplaining. I'm still processing everything, but I can't help thinking that Cipher *definitely* had a point about us.

But Cipher doesn't exist anymore—at least as far as we know. Most of the cultists, along with their initiates, were rescued from the harbor by the Coast Guard, but no one knows what happened to Brad and the twins. Maybe they're dead. Maybe they've scuttled off somewhere to regroup. As for Cipher Mourn? Apparently, there's no trace of him either.

Eventually, the Dragonsong students empty out of the garden. As Yuna leaves, she gives me a subtle wave, and I return the gesture. Things between us still aren't as good as they were before I became a spell sweeper, but they're getting there. (For the record, I finally admitted to stealing her manticore venom, which resulted in a couple of difficult days between us.)

It takes me a moment to realize that Harlee has drifted over to sit next to me on our favorite bench, sketchbook in hand. I can only imagine the things she's been drawing after everything we've been through.

Harlee leans down, scratches Zuki between the ears, then sits back and trains her eyes on the statue of Riva Dragonsong. "Members of the High Council arrived last night," she says. "You get called before them yet?"

"Not yet. You?"

She shakes her head. "It'll be an interrogation."

"Are you going to tell them about Nova?"

"Why would I?"

"Because you might *need* to? You know, uh, out of loyalty."

She whirls on me, eyes flaring. "The only one I'm loyal to in this situation is *you*."

"Awww," Zuki says, tails flicking.

"Behave, Spooky," she warns, wagging a finger at him before

turning her gaze back to the statue. "Look, I still don't want a BFF. But I'm not blindly following our masters anymore."

"What does *that* mean? Are you leaving?" I have to admit, it's something I've seriously considered myself since talking to Singh. Yes, I'm finally starting to figure out who I am in Dragonsong's giant magical mural, but . . .

"I've felt the way you do," Harlee says, reading me. "You *know* I have."

I nod, thinking back to our conversation in my room at the Drowsy Druid. Harlee has been wrestling with her feelings about wizardry for a long time, much longer than me.

"It's complicated, being us, dealing with . . . all *this*," Harlee continues, gesturing at the garden walls. "It's tempting to run off. That's what Trick did, and it didn't help anything." She draws in a deep breath. "I'm staying at Dragonsong. I'm going to work hard. I'm going to become the youngest wizard to ever join the High Council. I'm going to make things better."

"Better?"

"Look, I get keeping us hidden from Blisses," Harlee explains. "But why are we being secretive toward each other? So . . . manipulative? We need to be more open. Stop sweeping everything under the rug—maybe we need to *throw out* the rug."

I gape at her. I don't say it out loud, just in case she feels the need to melt me (rules or no rules), but I've never been more convinced than I am at this moment that she *is* the Chosen One. She isn't going to save us from some insidious outside force. She's going to save us from *ourselves*.

"One thing, though," Harlee says as she stands up.

"Yeah?"

"I could really use some support. An *ally*." She turns and gives me what can almost be construed as a smile. "I get it if you want to jet from this place, Cara, this wizardly life . . . but at least consider sticking around. Okay?"

Then she leaves with a swish of her robes, cool as always.

"I want you to stay, Cara," Zuki says. "Especially now that . . ." His voice catches. "The spell sweepers are the only family I have left."

Crouching down, I wrap my arms around his glorious white fur and hug him. "Come on," I say as I stand up.

"Where are we going?"

"Class—we're already late. Don't want to get on Madame Gloome's bad side already. She's only been teaching spell sweeping for a week."

"I hope she doesn't last one more day," Zuki says as he follows me into the Crucible. "You know, because Master Quibble comes back."

I nod. My feelings about the Q-Man are as thorny as the ones I have for my sister and Singh, but I will admit it gives me the shivers to think about him sitting there, solid stone, at the bottom of the sea. Singh assured me the Council will search for him, though they aren't sure whether they'll be able to revive him. The hairpin occuli might be able to do it, but it went down with the ship, along with the Wizard Whistle and the other stolen talismans. It's going to be a long, ongoing recovery operation, and the truth is that spells aren't so easy to reverse.

It's like Dad told me when I was a little kid (and what inspired my favorite analogy of the Magical Field): "Easy to squeeze the toothpaste out of the tube, Cara. Not so easy to put it back in."

Of course, he wasn't talking about spellcasting, or the life of a wizard—but he could have been. Because it's like I've always said.

Magic is messy.

There's something magical
about a broom

I still think about her, that old lady sweeping the street, the one I saw on my way to school when I was only four or five. The picture of her remains in my mind, as sharp as a fox's wit.

When I was young and naive, I thought she was a wizard who flew away on her broomstick. Then I went to Dragonsong, reality crashed in, and I decided she was just a pathetic old woman, the kind you can find anywhere in the world: sweeping a street corner in Seattle, whisking a doorstep in Florence, brushing away the rubbish of a market square in Shanghai. We've all seen this woman, though we rarely pay her any care or attention. She doesn't have a legion of followers on TikTok or a kajillion likes on Instagram. She's not popular, famous, or special—not by any modern definition.

Remind you of someone?

I'm not the Chosen One, the Queen of Dragonsong, or the "somebody" of the wizarding realm. Heck, as Su pointed out, I'm not even the somebody of my family.

But that doesn't mean I'm insignificant. Brooms will never be for flying, but that's okay. As I've learned, they're for something much more important. The truth is that I'm living a pretty amazing life; I've ridden magical creatures, battled dark spells, maybe even played a small part in saving wizardkind. Hardly anyone knowing it doesn't change those facts.

Which means I was right the first time, I think. That old woman *was* a wizard—just a wizard of a different sort.

A wizard like me.

AUTHOR'S NOTE

In the summer of 2019, this book felt like a mere spark in my imagination, a question flickering in my mind: "What if brooms in the magical world were still for sweeping?"

From there, the spark burst into flame, and this book spilled out of me in less than a year—though now I realize that I've been writing it in one way or another for a lot longer than that.

In 2004, I met a like-minded dreamer named Joon-hyung Park who was seeking a writing program for his daughters to take. He couldn't find the right type of workshop, so he decided to invent one—and he wanted my help. The next thing you know, Joon and I had started a creative writing program in Vancouver for immigrant kids from Asia (our own school of magic!). Our workshops blossomed and bloomed, and now we host many programs for kids from all walks of life. We write stories, draw pictures, brew potions, build dragon eggs—you name it! My wife and I have enjoyed an additional privilege— the opportunity to visit Asia to teach creative writing at schools, libraries, and education centers (I've been to Korea over twenty times!). Reading the stories by these creative kids—and about their dreams, desires, and fears—has definitely played a role in the creation of Dragonsong Academy. (By the way, it's no exaggeration to say that our teaching experiences led us to Japan, and our son Hiro, in 2018.)

Something else happened during my many trips to Asia. I began seeing brooms. *Everywhere.* There was always one leaning against a park bench or in the corner of a temple, as if impatiently waiting for its owner to return. I started photographing these brooms because—well, that's what I do. Something catches my interest, I take a photo, make a sketch or note in my brainstorming journal, just in case I need it down the road. I began imagining that these brooms contained hidden and unusual magic—my second strand of inspiration.

Coming back from a trip to Vietnam and Cambodia, I remembered something else: my grandfather used to make his own brooms! He grew the broomcorn, harvested it, and bound it to broomsticks. I never saw my grandfather build a broom (I really wish I had), but I realized I had one of his creations in the dusty corner of my closet. I had never dared to use the broom, but I dug it out as inspiration. Then, on a subsequent visit to my parents, I scavenged their house to find they had their own collection of my grandfather's handmade brooms. They all have the same humble construction—and, if you ask me, their own type of magic. Clearly, these brooms have been lingering in my subconscious all these years, waiting for me to tell their story.

The final bit of inspiration for this book came from an exchange that I've had many times with students. It happens almost exactly the same way each time; I'm wrapping up a class or a school visit and a student approaches me and asks, "Are you famous?" I always answer the same way: "I think the answer is in your question!" They inevitably press me on the matter: "But don't you *want* to be famous?"

"No!" I cry with the passionate zeal of an introvert. "I want to be a writer."

I have always asked my students to focus on craft over reward—but who can blame them for their yearnings? Every writer, artist, or actor I know (including me!) has craved accolades and recognition, has experienced those "why not me?" or "when is it my turn?" moments. My time as a teacher and speaker has prompted me to ponder our personal definitions of failure and success—and from these musings came the character of Caradine Moone. It is my hope that her journey (even though it involves *not* flying on a broom) rings true for readers.

By the way, while Dragonsong Island exists only in my imagination, the Seattle Underground and the Whistler Train Wreck are real!

ACKNOWLEDGMENTS

Magic is messy—and so is writing! Which means I could not have conjured this book to life without my own spellbinding crew.

Thank you to my agent, Rachel Letofsky, who fell in love with my idea for *Spell Sweeper*, and who has been the champion of all champions. I so deeply appreciate you sticking with me through all the ups and downs.

Thank you to HarperCollins and Stephanie Stein, editor extraordinaire. I was so thrilled that you fell in love with Cara's voice and personality. You brought love to this project, but also your keen story expertise. I view every book as a sort of puzzle, and you have a wizard's touch when it comes to taking all those scattered pieces and assembling them into something coherent and—dare I say—magical.

Thank you to the rest of the HarperCollins team: assistant editor Louisa Currigan, production editor Caitlin Lonning, and copy editor Jessica White. Thank you to Robby Imfeld, Lena Reilly, and Maeve O'Regan for marketing and publicity. Thank you to Jessie Gang and Alison Klapthor for a beautiful book design, and to the production team, James Neel and Nicole Moulaison.

And the cover! What can I say? Maike Plenzke, I have been a fan of your gorgeous artwork for a long time and the moment

I saw your concept for *Spell Sweeper*, I was ensorceled.

Thank you to all my "consultants" (many of you students past and present). Kathleen Zhang, Yali Xing, Emylie Choi, and Kanako Miyamoto provided their perspectives, knowledge, and opinions about fox spirit lore. Sarah Suk, Nadia Kim, Chloe Kang, Dona Park, and Charlotte McAren either pre-read the manuscript or listened to my ideas and provided many helpful perspectives. Sejin and Yujin Kim described their in-depth experiences of attending a boarding school far from home.

Thank you to Mary Schwieger of Granville Island Broom Co. for patiently answering all my questions about the traditions of broom making, and for letting me observe the process. (Seriously, this shop makes and sells GORGEOUS brooms. Check them out online.)

Thank you to my sensitivity readers—your honest assessments and appraisal of the manuscript improved it and helped correct its course.

Thank you to my author and literary crew for listening to me drone on about this book, or for simply being my cheerleaders along the way: Kallie George, Jeremy Tankard, Stacey Matson, Rob Stocks, kc dyer, Holman Wang, Mahtab Narsimhan, Sarah Bagshaw, Dov and Renuka Baron, Heather Fitzgerald, Carrie Bercic, Jeff Porter, Jennifer Newman, James McCann, Tanya Lloyd Kyi, Jina Kim, the crews at CWILL BC and MG Book Village (especially Kathie MacIsaac and Laurie Hnatiuk), and to Joon Park, Sarah Hong, and my many, many book-loving students.

And, finally, thank you to my family for your ongoing and continuing support—my parents, my siblings, my nieces and nephews, and especially Marcie and Hiro. It's probably easier living with a wizard than a writer!